'If poetry was the supreme literary form of the First World War then, as if in riposte, in the Second World War, the English novel came of age. This wonderful series is an exemplary reminder of that fact. Great novels were written about the Second World War and we should not forget them.'

WILLIAM BOYD

'It's wonderful to see these books given a new lease of life [...] classic novels from the Second World War written by those who were there, experienced the fear, anguish, pain and excitement first-hand and whose writings really do shine an incredibly vivid light onto what it was like to live and fight through that terrible conflict.'

JAMES HOLLAND, Historian, author and TV presenter

'The Imperial War Museum has performed a valuable public service by reissuing these absolutely superb novels'

ANDREW ROBERTS, author of *Churchill: Walking with Destiny*

'Witty, warm and hugely endearing, Barbara Whitton's *Green Hands* is full of engaging characters, burgeoning friendships and pure hard-graft. A lovely novel for anyone interested in wartime Britain, it leaves the reader with renewed admiration for the indefatigable work of the Women's Land Army.'

AJ PEARCE

'Tales from the home front are always more authentic when written from personal experience, as is the case here. Barbara Whitton evokes the highs and lows, joys and agonies of being a Land Girl in the Second World War.'

JULIE SUMMERS

GREEN HANDS

Barbara Whitton

IMPERIAL WAR MUSEUMS

First published in Great Britain in 1943

First published in this format in 2020 by
IWM, Lambeth Road, London SE1 6HZ
iwm.org.uk

© The Estate of Barbara Whitton, 2020

About the Author and Introduction © The Trustees of the
Imperial War Museum, 2020

ISBN 978-1-912423-26-2

A catalogue record for this book is available from the
British Library.

Printed and bound in Great Britain by CPI Group (UK) Ltd,
Croydon

Every effort has been made to contact all copyright holders.
The publishers will be glad to make good in future editions
any error or omissions brought to their attention.

Cover illustration by Bill Bragg
Design by Clare Skeats
Series Editor Madeleine James

About the Author

Margaret Hazel Watson (1921 – 2016)

MARGARET HAZEL WATSON (writing under the pseudonym Barbara Whitton) was born in Newcastle-upon-Tyne in 1921. She was educated at the Church High Girls School in Newcastle, and later sent to St Leonards School in St Andrews. Due to study Art in Paris, her training was curtailed by the outbreak of the Second World War.

Having volunteered for the Women's Land Army (WLA) in 1939, she worked as a Land Girl for around a year before moving to the First Aid Nursing Yeomanry (FANY) and later joining the Auxiliary Territorial Service (ATS) as a driver, where she remained for the duration of the war. Her novel *Green Hands* is a fictionalised account of her time spent as a Land Girl, detailing the back-breaking hard work and intensity of her experience with good humour and an enchanting lightness of touch. During her time with the ATS she met her husband Pat Chitty and they were married in 1941. After the war, she wrote a number of accounts of her wartime experience and retained an interest in art, literature and horticulture throughout her life. She died in 2016.

Introduction

The literary legacy of the First World War was a proliferation of war novels, with an explosion of the genre in the late 1920s. Erich Maria Remarque's *All Quiet on the Western Front* was a bestseller and was made into a Hollywood film in 1930. In the same year, Siegfried Sassoon's *Memoirs of an Infantry Officer* sold 24,000 copies. Generations of school children have grown up on a diet of Wilfred Owen's poetry and the novels of Sassoon. Yet the novels of the Second World War – or certainly those written by individuals who had first-hand experience of that war – are often forgotten. It could be argued that female voices of this experience, in particular, have been unfairly overlooked.

Green Hands by Barbara Whitton (Margaret Hazel Watson writing under a pseudonym) is a fine example of this first-hand experience translated into a fictional work. First published in 1943, the novel concerns the experiences of three young and inexperienced Land Girls and their time with the Women's Land Army (WLA) during the Second World War. The book displays a lightness of touch that renders it an enjoyable reading experience, whilst shining a light on a key aspect of the British home front.

In terms of historical backdrop to the novel, the total mobilisation of the population during the Second World War meant that women took on a wide variety of jobs hitherto performed by men, who had now been conscripted into the fighting services. Conscription of women began in 1941 after the Minister of Labour, Ernest Bevin, realised that over 1.5 million women were needed in the Auxiliary Services and industry for essential war work – work that could be done by the female population. It was the first time in British history that the conscription of single women was made compulsory, indeed only the Soviet Union mobilised a higher percentage of women for the war effort. When conscripted, women could opt to join the military services – the Women's Auxiliary Air Force (WAAF), Auxiliary Territorial Service (ATS) or the Women's Royal Naval

Service (WRNS) – take up a post in a wartime factory identified as vital for war production, or join the 'Land Girls' as a member of the Women's Land Army (WLA).

The WLA had originally been formed during the First World War. It was re-established in June 1939 when it was identified that if war came, an extra two million acres of productive agricultural land was needed to offset the loss of imported food from the Empire. Without a substantial number of women helpers this would have been impossible. To make up the labour shortfall (although being a farmer was a reserved occupation, being a farm labourer was not) Land Girls found themselves working alongside older male labourers, German and Italian prisoners of war, and even schoolchildren, who were allowed up to 20 days off school each year to help on farms. (Indeed, in some of the early scenes of the novel, schoolchildren are set up as rivals for productivity to the protagonist Bee and her fellow Land Girl.)

By the outbreak of war 17,000 women had volunteered and in 1943, supplemented by conscription, there were just over 80,000 members. At this point recruitment ceased, as the government began to worry that women were choosing to labour in the fields over vital factory work. Some put this down to the way WLA recruitment posters promised a happy, healthy outdoor life, invariably in the sunshine (something Bee and her friends do enjoy in the second half of the novel, albeit replete with continued back-breaking work and early starts – more of which later). Others liked the WLA uniform, which although practical; corduroy trousers and aertex shirt, was also stylish and distinctive, with its pork pie hat and jodhpur cut breeches (women wearing trousers was considered rather revolutionary at the time).

The author of *Green Hands*, Hazel Watson, volunteered for the Land Army in 1939, working on farms in North Northumberland and the Berwickshire Borders, and then in the South Tyne valley – locations reflected in the novel. She then joined the First Aid Nursing Yeomanry (FANY) and later the ATS, where she worked for the duration of the war. Watson reportedly loved her time spent as a Land Girl and her evident enjoyment of this period in her life shines through in the latter part of the novel – nonetheless it is not an entirely rosy picture of time spent 'lending a hand on the land', with issues such as sexism, the nature of the work and general attitudes towards the Land Girls themselves all playing a part.

Being a Land Girl could, without a doubt, be backbreaking work. A Land Girl was supposed to work a 48-hour week in the winter and 50 hours in the summer, but in reality a 12-hour day, six days a week was not uncommon. Contemporary accounts held in IWM's sound archive recall working such long days – one and half hours even before breakfast. This is borne out in the early scenes of labour in the novel, in which Bee and her fellow Land Girl Anne rise at 6am for their first morning and are both at breaking point before their morning meal:

> *The sleet slackens, and a few beams of anaemic sunlight struggle through. We go back to our labours, stiff with cold from standing. I decide that tonight I shall quite certainly die of pneumonia.*
>
> *Anne is beyond speech.*
>
> *One-two; one-two; mangold, cart; mangold, cart. My head spins and there is a sick feeling in the pit of my stomach. As I stoop the ground rushes up to meet me, and as I rise the sky wheels about my head. We seem to have been working all day when at last nine o'clock arrives...*

* * *

Despite the name, the WLA was a civilian service, with the Land Girls undertaking a variety of agricultural tasks such as milking cows, ploughing, managing poultry, picking crops, shovelling pig manure – basically whatever the farmer wanted them to do – in all weathers. There were training courses, but most learned on the job. The volunteers were essentially there to do any of the work the farmer asked of them, and this could certainly be a shock to the system. Bee's friend Anne in particular struggles with this, and there are several rather bleak scenes in their early days at Spital

Tongues farm (though none without humour entirely, it must be said). Notable is the first morning, as mentioned above, and Anne's repeated complaints that she will do 'a roaring pass out'. Later on, the women are set the unenviable task of shovelling manure, again described in a vivid manner by the author:

> *The manure is in a hemmel at the back of the farm. The hemmel has had pigs in it for two years without ever having been cleaned out. The manure is upward of two feet deep.*
>
> *We have met manure before in our farming experience, but never manure like this. Instead of a fairly tolerable commodity, keeping itself to itself in regulated clods, this manure is more suitable for lifting with spoons, than with the forks we are provided with. It is unbelievably unpleasant and smells overpoweringly of ammonia, and as we heave it up into the cart, it splashes all over us, spattering our faces in disgusting spots. The hemmel is enclosed from the air except for a small opening at one end, and it is not long before the heady ammonia has its effects. It begins to make us feel sick and dizzy, and we constantly have to stagger out into the rain to draw in deep refreshing breaths [...] I have long ceased to care whether the manure splashes into my hair or not.*

Eventually Anne has simply had enough, and makes good on her repeated threat to leave the service.

These early scenes of the novel also pull out another theme which is interwoven throughout the book – namely the prevailing social attitudes of the time that, although women have been specifically conscripted to these jobs, this is not 'women's work'. Bee, Pauline and Anne seem happy to brush off such comments and the relentless teasing depicted (particularly of Pauline) does little to phase them, nonetheless it is striking to the modern reader how often these scenes occur. Notable is Bee and Anne's initial meeting of the farmer Mr Thompson at Spital Tongues:

> *'Well,' he says in a sort of doleful chant, 'how do you think*

you are going to like the land? I doubt if you will last long.'

There doesn't seem to be much one can reply to this. It is hardly a promising opening and we stare back at him helplessly.

'We had land girls in the last war,' goes on the voice dolefully. 'They weren't any good at all. Fainted like cut grass, one after the other, propping each other up against the hedge.'

[...] 'It's hard work, very hard work. It's no work for a woman. I'll never let our Mary work in the fields. Hens – that's all she's fit for.'

The main initial objection to women working on the land was that they would not be able to carry out the heavy manual labour which was required, and contemporary accounts mention instances where some women were sent home as they weren't seen as being physically strong enough – indeed Anne does eventually give up and go home.

However in many places productivity on the farms in fact increased, and in the novel Bee and Pauline are stoic in their acceptance of the work, and their enjoyment in some of the tasks is evident (particularly in their second posting at a dairy farm). Nonetheless throughout the novel the girls are teased mercilessly, including when Bee is sent to the local market to sell some of Mr Smith's calves:

I am the only woman in the room, and I am uncomfortably aware of the interest I am arousing. I am increasingly grateful for the moral support of my fellow-milkman, but even he cannot prevent me from feeling a little like a prize heifer myself.

I begin answering questions as to my calves' ownership and place of residence. I am rather at a loss, however, when the unpleasant man behind the counter asks me what colour they are. I rack my brains. To me they are just calves, but in the end I hope for the best, and say that I think they are both brown and white.

[…] 'Don't you know nothing?' he says. 'Red is brown – same thing, see?'

I am silenced.

'Sex!' says the man, consulting his ledger.

'I beg your pardon?'

'I said sex,' says the man. 'Sex of calves. What sort are they?'

Silently I curse Mr. Smith with all my heart. How could he let me come all innocent and unprimed into this den of thieves! He must have known that I should have to face this awful inquisition. He must have known that I wouldn't have the slightest idea what sex his wretched calves were. I am absolutely at a loss.

Indeed unlike the women who served in the forces or civil defence, Land Girls were not eligible for business schemes, education or training at the end of the war, although the Ministry of Agriculture eventually conceded on training. The outspoken Labour Party Member of Parliament Edith Summerskill (who had herself established the unofficial Women's Home Defence organisation when she found out that women were not permitted to the join the Home Guard), and who had been lobbying on their behalf, described this an incredibly mean offer.

Considering the large number of women mobilised during the Second World War, the impact on employment patterns after the conflict was rather limited, as the majority of women continued to work in largely female dominated occupations and the average wage was 53% of the male wage. The consensus of historians is that the wartime role of women working across the different sectors was not a catalyst for change, but that the war did bring a new economic and social freedom for women.

***

Despite these challenges, the deep friendship and camaraderie between the girls is the real heart of this novel (by the end, inseparable as they are, it's easy to forget that Pauline was initially an unwanted companion for Bee). Throughout the difficult physical work and various romantic trials and tribulations, their friendship remains steadfast – even when Bee herself sometimes sees Pauline as a comical character: 'She is the most teasable person I have ever known. Her very appearance asks for it, with her absurd hat, which she wears perched on the back of her head; her shirt tails which constantly work out of her trousers, and her fine hair which hangs in a shaggy fringe about her face.'

Anne and Pauline were in fact the names of Hazel Watson's fellow Land Girls in real life, and they remained in touch after the war despite changes in circumstance and geographical location – in true testament to the bonding nature of their wartime experience, Pauline and Hazel were still writing letters and exchanging news well into their nineties.

After her time in the WLA, the author briefly served in the FANY, followed by a couple of years in the ATS as a driver (echoed by Bee's driving experience in the novel, first of a tractor and later of the milk van). It was here that she met her husband-to-be Pat, and they were married in 1941. After the war they settled in Newcastle-upon-Tyne and later Newbrough, near Hexham. The author claimed the first draft of *Green Hands* only took her only a week to write. Whatever the circumstances of its genesis, this charming and engaging novel of her time as a Land Girl brings vividly to life this important aspect of Britain's home front during the Second World War.

Imperial War Museum, London
2020

CHAPTER ONE
Going Native

THE PUFFING ENGINE runs a sweating finger round its collar; then breathing heavily, it shoulders its burden of two coaches and once more shuffles off into the night.

'Well,' says Anne, 'we've arrived.'

I turn and regard somewhat apprehensively the toppling stack of our luggage on the platform beside us. There suddenly seems to be a great deal of it.

'I hope they don't think we have brought too much stuff,' I say. 'Couldn't you have left any of it behind?'

'There is rather a heap,' says Anne, 'now you come to see it all at one time. But I do so believe in having everything I want when I want it. And I did leave my gas-mask behind. I thought it would make one less package.'

We look about us expectantly, and hope that the shadows will part to disclose someone to meet us. The journey has been long and dirty, and we are both weary.

Suddenly a voice speaks from behind us. It is the sort of voice one instinctively expects to belong to someone dressed in a plaid and sporran, but it is too dark for us to see its owner clearly.

'Hullo! Are you the land girls for Spital Tongues?'

Anne agrees eagerly that we are.

'Good,' says the voice. 'I'm Miss Thompson. What a lot of luggage you have! I hope we can get it all into the car. Can you find a porter anywhere?'

We find that the guard (or station master) also acts in the capacity of a porter, and he piles our cases skilfully on to a barrow. We are rather hesitant as to whether or not he is sufficient of a porter to accept a tip, but it seems he is, and after a few minutes we find ourselves huddled with our baggage in the back of a very small and ancient car. There is a sack of potatoes on the front seat, so, as Miss Thompson has said, there isn't very much room for us. I can only see Anne's face appearing dimly over a mound of parcels. On her lap is a suitcase, an eiderdown, and a ukulele. On the floor at my feet are a couple of pairs of large rubber boots, a bulging case, a cardboard hatbox and a sheep dog.

Miss Thompson switches on her lights, lets in her clutch with a bang, and the car leaps in the air. However, it seems to be pinned to the ground by the back wheels, for after another more feeble leap and a strangled gasp or two, it stops.

After the third attempt to start has failed Anne whispers to me that I ought not to be so heavy. I am too hemmed in to be able to swell with indignation, but fortunately at last the car manages to stagger off. We can almost hear its knees knocking as Miss Thompson sets it at the hill outside the station.

'Well,' says Miss Thompson in her broad Scotch, 'and how do you like land work?'

'I think I like it,' I reply a little doubtfully, vainly attempting to prevent the sheep dog from digging its claws into my silk stockings.

'We've only done a month so far,' says Anne. 'I dare say there are still a few shocks in store for us.'

'There is another land girl arriving on Friday,' says Miss Thompson, 'perhaps you know her. She calls herself Pauline Gardener. She comes from your part of the world.'

Anne and I gasp.

'Good heavens!' says Anne, moving her ukulele into a more comfortable position so that it bites angrily into my third rib. 'I should just think I do know her. Barbara and I used to go to school with her. She was a beastly little girl. I used to hate her. Do you remember her, Barbara?'

'Yes, she was pretty awful.'

'Oh, dear,' says Miss Thompson. 'How very unfortunate. But perhaps you will find she has changed.'

At that moment the car turns in through a gateway and stops with sudden decision before a long dark building. Miss Thompson turns off her engine and switches out her lights so that we are left in total darkness.

'Well,' she says brightly, 'here we are.'

Anne picks herself up off the sheep dog, on whom she had

descended when the car stopped, and gathering up as much luggage as we can carry, we follow Miss Thompson through the back door into the farmhouse. Inside we stand blinking in the sudden light of the kitchen. We get a fleeting impression of miles of large iron ranges and of pendant dishcloths suspended on rails over our heads. Then we find ourselves being introduced to Miss Thompson's mother. Miss Thompson's mother is a wizened old lady with peering short-sighted eyes and wisps of grey hair. She wears wire-rimmed glasses, and as she beams a welcome to us she discloses the fact that she is all gum and no teeth.

'Ah, come in, come in,' she says. 'So Mary found you all right? Did you have a good journey?'

Mary leans down towards her mother and suddenly emits a shrill shriek in her ear. It seems she is deaf.

'Show them up to their room, Mother,' she shouts. 'They will be wanting to get their supper.'

'Oh, yes, that's right, dear,' says Mrs Thompson, and picking up a small lamp from the kitchen dresser, she turns and we follow her out into the hall.

She is a weird sight with her old grey dress hanging in loose folds about her, the skirt hitched up in front in her knuckled hand. She holds the lamp high above her head so that her shadow distends and sprawls upward over the staircase wall.

'My sainted aunt!' whispers Anne. 'No electric light! We are going back to the land!'

Our room, however, proves to be a palatial affair with a huge expanse of faded carpet and a quantity of large pieces of mahogany furniture. But the bed leaves Anne momentarily speechless. It is vast and double; a four-poster with a red velvet canopy and a fringe of tassels. On the walls there are some prints, chiefly of death scenes in Shakespeare, and on either side of the mantelpiece there are texts written on green cards and decorated with white roses.

'There you are,' says Mrs Thompson. 'I hope you will be comfortable. There is a drawer for your things over there.' She sets the lamp down carefully on the dressing-table. 'The bathroom is down the passage. Come down when you are ready. Supper will be set for you in the sitting-room.'

The door closes behind her, and Anne and I look at one another with raised eyebrows.

'So far not bad,' I suggest. 'At least we've got room to turn round in and even the possibility of a bath. I wonder if we will get one tonight. I feel terribly dirty.'

'The room's certainly big enough,' agrees Anne, 'but, oh, Bee, what furniture! Did you ever see anything like it? I feel as if I had strayed into the pre-view of an auction sale.'

We set down our bundles and descend to the kitchen for the rest of our luggage.

'Do let's get settled in tonight,' says Anne. She opens her bag and taking out Gary Cooper's photograph she stands it on the dressing-table. Thus she stakes a claim of ownership. 'I do so like to feel I belong to a place. Which drawers will you have? I'll take the chest and you can have the dressing-table.'

She goes over to the chest of drawers and tries one drawer after another. Each time she fails to open one her eyebrows rise a little higher.

'Well, I'm hanged,' she says. 'I believe they are all locked!' She wrestles speechlessly with the knobs. 'They are, Bee – every one of them locked!'

'I'll try these,' I say, but even the meagre two in the dressing-table allotted to me by Anne as my share, prove to be equally fruitless.

'This is becoming silly,' says Anne. 'There must be a drawer somewhere. She said there was.'

'Try the one in the wardrobe!'

Anne tries it. 'Yes! it's open all right, but honestly, Bee, it hardly holds a thing! We shall just have to live in suitcases under the bed.'

Sadly we turn our backs on the rows of tantalisingly locked drawers, and with disillusion in our hearts, we pick out the few real essentials from our luggage and begin to arrange them in the one wardrobe drawer. Somehow, Anne's belongings become more and more spread out until they finally topple over on to mine. Only I appear to notice this, however.

The light from the lamp casts shadows over the fly-blown

looking-glass, and try as I may, I cannot arrange it any better. I peer at my reflection uselessly, and after a few blind dabs with my powder puff, I abandon the attempt.

'Let's go and find supper,' I say.

'Lead on, MacDuff,' says Anne, and holding the lamp high above my head, and feeling a little like the Statue of Liberty, I cautiously descend the coconut matting stairs.

We find supper set on a small table beside the fire in the sitting-room.

'Lord,' says Anne, unable to believe her eyes. For instead of the succulent plates of hot soup that we had hoped for, followed by perhaps a fried egg on toast and an apple, there is set on the table one plate of wafer biscuits and a hunk of cheese. On the hearth stands a jug of cocoa.

Silently we sit down, our stomachs clamouring for sustenance. Silently we begin to eat.

After a few minutes Miss Thompson pops her head round the door and asks brightly if we have everything we want. We long to tell her that this is indeed far from the case and to beseech her for a loaf of bread. We find, however, that we are suddenly overcome with shyness. After all, she has only been our hostess for a very short time. Miss Thompson departs, unmolested.

'H'm,' says Anne, gathering up the last crumbs of her biscuit and popping them into her mouth. 'I must say they are a bit frugal with their fare, Bee. Look at the fire!' The fire is built half-way up the grate in a sort of bracket, only wide enough to burn one piece of coal at a time. There is an area of about nine inches of hot air in its immediate vicinity. Beyond this circle the room is as cold as the tomb. We look at it with disgust. 'It is positively paralytic,' says Anne.

We finish our supper far too soon and Miss Thompson returns to ask us if we are ready to meet her father. Reluctantly we agree that we are, and settle ourselves nervously to face the coming ordeal.

The family file into the room: first Mrs Thompson, still beaming with the rather vacant smile that the hard of hearing sometimes have; then Mary, smiling as brightly as ever; then a tall drooping young man with red hair whom we haven't seen before; and finally Mr Thompson himself.

Mr Thompson is a very long thin man with a small stained, drooping moustache. He wears tweed knickerbockers, and he has a habit of fiddling with the watch in his waistcoat pocket. The whole family sit when he sits, and he regards us for what seems an interminable time, in complete silence. (Even Anne becomes uneasy in the end, and I know that she is wondering if she has smudged her lipstick during supper.) I am just beginning to feel a blush spreading upward from my neck, when at last he speaks. It is like the crack of doom.

'Well,' he says in a sort of doleful chant, 'how do you think you are going to like the land? I doubt if you will last long.'

There doesn't seem to be much one can reply to this. It is hardly a promising opening and we stare back at him helplessly.

'We had land girls in the last war,' goes on the voice dolefully. 'They weren't any good at all. Fainted like cut grass, one after the other, propping each other up against the hedge.'

A cinder falls in the grate and I begin to wonder if this is his way of preparing us for the sack merely on sight. I feel this is a little hard.

'It's hard work, very hard work. It's no work for a woman. I'll never let our Mary work in the fields. Hens – that's all she's fit for.'

Apparently it is the sack. I dare not catch Anne's eye, and privately decide to look up the time of the milk train.

'The fourth one isn't coming at all. She drove over to see me last week, and when I took her out and showed her the sugar beet she would have to lift if she came she said she would rather stay at home.'

We ponder on the fate of the fourth land girl in silence. We begin to feel she is the wisest of us.

'Well, what experience have you had? Only a month I hear!'

Anne finds her voice. 'Well, I think we've done most things, Mr Thompson,' she says brightly. 'Cutting thistles, manure, and of course the harvest. I drove the tractor once or twice, and I can nearly milk.'

'That's no good to you at all. It's sugar beet I want you for – sugar

beet, and maybe a week or so at mangolds. It's hard work I tell you –
very hard.' He shakes his head and we feel he is abandoning fools to
their folly. 'Ah, well, we'll see how you get on.' Mr Thompson gets
to his feet, giving a little bow, and he and his family file out again in
mournful silence. The interview, it seems, is ended.

'He's a cheerful bloke I must say,' says Anne when the door has
closed behind him. 'Perfect little ray of sunshine.'

She goes over to inspect the books in the small bookcase. She
runs her finger along the shelves, reading out the titles one by one.
They consist chiefly of bound volumes of John Bull and a few novels
by Jeffrey Farnol.

The door opens and Miss Thompson returns. Her smile is still
encouraging.

'Would you like to come and see where you will eat? You're to
have this room for yourselves. We live in the morning-room next
door. You will be able to hear the wireless if you leave your door
open. Of course it does make it rather cold, but you will find you can
hear it quite plainly. I do hope you will be quite comfortable. Did
you have enough supper?'

We agree politely that we did, and can hear our stomachs
shrieking at the lie. We follow Miss Thompson out of the room and
down the passage to a small square room where we are to have our
meals. It has a stone-flagged floor and a kitchen table. It is even
colder here than in the sitting-room. However, we admire it with
suitable comments. Then we murmur that we think we had better
go to bed.

'That's right,' says Miss Thompson, 'it will be an early start for
you in the morning I am afraid. Mother will call you at half-past
five. You will find candles on the hall dresser.'

I find the candles and lighting them we mount the stairs, shielding
the flames carefully from the draught.

Silently we unpack the clothes that we will put on next morning
– shirts, socks, thick woollen pants and dungarees. Anne is short in
stature and very round. I am tall and broad. However, owing to the
fact that there is only one size in dungarees so far supplied to the
Land Army, we both have somehow to squeeze ourselves into the

same medium stock. I am decidedly better off than Anne, across whose stern they fit with a creaking protest, for I can at least dispose of my three inches or so of bare ankle by cramming my feet into rubber boots.

We blow out the candles and climb wearily into our vast fourposter bed. We start on our own sides, but before long we find that the mattress slopes decidedly down into the middle and that we have to slide downhill with it. There is a strong smell of camphor and lavender, issuing no doubt from the mysterious depth of the red velvet canopy overhead. Outside our room there is the deathly quiet of a country night. We struggle back on to our own sides of the bed repeatedly, and at last by the shaking in my immediate neighbourhood I know that Anne is laughing.

'What's the matter?' I say crossly.

'Oh, dear,' Anne gasps, 'I was just thinking of old Mr Doomsday. No wonder the rest of the family look so tragic. Did you see the son? The red-haired one?'

'Yes, he sat on the back of the couch and never said a single word!'

'He's got the biggest brown eyes I've ever seen. And Mary! What a disappointment it was when she got into the light. I did so hope she'd be wearing kilts.'

'She's not bad-looking you know if she would only let herself live. Still, in a family like this, one can't really blame her. It must be a case of living as the Romans do, or, as one might say, as the Romans don't.'

'It's rather a blow Pauline coming, Bee. It means that you and I will have to bear with her. If only there had been four of us we could have left her with the other one and gone off by ourselves.'

'Oh well, perhaps she will have improved. I used to be pretty beastly too when I was at school. She used to dislike me just as much as I disliked her.'

We lie and stare up at the darkness, each busy with her own thoughts.

'Five-thirty,' says Anne suddenly. 'What an ungodly hour to have to get up. On the other farm we didn't have breakfast till eight.'

'Ah! but you were only training then. Your farmer was being paid by the Government to have you. They didn't care how little you did because you were only there as an extra hand. But we are here to work, and I bet they will expect it. I can't see Mr Doomsday as you call him handing out money for nothing.'

'I suppose so,' says Anne sighing. 'Oh well, I daresay we had better try to get some sleep. Although how I shall be able to, when I am being continually flung into your arms by this confounded bed, I really don't know.'

'You don't mean "flung",' I tell her unkindly, 'you mean "rolled". You ought not to be so round.'

'Oh shut up!' says Anne. She hitches herself once more out of the communal valley and the darkness and silence close in upon us. We sleep.

CHAPTER TWO
Comes the Dawn

WE ARE WOKEN next morning by a gentle but persistent tapping on our door.

'Thank you,' I shout.

'Thank you,' murmurs Anne; but the tapping continues, and suddenly I remember that Mrs Thompson is deaf.

'Damn,' I say, still stupid with sleep. 'She can't hear. I shall have to get out and open the door.' Swinging my feet out of the high bed, I feel cautiously for the floor. It is pitch black in the room and I suddenly realise that I haven't the slightest idea where the door is. Fumbling wildly about I crack my shin hard against a piece of furniture. I reel in agony, clutching the injured part. The knocking continues.

'All right!' I yell at the top of my voice.

'Do hurry up and stop her,' says Anne from the bed. 'She'll have the whole house aroused in a minute.'

'Find the candle, you chump. I can't see a thing. It's on the table by the bed.'

I hear Anne sigh and heave herself into reluctant activity. There is a rattle, a bump and a fruity curse, and I hear the candle roll across the floor.

'Curse,' says Anne. 'I've knocked it over. Why can't they have electric light?'

A strong desire for murder mounts in my throat, but fortunately the knocking stops and the door is opened from outside. Mrs Thompson appears in the aperture, bearing a lamp and the light flashes on her vacant smile and is reflected in her glasses.

'Time to get up, girls,' she says reproachfully.

'Thank you!' we answer in unison.

She withdraws, taking the lamp with her.

'Hurry up, Anne, and find the candle. We simply can't be late the first morning.'

'Well, I can't find it,' says Anne crossly. 'I think it rolled under the bed. Do come and help, Bee!'

We crawl about miserably in the icy room, our hands sweep in the carpet in seeking circles. I am cross enough to hope that Anne's teeth are chattering as much as mine. I finally run the candle to earth, lodged behind the china chamber, and after a further search for the matches (which Anne has put down somewhere in her agitation and can't remember where) we get the thing lit and back into its blue enamelled candlestick.

'My God!' chatters Anne, 'I've never been so cold in my life.'

We begin to dress as fast as we can, pulling woollen jerseys over our flannel shirts and struggling into our dungarees. I have brought with me a bright scarlet scarf which I secretly have decided is rather fetching with my khaki. This I tie about my head. Anne has a woollen Balaclava helmet which leaves only her nose visible. At last we are ready, and we stump off in our rubber boots downstairs. These rubber boots are also only provided in one size. Anne's are far too big for her and mine are too small.

Mrs Thompson meets us in the hall and tells us that there is a plate of sandwiches and some tea set for us in our dining-room. She says we are to take our breakfasts with us in a leather satchel.

We stuff our mouths with blackberry jam and brown bread, and gulp down scalding tea. Both of us are silent. Neither of us feels at our best at six o'clock in the morning. We are just draining the last of the tea when Mrs Thompson hurries in and tells us that the farm steward is waiting for us at the back door. I am too sleepy to remember that I am in Scotland, and I vaguely wonder whether a steward is some sort of conveyance. It proves, however, to be a burly individual with an even more indecipherable accent than the Thompsons', and who appears to be known as 'Tam'.

Tam greets us kindly with a hand grasp that is so agonising I have to flex my fingers to regain any feeling in them.

'Come along to the stable,' he says, speaking as if his mouth is filled with hot potato, and getting more r's rolled into an r-less sentence than I would have believed possible. 'You'll get a ride down to the fields in the carts.' He carries a storm lantern in one hand and in the other is a gnarled walking-stick with a carved handle. The night is still black and I can see no sign of any dawn.

'How on earth do we work in this?' Anne whispers. 'I can't see a thing.'

We follow Tam with squelching feet and our skins shrink from the freezing air. Round the edges of the puddles where the mud is crisply crusted with frost I can hear the tinkle of cat-ice. By the stable there is a bustling of people. A stream of carts are creaking away down the road and the clump of horses' hooves rings out in the silence. One cart remains and Tam takes us over and introduces us to the driver, who, it seems, has been detailed to wait for us.

'This is my son, Ian,' Tam says. It is still too dark to see Ian clearly but we glimpse by the swinging light of the lantern a tall, gaunt man with hollow cheeks.

'Pleased to meet you,' says Ian, and turns his back while he does something to the harness on his horse's head.

There are several people in the stableyard, and although they seem busy about their work, we are conscious that we are under an intense scrutiny. It is most disturbing, and we are thankful when Tam tells us to get up into the cart. We are stiff and we struggle up awkwardly, slipping with our rubbery feet on the frosty hubs of the wheels. Ian swings himself easily on to the front and the horse moves forward.

'Ian will show you what to do,' calls the steward, and we watch the light of his lantern growing smaller and smaller as the cart turns out of the stableyard and follows the others down the road. Ian sits silently clicking to his horse, and Anne and I are too shy to attempt to talk to him. We perch uncomfortably on the sharp edge of the cart and vainly try to ease our sterns against its persistent jolting. The ride is long. It seems to us to be going on forever, and we are amazed by the apparent size of the farm. We watch the sky lighten in a blue band towards the east and gradually the sun hangs out its golden flags of dawn. It is bitterly cold and I blow through my woollen gloves in an attempt to warm my fingers, but I only succeed in making them clammy.

'I haven't got on nearly enough clothes,' says Anne. 'I am going to be absolutely frozen.'

'Put it in the present tense,' I reply, and miserably beat my feet on the hollow floor of the cart.

When we eventually arrive at the scene of operations it is quite light and the other workers are already busy. There is a line of men and girls spread out over the field pulling up mangolds and laying them in a neat row with their green leaves trimmed off neatly. They work with an easy rhythm, holding the leaves in one hand and then severing off the pendant root with a flash of thin, oddly curved knives. This process is called shawing. We get down from the cart and with one accord they stop working and stare at us across the field. To my amusement I see Anne flushing scarlet. I mentally congratulate myself on my choice of headgear, and decide I look slightly less silly than she does. This, however, is slender comfort, and still pink under their intense scrutiny, we set nervously to work. Under Ian's direction, we stand one on either side of his cart, each with a row of severed mangolds at our feet. Our task, it appears, is to go along the rows tossing the mangolds into the cart as the horse moves forward. This seems to be a simple enough operation, and we set to with enthusiastic relief. Our morale, however, is soon so shattered by the forty pairs of eyes watching us that we lose our heads and begin to fling the mangolds wildly about, missing the cart almost every time. Either they fall short and bounce off the tailboard with a bang, or they hurtle into the bottom, spin giddily, bounce up the wooden sides opposite, and out again on to the ground. A well directed one from Anne leaps off the cart and hits me on the head. Mangolds are not light. My head reels and my knees sag beneath me.

'Sorry, Bee,' says Anne from a hazy distance.

'Steady – steady!' says Ian reproachfully. 'Take your time now, take your time.'

With desperate care we try once more to hit the cart, this time with more success.

'This is as difficult as playing golf,' gasps Anne.

I dare not look at the watching workers for fear of the mirth I know must be in their eyes. When I do look, however, I find they have returned to work and are continuing placidly up their drills as if nothing peculiar had happened.

We work with a will. There is a second cart beside ours being filled by two small boys, and immediately we become conscious of them a feeling of inevitable competition is born. It becomes absolutely imperative for us to get our cart filled before they fill theirs. Ian is a gentleman. He patiently shows us how we can best and most quickly pick up two of the big roots at a time instead of singly, as we are doing. He is still silent, but we feel he is a little less aloof, and that in a certain measure he has adopted us as his protégées.

At last our cart is filled, and Ian ties the horse to the tailboard of the boys' cart and leads the caravan off to the other side of the field. Here a party of men are building the mangolds into a pit and covering them over with straw.

Anne and I remove our scarves and unbutton out tunics. Gone is the bitter cold, and we are both pink and shiny in the face.

'I'm getting good, Bee,' says Anne. 'Quite one in two go in the cart now.'

'It was awful at first,' I say. 'I never felt more silly in my life.'

Two more carts have appeared and we set to work once more. This time the driver is red-haired with a ginger moustache. His name is Mr Wren. He has twinkling blue eyes, and he wears a blue postman's jacket over his brown corduroy breeches. His waistcoat is brown tweed, and set in the middle of his chest is a large patch of pink rosebud chintz. I wonder fleetingly whether his wife is colour blind or simply of a gay disposition.

The carts filled, Mr Wren leads his horses away, and we wait for Ian to return.

'All this stooping must be pretty good for the figure,' puffs Anne.

'That's the only comfort – and when I remember that I used to touch my toes ten times before breakfast and think I was doing well! We must have touched them at least a hundred times already.'

We return to work and presently Ian asks us how we are doing.

We are working neck to neck with the small boys alongside us and we haven't much breath to spare for an answer.

The mangolds fly in a gold arc through the air.

The carts come in an unending stream and I begin to ache in muscles that I didn't even know I had.

Between carts we learn the trick of perching ourselves like hens with a mangold for a seat, so that we can snatch a few minutes' rest. We become slower and slower however and discard more and more clothing. The small boys race ahead, and their driver has to tell them to give us a hand when their cart is filled so as not to keep him waiting. We are bitter with mortification and are filled with a strong desire to knock the small boys' heads together but we are too weary to put on another ounce of steam.

'I'm dying,' gasps Anne, drooping like a plant on a hot summer's day, as she sinks on to her mangold seat. 'Any minute now I shall do a roaring pass out. Honestly, Bee, I can't keep this up much longer.'

I agree with her.

At about eight-thirty it starts to rain; or rather it starts to sleet but it is wet enough to soak us through. Back go Anne's jacket and scarf, and she closes her eyes with an expression of abject misery. She becomes slower than ever, for with all the clothes she is wearing she finds it almost impossible to bend. As a result she gets steadily colder and her shiny round face grows scarlet with the lashing sleet. I have piled my jersey with my scarf and jacket in the leeward of the dyke, and I hope that they will be dry enough to warm me during breakfast. My flannel shirt is soon wet through and my arms and face feel as if they are scalded; but I suspect that I am warmer than Anne, who is a picture of mute dejection. At last the sleet comes in a perfect storm and we all stop work, and scurry into shelter behind the carts. The other workers are a healthy-looking lot with tough, weather-beaten faces. They wear no gloves, and aprons of sacking are slung about their waists; the women have silk scarves pinned on their heads in a fashion all their own. There is a tall, lean girl there with a face the colour of a tomato, and she beams at us with laughing eyes. She is obviously a member of the modern school of thought, for on her head is a black beret set at a rakish angle, and while the storm rages she makes a screen of her man's jacket and lights the butt of a cigarette. Anne is very impressed. This is obviously a professional.

The sleet slackens, and a few beams of anaemic sunlight struggle through. We go back to our labours, stiff with cold from standing. I decide that tonight I shall quite certainly die of pneumonia.

Anne is beyond speech.

One-two; one-two; mangold, cart; mangold, cart. My head spins and there is a sick feeling in the pit of my stomach. As I stoop the ground rushes up to meet me, and as I rise the sky wheels about my head. We seem to have been working all day when at last nine o'clock arrives, and Ian, who is becoming more and more matey, tells us that it is now lousing time. Anne's eyes pop. We have no idea what lousing time may be. I have a wild desire to giggle as I visualise a universal searching in one another's heads. It seems, however, to be nothing so exciting. The others stop work and we all make our way to the hedge where our breakfast awaits us in a row of leather satchels. We sit in the lee of the dyke. I put on my jumper and jacket and wind my scarf about my neck. A motherly woman lends us an old sack, and this we spread beneath us. Our gloves are a saturated mass of mud, and we take them off and carefully lay them on one side. I open the satchel eagerly, for now that my stomach has come the right way up, I realise that I am hungry. The first package, however, proves to be cold bacon sandwiches, cut thickly and spread with margarine. The fat on the bacon is white and congealed, and at the sight of it my stomach turns right over and puts its face to the wall. I offer the sandwiches to Anne, but after a shrinking look, she turns slightly green and shudders.

'Put them away, for goodness' sake. Haven't I endured enough?'

I put them away. Then I decide that I had better not offend Mary by taking them home again so I hide them carefully in the hedge. This proves to be a tactical error as Mary apparently decides that we like bacon sandwiches, and we duly get them every morning for the rest of our stay.

The next package proves to be better, and we dispose of the blackberry jam and bread with all possible speed. There is also a thermos flask filled with tea. At least we think it is tea, although it neither smells nor tastes like it, having indeed a very definite character of its own.

While we eat, the sleet begins again and it is unbelievably cold. I am frozen through and through, and I can feel my wet shirt sticking coldly on my chest and back.

'Oh, misery, misery, misery!' says Anne bitterly. 'If you had told me a little while ago that the day would come when I would sit in a ditch eating my breakfast in a snowstorm, I should have thought you were mad. But here I am, just the same. Fate is a cruel jester.'

'Do you remember picking strawberries last summer?' I remind her. 'Do you remember what a fuss we made because it was so hot, and because the net kept on getting entangled in our buttons and because we had to bend our backs?'

'Don't,' says Anne, 'I shall dissolve into tears in a minute. It's more than I can bear.'

When breakfast is over we follow the example of the other girls and leap up and down, beating our shoulders with our hands. Our feet are solid blocks of frozen pain, and my boots pinch my toes unbearably. Our gloves have become frozen too, and in their wet and sodden condition they are too unpleasant to put on again.

By ten o'clock the sun is out once more, but the clouds are massed overhead threateningly.

'Going to be more rain I doubt,' says Mr Wren. We gather he means that he is afraid there will be more rain, not that he doubts the possibility of it.

As we perch on our mangold seats waiting for Ian to return, we notice that the women workers all seem to be looking at us with a new persistence. This puzzles us until Ian arrives. Then he draws me to one side with a conspiratorial air.

'I know it's not a very nice thing to say to a young lady,' he says apologetically, 'but if you and Anne want to relieve yourselves, the other women are going now.'

'Oh, thank you,' I stammer and clutching a startled Anne by the arm, I haul her off to join the party of workers who are slowly going out through the gate into the next field. Once through the gate there is a high hedge admirable for our purpose. Here the party halts. The women look at us and we smile bleakly back. They ask us kindly how we are getting on, and tell us encouragingly that we are not doing so badly. Then there is a silence; an awkward pause filled with expectancy. I long to make a move in the desired direction, for the cold and my breakfast are having their inevitable effect. Somehow, however, my heart fails me, and I mutter to Anne that I won't go unless she does. Anne mutters back that no doubt the others will make a lead in a minute if we give them time.

It seems, however, that the women are as embarrassed by us as we are by them. They look at each other and shuffle their feet and stamp on the hard ground. Once the girl in the black beret takes off her sackcloth apron. Hope rises in the breasts of the two land girls, but she only ties it on again elaborately. I have just decided that come what may, I must make a move when somebody produces a bag of toffees and hands them round. We stand and munch and look at the ground.

'Oh, well,' says the girl in the beret at last, 'we had best be getting back I suppose.'

'Uh-ha,' says the crowd, and mutely following them Anne and I find ourselves once again back in the field. Too late we realise we have missed our chance.

'That was a lot of use, I must say,' says Anne.

'Anne, I shall die in a minute. How long is it till lunch time?'

'I haven't the slightest idea. Time doesn't mean a thing to me any more. My minutes are numbered.'

We make our way knee deep through the saturated turnip tops, back to the two carts.

'Anyway,' says Anne bitterly, 'I doubt if they would notice if we did die. I'm sure they wouldn't care.'

Mr Wren greets us with a smile and his blue eyes twinkle.

'Well, now,' he says, 'and how are you doing?'

'Mr Wren,' says Anne solemnly, 'I'm a broken woman, I'm going to do a roaring pass out.'

'Is that so?' says Mr Wren. 'Come now, that's bad.' His eyes flash blue fire, and he clicks to his horse. 'Gid up there, Dint.'

'What did I tell you?' says Anne disgustedly.

Soon the rain begins again. The black clouds have laced the sky, and it pours down as if the sluice gates of heaven have been opened. I see Anne's bobbing face shining with rain on the other side of the cart. Long ago she has given up loading with two hands at once.

Now she picks up one turnip at a time, and throws them singly and with a mighty effort from her shoulder. Her hair hangs about her face in a lank curtain, escaping in tails from the sodden mass of her Balaclava helmet. My own shirt is so wet it hugs my form with an embarrassing faithfulness. I can feel a damp strip of vest clinging to my spine and across my shoulders. The rain hangs in drops on my eyelashes and trickles down into my eyes.

'If it's as wet as this after dinner, you girls will not be out this afternoon,' says Ian.

We can hardly believe our ears, and I can see Anne's lips moving in sudden earnest prayer.

At last the morning is over. It is lousing time again, and clinging to the tailboard of the cart, we drag our weary feet behind it to the pit. The horse is backed. The cart is tipped, and the mangolds descend in a tumbling golden cascade into the trough of wet straw. Mr Wren is standing there holding the horses' heads. He sees us, and a wet and bedraggled sight we must look for he suddenly tosses back his head and roars with laughter. I master a passionate longing to pull his ginger moustache.

We clamber into the carts, and as many workers as can climb in too. I find myself next to the girl in the black beret. She smiles at me and taking off her sack apron she offers me half of it to hold about my shoulders. I learn that she is the daughter of Mr Wren, that she is called Sally, and that she is seventeen.

Anne huddles in the bottom of the cart, and is too dejected even to try to protect her stern from the jolting. The journey home seems even longer than it was coming, and the horses' hooves splash along the puddled road.

We are met in the stable yard by Tam, who wants to know how we have got on. We tell him we are both potential corpses and he laughs and tells us to go in and get changed. He promises to come and tell us if we need go out again after dinner.

We pull off our boots on the step of the kitchen door. Mary meets us in the kitchen and asks if we would mind washing our boots under the stable tap before we come in as the mud does make such a mess. We say nothing, but look many things.

We put on our boots again with a struggle, our damp stockings sticking to their wet insides, and hobble painfully to the tap. There is a large broom there to brush off the mud. We hobble back to the kitchen step and prise off our boots once more.

Staggering upstairs, we drag off our saturated clothes, leaving them in a heap on the bedroom floor. We dry ourselves. The towels are little bigger than large handkerchiefs. Wearily we get into dry clothing. We manage to hang up our wet things in the kitchen before collapsing inanimately on to the sitting-room floor.

The fire has been lit in the little bracket but there is not much heat in it. We sit on the fender so near to it that our backs are in imminent danger from the flames. Still we are not warmed. We chafe each other's hands and sit on our feet.

The gong sounds and we go into the dining-room for lunch, here there is an oil stove lit, a shiny new affair with a little glass window, giving off a certain amount of heat. We crouch over it gratefully.

For lunch there is cold meat and rice pudding.

All through lunch the rain beats in a torrent against the window and streams in a silver river down the glass. The window looks out on to a grass bank and an apple tree, but it faces north, so that there is never any sun in the room. Today it is unbelievably dark.

We watch the rain delightedly with thanksgiving in our hearts.

'My dear, I honestly don't think I could have possibly survived the afternoon,' says Anne. I believe her, for I don't think I could have survived the afternoon either.

But the rain stops. We become aware of the ominous silence at the ceasing of its cheerful patter and we look at one another in horror. We rush to the window and peer out.

'Oh, dear God! Dear God!' breathes Anne.

The sun, watery but persistent, is striving to fight its way through the sodden sky. Every moment it becomes stronger.

'No! No! No!' says Anne, shaking her fist at it. 'Go away you idiot! I hate the very sight of you.'

'It's no use, Anne. He's determined to shine all right.'

'Can't we whistle for the rain, or whatever it is you do? I'm not going out again! I simply won't!'

'It looks as if we will have to.'

'I'm an ill girl! I've got a pain! My back is broken and my head aches!'

'It's no use. Come on. We'll have to go and get ready.'

Dejectedly we climb the stairs and change into our other pair of dry dungarees. We wind dry scarves around our necks and pull dry jerseys down about us. But in the kitchen nothing can disguise the fact that our rubber boots are wet through.

'I can't think why they should be,' says Anne, miserably striving to spread her toes in her twisted stockings. 'The wet ought not to come from without, and I hope it doesn't come from within.'

We get as far as the stable yard before the rain starts again. There is no mistaking it this time. We stand in the stable doorway with the other workers and watch the drops spurt up from the saturated ground in little silver umbrellas.

'All right,' says Tam at last. 'Get you away in. The lasses can stay at home this afternoon.'

Sally lets out a whoop of joy and immediately begins to make plans to spend the afternoon at the pictures.

Anne and I also let out a whoop of joy and plan to spend the afternoon in bed. I have a strong desire to throw my arms about Tam's robust neck.

We run for the house with our heads down, our satchels of tea swinging between us. We rush into the kitchen laughing and singing, and even include Mary in our all-embracing smiles of goodwill. We bound upstairs and slam the bedroom door behind us. We fling ourselves on to the bed, panting. All is well with the world.

CHAPTER THREE
Merciful Heavens

'I'M GOING TO have a bath,' says Anne.

She flings her clothes about the room in glorious abandon. She snatches up her ukulele from the mahogany chest of drawers and twangs it joyfully as she leaps about. She is quite naked. She stands in front of the mirror, striking a posture with her stern thrown out in absurd distortion. She pulls a face at her own reflection, and then catching my eyes in the glass, she laughs delightedly and begins to chant, 'Oh, I'm a wow,' over and over again, to the tune of, 'Oh Mr Woo.' She gathers her dressing-gown with a sweep and slings it round her shoulders. I lie and watch her lazily from the bed as with another swoop she snatches her towel and her sponge bag.

'Don't be long,' I say, 'and I'll come and have one too.'

'I'm going to be hours,' she says, 'positively hours. I'm going to lie and wallow like a hippopotamus.' She spins to the door. 'I'm even going to blow bubbles like a hippopotamus,' she says, and the door slams behind her.

I smile to myself as my eyes wander over the disorder she has left in her wake. A stocking hangs from a rail on the bed while another dangles from the seat of a chair. Her jersey, dungarees, and underclothes lie in a scattered heap on the floor. Her Balaclava helmet has been tossed into the middle of our aspidistra. Anne loves this aspidistra. She calls it 'Spital's Pride', and has already given it one treatment of aspirin. George – the ukulele – smirks flatly from the seat of the horsehair armchair.

Suddenly the door opens again and Anne whisks in. She shuts it behind her with an elaborate gesture, her stern stuck out at the same ridiculous angle. Whistling tunelessly through her teeth she slings her towel on to one chair and her sponge bag on to another. She gets a cigarette and puffing vigorously she minces over to the bed, tossing herself down beside me. She sighs happily.

'Goodness me!' I remark mildly. 'What speed! It must have been more of a promise than a lick. I thought you said you were going to wallow?'

'Oh!' says Anne casually. 'It wasn't possible. The water is cold.'

Suddenly she throws her head back and shakes with laughter. Her voice comes in a stifled gasp and tears stream from her eyes. 'Stone cold,' she giggles. 'Colder, much colder than stone.'

For no reason at all I begin to laugh too. My overwrought body relaxes weakly and shakes with mirth. I don't know what is so funny; I only know that I must laugh. I do so, long and feebly, and I am aware that I am not very far from tears.

'Oh dear!' gasps Anne. 'What a life! Any minute now you may stand by for a roaring pass out.'

We recover slowly and lie exhausted on our backs staring at the ceiling. Anne puffs at her cigarette. She hasn't been smoking for very long and she is not very good at it, but she does it with a great air.

Eventually we dress. I make Anne tidy the room. She does this by gathering her things into a bundle and then shoving them into her suitcase. She sits on the bulging lid, squashes it shut, and shoves the suitcase back under the bed. She puts on a maroon siren suit with a zip fastener up the front, carefully sets her damp hair and ties a scarf about her head.

We stagger down to the sitting-room, our arms filled with books, boxes of sweets, writing pads and ink bottles, and of course, 'George', the ukulele. We squat in front of the hearth. We pile cushions on the floor and languish deliciously. Anne produces some pink marshmallows from a rather sticky paper bag, and using a knitting pin as a spit, she begins to roast them over the fire. The room fills with a delightful smell of toasting sugar, and outside the window the rain lashes down.

I begin a letter to my family, but my fingers move slowly. I am filled with a drowsy lassitude.

'Dear family,' I start –

'Have a marshmallow!' says Anne.

It grows dark early and the maid comes in and wrestles with the blackout. The lamp is lit. Its wick is turned up and the spiral of smoke curls up seductively in the glass chimney. The maid returns bearing a tray of high tea, which she sets down on the little table.

This time there is an egg and biscuits and cheese as well.

'Watch that lamp, will you?' she says. 'If the mantle becomes black, turn it down for a bit.'

We promise we will. Lunch seems a long time ago, and in spite of the marshmallows we eat hungrily.

After tea Anne picks up 'George' and begins strumming softly to herself.

'You will now hear,' she says, 'a talented performance by Miss Anne Wilcox, that famous finger-wizard, the Mrs Formby.'

She breaks into a strumming and her foot taps in harmony. She has had to remove her cigarette while she strums, as to smoke and play and keep her eyes from watering is as yet more than she can manage.

She is in the midst of her repertoire when the door opens and in comes the lanky, red-haired youth with the brown eyes. We smile politely and he smiles broadly. He wanders into the room and begins feebly to twitch the curtains at the already adequately blacked-out window.

'Just to see if it was blacked out,' he explains.

He perches himself on the corner of the sofa and regards Anne and her ukulele with calf-like eyes. Anne stops playing, picks up her cigarette, puffs a long stream of smoke to the ceiling, and then begins to play again.

'H'm, you're quite good,' says the young man tolerantly. 'What else can you play?'

'Give me time, give me time,' says Anne.

This is approximately at six o'clock. At half-past eight the young man is still with us, and we are feeling less and less hospitable. He is still perched on the corner of the sofa, and he is running through his repertoire of conversation for the third time. We discover he is called Walter, and somehow once we know this we see that no other name would have been possible for him.

He says he will try to fix up a loud speaker for us, so that we will be able to hear the wireless with the door shut. For this we are grateful, but after he has repeated his promise for the third time we begin to wish he would get on with it and not talk so much. He also tells us that we ought to see him playing football. We accept the statement non-committally. He also tells us which horse will win the Derby. We take more interest here, but even this statement after the third repetition, loses its kick. We begin to wish heartily that he would go.

Anne looks at me and I look at Anne. We make several remarks of the 'how nice it was of them to let us have a sitting-room to ourselves' type, but Walter remains immobile. Anne has stopped playing 'George' long ago and is knitting a startling jersey of violet wool. I am still trying to write to the family.

As Walter seems impervious to hints, we attempt direct rudeness. Anne stops knitting and begins to read. I write intently. Still Walter talks on. He tells us that we just ought to see him playing football, but nobody listens.

At last, after ten minutes or so of pointed silence, Walter sighs and says that he thinks he will go and listen to the news. Anne and I brighten up at once and say that we think that a very good idea, and quickly return to our pursuits before he can begin talking again. He reluctantly goes.

The door has no sooner closed behind him than I toss aside my letter, and Anne her book. She flings herself back into her chair in a posture of exhaustion.

'My dear!' she says, 'what a man! What a truly awful man!'

She strums a liberated little ditty of gladness on 'George'. Then she gets to her feet. 'Come on,' she says, 'let's go to bed. I've never been so tired in my life. I'm aching all over.'

'What do you think it will be tomorrow?' I say. 'Mangolds again?'

'Please God – no!' says Anne. 'Never no more – no more.' But it was; and for many days to come.

We turn out the lamp, and collecting our candles from the hall dresser we go up to bed. The bedroom is, of course, freezingly cold. So is the water in the bathroom tap.

'Do they never bathe here?' says Anne. 'What's the use of having a bath if you never use it?'

We undress with all possible speed and I carefully set the candle on the table by the bed, where we shall be sure to find it in the morning. Anne produces the most incredible pair of pink meridian pyjamas, and some white woolly bed socks.

'Gosh! It's cold,' she chatters as she rolls downhill into bed. 'I never thought my old school pyjamas would see the light of day again. You never know, do you?'

I agree that one never does, and I blow out the candle.

'And tomorrow', says Anne as she turns over, 'we will have little Pauline with us.'

'Bless her little heart,' I say. Almost before the words are out of my mouth I know by Anne's regular breathing that she is asleep.

Next morning it is just as cold but there is no rain. Instead, a wind is blowing, chasing the rolling clouds across the sunlit sky. The wind teases the horses' tails, rushing across the wet fields and carrying with it the scent of leaves, wood smoke, and wet heather.

We are so stiff at first we can hardly stoop at all. We feel as if we have been beaten all over. Our rubber boots are clammy about our feet but, although our bodies are soon sore and aching, we are somehow in better form than we were yesterday. Perhaps it is that we do not exhaust ourselves with one wild rush but work more slowly and steadily. Perhaps it is that the rain has stopped so that physically we are more comfortable. Anyway we plod on less desperately, and Anne only occasionally murmurs that any minute now she will do a roaring pass out.

At breakfast we learn several tricks of the trade. We learn to pull our feet up into the legs of our rubber boots, where, for some reason, they keep warmer. We learn to save a little tea from our thermos flasks to pour over the outside of our rubber boots so that the warmth penetrates through. We learn that Sally is head woman, a fact seemingly accepted by the older women without resentment because she is the fastest worker.

Five of the men sit aloofly in the corner of the field, keeping themselves to themselves with lofty seclusion. These, it seems, are five Irishmen – seasonal workers – employed by the piece, who come to England for work during the winter and return to Ireland in the summer to sleep off their well-earned fortune. They are quite friendly and pleasant, on ordinary occasions, but at mealtimes they prefer to eat by themselves.

The day seems unending, and we become steadily stiffer. Everyone tells us that our muscles will soon become used to it, but we begin to wonder if the end won't have come long before then. We return to the farm for dinner, which this time consists of cold meat and prunes. We have tea in the field; there is a thermos flask of the same brown liquid that we have had for breakfast, also the same kind of sandwiches of brown bread and blackberry jam. For many years to come I am never going to be able to face blackberry jam without thinking of Spital Tongues.

We are depressed by the knowledge of Pauline's arrival in the evening. We are already possessive about our sitting-room, and resent the thought of having to share it with anyone else.

It is dark before we stop in the evening and, as we sit in the cart on our way home, we see the black mass of farm buildings looming stolidly up before a stormy sky.

'I hardly ever see the place in daylight,' says Anne bitterly. 'Dark when we get up: dark when we get back.'

We wearily wash our rubber boots before we pull them off at the back doorstep. We toss them into a drunken row on the scullery floor, and ignore Mary's reproachful look. We lay our saturated and muddy gloves on the top of the boiler. The boiler is, of course, cold, but we have a forlorn hope that one day it may perhaps at least become a little warmer than its surroundings.

Pauline, we gather, has arrived. We groan and take ourselves off upstairs. All day we had nurtured a faint hope that she too may have decided not to come.

CHAPTER FOUR
Pauline Arrives

WE TAKE OFF our muddy dungarees in brooding silence. We can hear someone moving about in the room next door. Anne suddenly stands in an attitude of acute listening. Her expression is bitterly resentful. 'Well, I'm damned!' she says at last. 'She's been given more than one drawer! Either that, or she is opening and shutting the same one over and over again.'

'Oh, well,' I say. 'The poor girl will need something to console her. Think of the horrors in store for her!'

'Do you think she might go home if we tell her all the anguish she will have to suffer?'

I can offer her no hope.

'Not if I remember Pauline rightly. She used to be a tenacious little beast.'

'Oh, well,' says Anne, helping herself out of my box of chocolates, 'I will grant her more than one drawer so long as she doesn't come and sleep in here. I must be allowed a little privacy.'

'What about me?' I say, removing the chocolates.

'Oh, you don't count,' says Anne.

We repair to the bathroom in gloomy silence and spray ourselves sparsely in cold water.

'Oh well,' says Anne at last as she rubs herself dry. 'I suppose what must be, must be. I dare say she will be bearable. Anyway, away, foul care! Banish all trouble!' She executes a little tap-dance with her bedroom slippers, flapping them on the bathroom linoleum. She begins humming to herself.

'Who's afraid of the big bad wolf,' she sings. 'Silly old Pauline!!!'

She minces back to the bedroom and pirouettes in the middle of the floor. Her blue flannel dressing-gown is caught tightly around her waist with a silk cord, and the result is strangely incongruous. So would one feel if one suddenly found a sack of beans dancing the polka.

'Dear old Bee! Silly old Bee!' she says.

She selects the maroon siren suit from the wardrobe. She holds it away from her on its hanger and brushes its folds tenderly. It droops and looks like a slightly bucolic ghost.

She pulls it round her ampleness carefully and zips it neatly to her chin. About her head she ties a bright green scarf, finishing it off with an impudent bow. On her lips she slashes a violent lipstick. Her feet are thrust into bedroom slippers and under one arm she sticks 'George' the ukulele. Nodding casually to me she pads out of the room.

'Bye-bye,' she says, 'I'll be seeing you.'

I cannot help smiling to myself as I picture the coming meeting between Anne and Pauline. Anne must be rather a startling sight to come across suddenly in a Victorian Scottish farmhouse, and I wonder if Pauline will be able to take it.

I dress more leisurely, and in spite of the cold I fling off my gown and stand naked before the dark mirror. I powder my body and stretch deliciously, my arms above my head.

In my own way, I, too, am determined to impress Pauline. I remember only too well my last encounter with her. She used to be a solemn little girl with large eyes and her hair cut in a heavy fringe over her brow. She had a big mouth and long skinny legs. In those days her heavy fringe had asked to be pulled, and, being a human small girl, I had, of course pulled it. Pauline promptly dissolved into tears. On being questioned by her mother on the cause of her woe, the truth came out, and, accordingly, next day Pauline brought to school with her a note of protest. This, our respected mistress had in due course received. I was a fat, plain little girl in those days, with a bush of mousy hair that hung in an untidy mass about my shoulders. I can picture all too clearly, the figure I must have cut as I was hauled out in front of the form, and soundly scolded. Nor have I forgotten Pauline's triumphant face.

Carefully, therefore, I select my most gossamer underclothes. I pull on my best pair of silk stockings, and triumphantly I adorn myself with a rather nice dress of a seductive blue. I look my best in blue, and in spite of the dull mirror, I am well satisfied with the result. My hair is matted thickly by the day's wind, but when I have brushed it, it curls about my head exactly as it should. I make my face up carefully, and finally pinning my best brooch in my bosom, I take up my candle and follow Anne downstairs.

I open the sitting-room door and sweep in. I can hardly restrain my mirth as my eyes take in the two occupants, but I manage to hold out my hand to Pauline with a lofty smile, before I sink into my chair with what I hope is quiet dignity.

Inwardly I am quaking with laughter. Anne is sprawled full length on the sofa, with one leg trailing on the ground. In her hand she has a cigarette in a long tortoiseshell holder, and this she is puffing languorously and tapping the ash abandonedly on to the carpet. Pauline is sitting forward in her chair, gazing into the fire. I see at a glance that she has become attractive since she left school. Her hair is no longer in a heavy fringe over her brow, but in long curls upon her shoulders. In spite of this, I find my fingers itching to pull it. No doubt this is from force of habit. She wears a scarlet jersey and a well-cut skirt. Her legs are still long but they are shapely with slim ankles. I am only comforted by the fact that my figure is now better than hers.

Pauline and Anne are regarding one another like a couple of terriers with raised hackles. Anne is being insufferably patronising, and Pauline is responding with a somewhat bombastic self-assurance.

'Done any farmwork before?' says Anne.

'Oh, yes,' Pauline retorts. 'Quite a lot. I like it.'

'How much have you done?'

Pauline is pinned down, and has to admit that she has only done a month.

'Oh, we've all done a month!' says Anne scornfully, and taps her ash on to the hearthrug. Pauline makes a comeback.

'Can you milk?'

'Of course,' says Anne, and I marvel at the misconstruing of fact.

'How many cows can you milk in half an hour?'

'I've no idea. I've never tried. How many can you?'

'Well, nearly three.'

I, at least, am impressed. I hope that Pauline isn't going to prove to be too earnest a worker. If she does, she will certainly put Anne and me to shame.

Pauline turns to me, 'Are you still living up North?' she asks. 'It's funny I never see you about. I don't think we've met since we were at school?'

I am stung. 'Oh, yes,' I say languidly. 'Still there. I should have thought we would have met at dances, or don't you ever go to them?'

'Of course I go to them!'

'How old are you?' says Anne, stabbing her in the back.

'Eighteen last week. How old are you?'

'Oh, nineteen,' says Anne, and blows a long stream of smoke. 'Barbara there, will be nineteen in the summer. I knew you were the youngest.'

Pauline is somewhat downcast. 'I was sure I was older than you,' she says, attempting to be cutting.

'Oh, no,' says Anne. 'We knew you weren't.'

We troop into the dining-room for supper. Now that there are three of us the maid refuses to let us have it on a tray. For supper there are sardines, biscuits, and cheese.

Pauline says she doesn't like sardines.

Anne and I say, 'What bad luck,' and divide them between us. Her biscuits and cheese are finished so soon, however, that I take pity on her and let her have some of mine.

'What is it like here?' she asks.

'Awful,' says Anne. 'You've no idea. I have never worked so hard in my life.'

'What are you doing?'

'Mangold-wurzels.'

'I didn't know there were such things outside P. G. Wodehouse. What do you do to them?'

'Put them in a cart.'

'Well, that sounds easy enough.'

Anne appeals to me. 'Did you hear that?' she asks. 'Did you hear that? She thinks it's easy. Poor innocent, you little know.'

'You go bouncing up and down all day,' I tell her. 'You stoop and pick them up so often your head spins.'

'And your back breaks – '

'And your stomach heaves – '

'And you only have cold bacon sandwiches for breakfast – '

'And all the time it rains – '

'And you get wet through – '

'And it's terribly cold – '

'And every minute you know that in the next you will be doing a roaring pass out.'

'Oh dear!' says Pauline. 'I think I had better go home.'

'You'll go if you are wise!' says Anne darkly.

After supper we go back to the sitting-room. We settle ourselves about the meagre fire and peace reigns. Anne looks at the paper. She groans.

'I wish we had a wireless,' she says. 'There is a wonderful programme on tonight.'

'Well, open the door,' I say. 'Miss Thompson says you can hear it all right.'

'Isn't it cold enough?' says Anne bitterly.

She gets up and begins to wander restlessly about. 'Oh, what a place,' she says. 'Look at it! Hideous wallpaper, a table with a green serge tablecloth and the inevitable aspidistra. Outside is nothing but the country night. The cows are ruminating in the byres, and everyone who can has gone into Auchterian to the pictures. I should like to go gay tonight and what can I do? Knit and read a battered edition of Jeffrey Farnell!'

'Turn down that lamp Anne,' I say. 'The mantle is getting black. Turn it down and it will burn itself clean.'

Anne fiddles with the lamp and at last the light fades into a gloomy blueness. The fire flickers feebly and Pauline huddles over it. She has yet to learn that no amount of huddling makes it seem any hotter.

'Do you play the ukulele?' says Anne to Pauline, picking up 'George' and setting it on her knee.

'No, but I can play the piano a little.'

'Play something,' says Anne.

'Yes, do,' I say. 'If you don't, Anne will.'

'I haven't any music.'

'I've got heaps,' says Anne. 'There you are, a whole bundle.'

Pauline goes over to the piano and strikes a chord. The aspidistra in its china saucer, dances on the top, and she lifts it down and sets it on the floor. She begins to play. 'It's flat,' she says.

We lie back and listen, occasionally joining in and humming the refrain. She is good. She sight-reads the music with ease and our feet tap in response.

'She sight-reads much better than I do,' whispers Anne.

The lamp light grows dimmer and dimmer. I happen to cast a glance in its direction and suddenly I let out a horrified yell. The chimney is blue and green, and the mantle is covered completely in black.

'Anne!' I say, 'the lamp! What on earth have you done to it?'

'I haven't done a thing,' says Anne in an injured tone. 'Only turned it down as you said.'

'Well, turn it up again quickly.'

We twiddle the knob anxiously and the light increases. From the lamp issues a cloud of smoke and fumes. The room is soon thick with it and our eyes begin to stream.

'I hope it won't explode,' says Pauline anxiously.

'If you ask me,' says Anne, 'the thing is going to do a roaring pass out.'

'I'll go and see if I can find Mary,' I say, and I hurry from the room. The kitchen, however, is empty of either Mary or the maid, and I can see no sign of them anywhere. In the scullery, however, polishing the barrel of his gun, I find the woeful Walter. In my anxiety even Walter is a friend in need, and I clutch him beseechingly by the arm.

'Oh, please!' I say, 'do come and look at our lamp. It is making the rudest smells.'

Walter grins agreeably and he comes with me all too willingly. He nods to Anne and Pauline and brushing them aside he gives a demonstration of a strong man taking over.

'Why, you've turned it full on!' he says. 'It gets as bright as it can, and then it gets dull again if you turn it too far.'

'Damned silly lamp,' murmurs Anne. 'Who with any sense would have a lamp like that!'

Walter turns it low and carries it out into the hall. 'Never mind,' he says, 'the mantle will clean itself and the girl can wash the chimney in the morning.'

He brings in the hall lamp, and we settle down once more. Unfortunately, though, peace has been banished. Now Walter is with us, and so far as we can see he shows no signs of going. Anne and I begin reading absorbedly, and Pauline wanders back to the piano. She plays softly and Walter goes and stands behind her.

'H'm! Not bad,' we hear him say, 'what else can you play?'

Pauline breaks into a Strauss Waltz, and Anne's eyes meet mine. Apparently, however, it is not long before even Pauline tires of having Walter breathing warmly down her neck, for she closes the piano and says she can't remember any more. She sits down in her chair and Walter goes to his old roost on the sofa. He fixes on her his large calf eyes. We hear him telling her that she just ought to see him playing football. Anne and I bury ourselves in our books, but apparently the conversation goes with a swing. Pauline responds by nodding and smiling politely. She even says that she is very interested in football, whereupon Walter asks her if she ever plays tennis – she just ought to see him playing tennis.

I glance up at this, and catch Walter with quite an amazingly animated look in his eyes. Obviously he regards Pauline as an enthusiastic audience. He has probably never had such an enthusiastic audience before.

In half an hour Pauline has undone all the good work that Anne and I put in the night before. Walter has obviously taken root.

At last we can bear it no longer. I yawn hugely and say I think I will take myself off to bed. Anne closes her book with a snap and agrees sleepily. Pauline, apparently reluctant to risk a solitary dose of the dashing Walter, begins to gather up her belongings. Walter turns out the lamp reluctantly, and we bid him good night.

We light Pauline's candle for her and she follows us up the stairs. We peer into her room. It is a huge affair, but Anne is delighted to discover that although Pauline has indeed two drawers, they are both considerably smaller than ours.

'Good night,' we say. 'We'll wait for you in the morning.'

'Good night,' says Pauline.

'I might have known it,' says Anne as soon as we are in the seclusion of our own room. 'She would go and encourage him!'

'Perhaps she found him a pleasant change from us. We didn't exactly welcome her with open arms.'

'Well, honestly Bee! She is the end! I resent the way she looks at me as if I smell. I probably do smell; but so would she if she could never get a bath. I can hardly remember what a bath is like. She and her two cows and a half! Just let her wait till tomorrow! That will show her what farming is!'

'She's got a half-day, anyway. She will have the afternoon to recover in.'

'She'll need it,' says Anne with satisfaction.

Next morning on her return trip from the bathroom Anne runs into Pauline already fully dressed. Like us on our first morning, she has bounced out of bed at once, determined not to be late. Anne and I have, of course, by this time worked out to a minute exactly how long it takes us to dress, and we stay in bed to the last possible second. Inevitably each day the second is a little more delayed.

Anne bursts into the room grinning delightedly.

'My dear!' she says, 'her hat! Just wait till you see it.'

The hat proves to be quite incredible. It is obviously Pauline's old school hat, and is a black velour with a curling turned-up brim. Pauline looks lost in it, her huge eyes peering out and upward with an infantile innocence. The hat is later to become a landmark of the farm. Pauline is unmercifully teased about it. Whenever anyone sees it, it is immediately regarded as something to be pushed down over Pauline's eyes, thus eclipsing her completely. Pauline gets very tired of this form of amusement, but everyone else loves it.

Anne and I watch Pauline closely as she sets to work. After her rather highly-coloured accounts of the night before, we are a little afraid that she may indeed be as experienced as she has made out. It is a great relief therefore, when she proves to be quite as slow and inefficient as we are. Indeed she works all day with a somewhat bemused air. It is as if she is in a daze, hardly being able to believe that this frightful labour can really be expected of her. She is working on the second cart, replacing one of the small boys. There is now no question as to which cart is filled first, and it is our turn for a change to go over to help the others out. It is well worth the extra labour for the satisfaction which it gives us.

Anne and I are probably as weary as Pauline by the time lousing time has come, but we would not admit it for the world. We comfort her patronisingly with the assurance that it is only a matter of time before her muscles become hardened. It is so very nice to be able to say this to someone else.

We are still a little guarded with one another, but during lunch our barriers are somewhat lowered. Being Saturday, we have a gala lunch. There is cold meat and not only rice pudding, but prunes as well.

Pauline's coming has caused an unforeseen complication in the matter of the stove. Anne and I have been used to standing it between our two chairs, and as close to us as possible, so that we get a maximum share of its warmth. There are now three of us to share the stove and the only solution seems to be to stand it in the middle of our legs underneath the table. This is altogether a satisfactory arrangement until we suddenly become aware of the most ominous smell of burning. On examination we find that the whole of the underside of the table is on fire. We quickly remove the stove, and hope that by saying nothing, no one will notice. After this mutual contretemps no one could really keep up any serious barriers, and during the remainder of the day, we are almost friendly. Anne and Pauline find a mutual bond in their admiration for Gary Cooper, although there is an awkward straining of the atmosphere when it appears that Pauline has a photograph that has actually been signed by Mr Cooper himself, whereas Anne's has only been enclosed with a letter from his secretary!

The friendship between Pauline and Walter also blossoms. Walter is with us practically all the day. In the evening he settles himself down with a large box of old photographs on his knee. He and Pauline pore over them together. They examine them from all angles, and apparently they fail to see the humour Anne and I find in snapshots of Walter lying naked on a bearskin, at the age of dot, grinning serenely, and closely resembling an infantile Mussolini.

Anne indeed remarks on this. Walter pretends to swell with indignation, and because Pauline laughs, he grasps the opportunity of pulling her hair. There is a decided difference between the way he pulls Pauline's hair and my own technique, and with a critical eye I decide that our Walter is becoming amorous.

CHAPTER FIVE
Giltless Gingerbread

DURING THE NEXT week Anne's roaring pass out becomes only a matter of time. In spite of all the assurances that we daily receive that in a few days our muscles will become harder, we grow instead more and more stiff and sore.

'I feel exactly like a deck-chair that needs oiling,' moans Anne. 'I shall never be able to stand upright again.'

The weather seems to be permanently broken, for daily we wake up to a grey and overcast sky. It is bitterly cold, and instead of the mealtime break being a welcome respite, it is only a period of minutes during which we become more frozen.

Anne daily piles on extra clothing. She ends by wearing everything she has got, and I begin to wonder why she doesn't add her meridian pyjamas. She is an incredible sight. Her own roundness of stature is increased tenfold by her assortment of jumpers, cardigans, coats and scarves, over all being the Balaclava helmet. She looks exactly like a cricket umpire wearing everyone else's discarded raiment, and still she stands shivering in the field. She is unable to stoop at all, and her immobility makes her colder than ever. In the evenings she complains of neuralgia in her legs. She refuses to sit upright in a chair and sprawls on the floor with her eyes closed, wearing an expression of martyred suffering. It is not often that she even has the heart to play her ukulele.

On the Tuesday following Pauline's arrival we have a change of occupation; but in spite of the change, Anne is no better pleased. The morning dawns so wetly that she has been momentarily elated by a wild hope that we may be allowed to stay indoors. Tam has other plans for us, however, and instead of mangolds, we find ourselves loading carts with manure.

The manure is in a hemmel at the back of the farm. The hemmel has had pigs in it for two years without ever having been cleaned out. The manure is upward of two feet deep.

We have met manure before in our farming experience, but never manure like this. Instead of a fairly tolerable commodity, keeping itself to itself in regulated clods, this manure is more suitable for lifting with spoons, than with the forks we are provided with. It is unbelievably unpleasant and smells overpoweringly of ammonia, and as we heave it up into the cart, it splashes all over us, spattering our faces in disgusting spots. The hemmel is enclosed from the air except for a small opening at one end, and it is not long before the heady ammonia has its effects. It begins to make us feel sick and dizzy, and we constantly have to stagger out into the rain to draw in deep refreshing breaths. My scarlet scarf, the pride of my heart when I first appeared in it, has already become sad and careworn: wind and rain have left their mark and it is bedraggled and spotted with mud. I find, however, that it can be made to act as an excellent gasmask, and I tie it tightly about my mouth; I have long ceased to care whether the manure splashes into my hair or not.

Our Wellington boots sink to the top in the mire, and at every step we take we are in danger of leaving them behind. When we do drag them clear they capitulate suddenly with a squelching suck.

The carts, as we fill them, are led away to a distant field, where the dung is emptied into little heaps preparatory to being scattered as fertilizer. They come in an unending stream, waiting two at a time outside the hemmel until it is their turn to be filled. Sally is with us helping to load at our end; she has a small kittenish woman with her who is surprisingly strong for her size. The men are in charge of the horses, and it is their job to lead the carts from the hemmel to the field where the rest of the women do the unloading. This seems to us to be a most unfair distribution of labour. We ponder bitterly on the old tradition that women are supposed to be the weaker vessels; so far on the farm we have met little to substantiate it.

We are in the midst of our misery when Mr Thompson arrives with Tam. He stands and watches us gloatingly as we work on. No words of encouragement pass his lips, and I am certain that he is longing for the chance to be able to tell us that he told us so. Tam's eyes fill with laughter as he catches sight of Anne, and really I can hardly blame him. In spite of everything, she still clings to every one of her garments. Not a coat has been discarded, and her face peers out from the circle of her Balaclava helmet, scarlet with perspiration. She stops working continually to wrinkle up her nose in an expression of unutterable disgust, and she constantly has to go outside into the fresh air to recover. I feel sure that the only thing that prevents her from prophesying her roaring pass out, is the fact that the hemmel with its floor of filth, is no enticing bed on which to subside.

Sally is a cheerful soul and the smell does not seem to affect her at all. She talks a lot, and we learn a considerable amount about her private life. She tells us she spends all her money and time at the local pictures, and she has an incredible knowledge of the life and history of various film stars. Even Pauline, who subscribes to a film chronicle, finds herself comparatively ignorant. Sally is also a dance enthusiast. She goes to the village hop at Auchterian every Friday evening, and we gather that she dances rather well. Her favourite partner is the baker's son, with whom she does the tango!

The small kittenish woman appears to be called Evie. She wears on her head the silk scarf that all the women, but Sally, seem to favour. It is pinned together under her chin, and on the top of it is a small black hat that has seen better days. She wears a neat black jacket, now sadly marked and torn, and some rather natty riding breeches. Her face is round with small regular features and it is shiny and pink from constant contact with the air.

She continues her work with an easy lack of effort, swinging up big fork-fulls of the heavy manure on to the top of the cart, well above her head.

Evie has been in service; and since her marriage to the dairy man, we gather that she considers she has come down in life. She is without any doubt at all, a decided snob. She constantly refers to 'my cousin, the schoolteacher', whom she regards as the only member of her family who has any 'class'. She also shows a pathetic interest in our own private lives, eagerly questioning us as to how many servants our mothers keep, and whether or not we run our own cars.

Sally is amusing and abundantly filled with life. She is tall and lean, and incredibly muscular. She seems to know every dance tune that has ever been written and she is constantly bursting into song.

She also knocks Pauline's velour hat down on to her nose more often than anyone else on the farm. She tells us that on the first morning the betting among the other workers had all been in favour of our going home again before the week was out.

'We never thought you would stick it,' she says frankly. 'It's hard if you've not been used to it.'

'There is still time for us to go,' says Anne darkly.

'Oh, come, Annie!' says Sally cheerfully. 'You aren't doing so badly at all.'

(Everyone on the farm always calls Anne, 'Annie', which is a further thorn in her side.)

The last day of mangold picking, however, very nearly does do for us.

We have been filling an average of forty-two carts each day, during the last week. On the last day of all, Tam is so eager to get the field finished, that the work is multiplied threefold. Extra carts are added to the caravan, and the dairy people come and work with us, so as to load as many as possible. Everyone works at full pressure. On our cart we have the added assistance of a small boy of the name of Willie. He is a hard worker, loading tirelessly at an incredible pace, but we are not long in deciding we would very much rather be without him. He obviously decides we are of no use at all, and he promotes himself to be master of ceremonies. He keeps up a ceaseless run of directions, ordering us about all over the place. It is with reluctance we resist the inclination to wring his neck.

'The back of the cart – the back of the cart – I must have them in the back of the cart!' says Willie. 'Hurry up there, Annie. Look where you throw them, now! That one came right over the top.'

A new pit is made; so close that it takes no time at all for the carts to dispose of their loads and be back again for refilling. There is no longer any time for a rest between loads. We seem to bob up and down unceasingly. The feeling of giddiness which lately has not troubled me, returns in full force, and I seem to hang in a black hammock, suspended between the earth and the sky. Instead of the usual forty-two carts per day, I count thirty-six during the morning session alone.

41

Tam seems to be bitten by a mad bug of urgency. He has cast aside his gnarled stick, and removing his jacket, he himself has taken charge of the stacking of the pit. His small black pomeranian, which follows him about unceasingly, sits disconsolately beside his jacket and howls with disapproval at the whole proceedings. Tam has become a friend of mine during the last few days. I have found that he is not unsusceptible to blue eyes, and I have rolled mine at him shamelessly. Tam, I feel, will be a valuable ally to have. It is he who is responsible for allotting us our daily tasks, and I have hopes that he will one day be persuaded to let me drive his tractor. He has already given me a ride on the pillion of his motor-cycle, rushing me back to the farm with incredible speed, and adding quite ten minutes to my lunch hour, even if taking ten years off my life.

When teatime comes therefore, Anne and Pauline draw me to one side. Anne is nearly in tears, and Pauline is so weary that she can hardly stand. My own body aches, and my feet are covered with blisters and horribly painful. None of us can bear very much more.

'For God's sake!' says Anne in a tremulous voice, 'make that beastly steward slack off a little. Sit beside him at tea, Bee, and keep him talking as long as you can.'

'Yes, do, Barbara,' says Pauline. 'If you can't no one can. I don't know what's come over the man.'

I settle myself beside Tam, therefore, and give him an engaging smile. I lead him on to talking. It is not easy, for at first he has a decidedly abstracted air. In the end, however, by a judicious display of my reclining self, he is led to forget the urgency of the moment, and with throaty chuckles he tells me of his memories of the land girls in the last war. They afford him much amusement, and from what I can gather his opinion of them didn't amount to much.

I manage, however, to get him well away, and by offering to fill his pipe for him I succeed in spinning out the fifteen minutes allotted for tea, first to twenty minutes and then to half an hour.

The soft straw about the mangold pit is littered with recumbent figures, all of them watching my efforts at vamping with amused eyes. I know that I shall suffer for this exhibition later, but the sight of Pauline and Anne, who are stretched out in complete and utter exhaustion, spurs me on.

'Well,' says Anne that night as she flings herself on to the bed. 'Thank the Lord that is the last of the mangolds! Honestly, Bee, at one time I really thought that I was going to collapse. And that awful little boy. I could have killed him! "The back of the cart – the back of the cart. I must have them in the back of the cart!" Murder would have been too kind!'

'What did Tam say we were going to do tomorrow?'

'Potatoes.'

'God! Well, at least they can't be any worse.'

A knock comes at the door. It is Pauline, who says she wants to spend a penny. No one can spend a penny at Spital Tongues without the whole house knowing about it. For one thing the lavatory has a demoniacal voice which echoes in all the four corners of the building. For another, it has a door handle only on the outside. Thus, once you are in it is impossible to get out again unless you have a friend standing by outside to open the door for you. The first day we discovered this, I was shut in there almost for half an hour before Anne heard my frantic bangings and came to my rescue.

On this occasion I oblige, therefore, and go along as Pauline's second.

When I return, I find Anne on her hands and knees crawling about on the bedroom floor. It seems she has been at my chocolates again, and there is a truant peppermint cream somewhere on the carpet. She holds the candle low and peers about under the bed. I drop down on my knees beside her.

We are so tired that neither of us is very far from hysteria, and in this state more or less anything appears to us to be vastly amusing. We giggle feebly and the search becomes increasingly urgent.

'It simply must be somewhere,' says Anne. 'We must find it. I don't want to leap out of bed tomorrow and step on it.'

Suddenly, an awful suspicion crosses my mind. Wherever Anne goes I notice the ominous crackling of paper. The truth dawns upon me, and, sure enough, on the sole of her shoe I see the truant chocolate already flattened to a sticky mess. Anne continues her search in ignorance, and the sight of her grovelling round the carpet

43

with the candle in her hand, is irresistibly funny. I give a howl of mirth and point helplessly to her foot.

'What is the matter now?' says Anne.

My laughter becomes abandoned. I am beyond words and can only point at her shoe weakly. My stomach aches unbearably and the tears stream from my eyes. Suddenly Anne sees her shoe too; her laughter mingles with mine and we roll about the carpet helplessly. The candle flickers grotesquely, sending long fingers of shadow dancing up to the murky ceiling.

Next day it is indeed potatoes. There are, fortunately, very few left to gather and, by dint of everybody helping, Tam hopes to get them finished in one day. It is to be another rush day – another twelve hours of ceaseless back-breaking labour.

We are divided into couples, and each couple is given a patch of twenty feet from which we are to gather the potatoes as they are tossed out of the soil by the digger. The digger must not be kept waiting at the top and each strip must be clear before a new lot of potatoes are uprooted. All the time, therefore, we are racing to be ready, frantically scrabbling in the soil and gathering the potatoes into battered buckets.

It is a glorious day with fleeting sun and shadow. The pair of horses pulling the digger arch their necks and pick their feathered hooves high with a mincing step. Their wise heads nod in unison, and their glorious coats gleam like satin in the sun. Tam loves his horses and it bodes ill for any man who turns out with his charges improperly cleaned. The two in the digger today are Dot and Dint, Mr Wren's especial pride. Dint is a young one which he is still training, and her real name is Dainty, abbreviated by one and all to Dint. They are black and white, and their markings are perfectly matched. The beauty of their powerful limbs, coupled with their graceful motion, fills me with wonder, and I long to trap it so that I can keep the picture with me always. Mr Wren has plaited their manes and tails in a complicated pattern, with strands of golden straw. I decide that I must extend my womanly wiles to include Mr Wren. I must certainly learn the secret of such artistry.

While we sit in the hedge eating our breakfast (the usual cold bacon sandwiches, followed by blackberry jam; we have long ago learned to swallow the bacon sandwiches rather than go hungry), my eyes seek further than the striped earth of the field, and I raise them to the chain of hills beyond. The hills hunch in a line of green shoulders, the grass cropped close to the earth by the mountain sheep. They look glazed like the tawny skin of apples. Here and there, a strip of fir trees, planted to give winter protection to the stock, bristle along the crest of the crags like the teeth of a toothbrush. Little white sheep like strings of pearls hang in festoons on the breasts of the bills, clinging with their nimble feet to the steep mountain pasture, and occasionally bleating with their solitary cry. The farm with its grey stone buildings, crouches behind me in the hollow; and beyond it in the valley are the spirals of grey smoke, curling up from Auchterian. The river winds there in incredible loops, curling back on itself for apparently no reason, and covering many miles in the short stretch of country that it has to cross on its journey to the sea.

As usual, the five Irishmen sit in the far corner of the field, eating their sandwiches, alone. They are a dark swarthy lot, but by now I have learned to tell one from the other. They are gay, cheerful people, living by themselves in an old converted barn, concocting strange brews in tins over their stove, and sleeping on the floor on sacks of hay. Sometimes, as we wash our boots at the stable tap, a smell of roast rabbit reaches us, as they begin to cook their supper. Sometimes we can hear Paddy singing in his deep melodious voice. Once or twice, I have seen our Sally disappearing in the stackyard with Paddy; once their disappearance was followed by shrieks of laughter, and Sally emerged with her face even redder than usual, and her beret all askew, vainly striving to retrieve the handful of hay which had somehow got into her blouse.

Anne and I are as usual working together. On one side of us is Pauline, gathering potatoes with the tough little Evie. On the other side are Paddy and Mike. Fortunately Paddy and Mike prove to have hearts of gold; and really if it wasn't for them, I do not think that we should have been able to last out the day. We should certainly have been disgraced by keeping the digger waiting while we disposed of the last few feet of our littered strip. As it is, the two Irishmen finish their own strip long before they need, and they work on and help us with the end of ours. By lousing time I have decided that never again will I hear another word said against the Irish. They are the salt of the earth!

Long before the day is out Anne and I are down on our knees crawling in the soil rather than stoop any more. There is a searing pain as of hot iron across our backs and behind our thighs. Potato picking is far worse than mangolds, where at least we stooped and rose alternately.

Anne announces, when we stop for lunch, that this really is the end. She has done her best. She has given her muscles time to become hardened, but they show no sign of doing so. Every day she has awakened with the hope that this day at least will bring less suffering. Each day she has suffered more. Very well; Anne has had enough! She feels that there are other walks of life to which she is more suited. She is resolved to seek them.

During the course of the afternoon, however, when the ebb of life is at its lowest and our misery is most acute, a car drives up to the field and a firm little figure in a neat tweed suit gets out. It proves to be our Land Army Secretary.

'Well, girls,' she says cheerfully. 'How are you getting on?'

I feel rather as if I am a girl guide again, and I smile wanly.

'We are nearly dead,' says Anne. 'I have never worked so hard in all my life. I am a solid lump of misery.'

Our Land Army Secretary clicks her tongue disapprovingly. She looks at Anne as if she is a small girl in the middle fourth who has let down the honour of the Old School. Anne, however, is frankly rebellious and is beyond caring.

'What's the matter, child?' says the Land Army Secretary.

'We've done nothing but stoop ever since we came,' says Anne bitterly, her hand clasping the small of her back as she painfully eases her aching bones. 'We've never been in an upright position once, and I for one have had enough!'

Suddenly the Land Army Secretary becomes human. Her face breaks into smiles, and she pats Anne's shoulders.

'Poor child,' she says, 'but I am sure you would find it easier if you didn't wear so many clothes. However, I'll go and see Mr Thompson. Perhaps he will put you on to another job for a few days until your backs recover. Would you consent to stay if I did that?'

Anne condescends to say guardedly that she might, and the Land Army Secretary bustles away with her white terrier trotting at her heels.

I have already met a number of Land Army secretaries, and they have all had white terriers. Whether they join the Land Army because of this, or the other way round, I have never discovered.

The outcome of all this however, is that she brings back Mr Thompson with her and they come over to where we are working. Mr Thompson can't resist the chance of telling us that he always warned us that it would be hard, and that he has known all along that we would not be able to stand it.

The Land Army Secretary, however, beams at us encouragingly, and places her hand bracingly on Anne's shoulder.

'I've talked to Mr Thompson, girls,' she says, 'and he has promised to give you a rest. You will have a new job on Monday. Isn't that lovely?'

'What are we going to do?' says Anne with noticeable lack of enthusiasm.

'Spreading manure,' says Mr Thompson gloomily. 'It's hard work. It's no work for women.'

The Land Army Secretary cuts in hastily with her cheery smile.

'There!' she says, metaphorically wiping away Anne's tears. 'I am sure you will find spreading manure a lot easier. Goodbye my dears. I'll be over to see you again soon.'

She picks her way briskly back to her car, her brilliantly-polished brogues twinkling brightly in the mud of the field. The terrier startles a rabbit from the hedge, but comes obediently to heel. The two of them climb into the car, and soon all that is left of them is the smell from the exhaust.

'Well, that's something,' says Pauline. 'At least we ought to be working upright spreading manure. It will be a change from this everlasting stooping.'

'I'll give it one day!' says Anne. 'I'll give it one day's trial, and if

47

that fails me too it will be the end. I really will go.'

And we know she means it. I hope earnestly that the manure will prove to be all the honey that our secretary seems to think, for I will be sorry indeed to lose my Anne. We have become so used to her with her Balaclava helmet, and her roaring pass out, not to speak of the maroon siren suit and 'George' the ukulele, that things would not be the same at all if she were to go.

The last drill of potatoes are gathered as the November sun sinks in the evening sky. Even the old-timers are weary, for the day bas been long and arduous. As for us? it is all we can do to clamber up into the carts and be carried home.

Tomorrow is Saturday. We eat our suppers (a shepherd's pie made in a teacup saucer, and hardly sufficient to satisfy one land girl with an appetite), and sprawl out over the sitting-room floor. There is a knock on the door. We know it cannot be Walter, because he has by now so adopted our sitting-room as his natural home from home, that he has taken his welcome long ago for granted. It proves to be Mr Thompson. In one hand he has a small brown attaché case, and in the other a roll of wages. Friday night is pay night, and he has come to deliver us our earnings. It is a big moment when he calls out our names in turn, and hands us a ten shilling note and few coins. It is still a big moment when we find we have to return to him one of the coins for dole and another one for our health insurance. We are left with eight shillings odd, and in the pride of wage earning we fail to realise that, in fact, all that our labours have achieved for us is our board and keep, and a little over a shilling a day for ourselves.

'Hard-earned money, eh?' says Mr Thompson with gloomy pleasure. 'I told you it would be no work for women!'

CHAPTER SIX
Out with Walter

THE NEXT DAY is Saturday and we spend the morning in going over the potato field with a fine-toothed comb, collecting all the potatoes that we missed the day before, and following the chain harrow as its teeth unearth them from partial burial in the soft soil.

At lunchtime we are free. It is a wonderful feeling to be able to linger over our meal, reading the letters which have come in by the morning's mail, and knowing that we have absolutely nothing that we are compelled to do for a whole day and a half.

Anne has received a letter from Mrs Formby enclosing George's autograph and a photo of him playing the ukulele. This cheers her up tremendously, and instead of sitting inanimately as she has done of late, her conversation regains a little of its old perkiness.

I have a letter from home, full of concern for my well-being, and urging me to 'tell them you are feeling tired. Tell them you are going to take a day off, and stay in bed,' and to 'be sure and give it up if it is too much for you'. I cannot resist a smile as the absurdity strikes me of confessing to Mr Thompson that 'I am a little overtired and I want to sleep it off'. Lately, my fingers have been too stiff and sore to be able to write home much, but I determine to do so after lunch. I decide I will draw them a lurid picture of our sufferings. After all there is no fun in being a martyr if no one knows that you are one.

The afternoon passes pleasantly. Anne and Pauline are still rather guarded with each other, however, and Pauline's chief way of annoying Anne is to join in with her ukulele, and sing the refrains of her songs all out of tune. She has found that this annoys Anne intensely. Although the neutrality is armed, therefore, we manage on the whole to get on together fairly well. If only Pauline had not struck up such an unfortunate friendship with the woeful Walter, we would willingly have met her more than half-way.

Sure enough, the day has not advanced very far before the sitting-room door opens and the gentleman in question looks in. For once, however, he has a trick up his sleeve that we have not suspected, and including us all in his sunny smile, he asks us if we would care to go into Auchterian with him to spend the evening at the pictures.

Spital Tongues is a desolate place with few buses passing through it, and so far we have not escaped from it during the whole time we have been there. An invitation to go out, therefore, even from Walter, is as manna for the starving, and almost embracing him in our joy, we dash upstairs to get ready. We dress hurriedly, putting on our best clothes and covering ourselves with scent. We feel the expedition is in the nature of a gala affair, and externally at least, we are determined to do it justice.

'Let Pauline sit in the front with him,' says Anne, dabbing her nose blindly with a liberal supply of powder. 'He only wants her really; he has had to ask us as well just as camouflage.'

By speedy manoeuvring, therefore, Anne and I plant Pauline on the front seat of the car, and happily we bowl out of the stable yard and away down the road. Walter talks unceasingly on his old topics but we even forgive him this. (We have discovered that it is he who is responsible for the bound copies of *John Bull*: also a shelf of prize books that can be obtained by collecting coupons out of packets of soap – a series of *Handyman in the Home*, *Handyman in the Garden*, *Handyman in the Office*, etc. If Walter has read half of these volumes he must be a handy man indeed.)

Pauline and Walter get along excellently. Anne and I think that their talk consists of a series of platitudes, but they both seem well content with one another.

'Pretty scenery,' says Walter.

'Yes, it's lovely.'

'Nice trees,' says Walter.

'Yes, they are pretty, aren't they?'

'Beautiful! Think the rain will hold off? Hope so – the Boys are playing a match at Willeston today.'

'Are they? How nice.'

Anne and I kick one another's ankles joyfully.

Suddenly Walter turns the car in at a farm gate, and stops it by a manure midden, next to a hen house.

'Do you mind stopping a minute?' he says. 'I want to see a friend of mine about something.'

Politely we agree, and Walter disentangles himself from the steering wheel and gets out. He is away for almost three-quarters of an hour. We are extremely bored. We have long ago exhausted the possibilities of the manure heap, and the hen house has lost its anyway doubtful capacity for entertainment. Momentarily we become more impatient.

Finally, however, just as we are pondering whether or not we should borrow the car and go on into Auchterian alone, Walter returns. He gives no explanation for his prolonged absence, but simply gets in and starts his engine.

'My friend says he may join us later on,' he announces casually as he turns the car out into the road. 'He's a nice chap. He plays a first-rate centre-forward.'

Auchterian is finally reached. By this time it is quite dark, and all the shops have their blackout shutters up. Walter suggests that we might like to do a little shopping before the shops close. We agree, and arrange to meet him again at the car in half an hour's time. Linking arms, we troop off happily into the night.

I have never before seen shops so well blacked-out as the shops in Auchterian. They have intricate screens of plywood arranged about their doors, and it is impossible to see what sort of a shop it is until one is right inside. We plunge into a butcher's, an ironmonger's, a draper's, and a cake shop, before we finally find a grocer who can sell us a packet of soap. It certainly makes shopping a prolonged affair, and with this solitary victory to our credit, our half hour has elapsed, and we seek once more the woeful Walter, whom we picture sitting morosely in the car awaiting our return.

Walter, however, is not in the car. The car is locked and there is no sign of Walter anywhere. We stand disconsolately on the pavement growing colder and colder, but afraid to go away again in case we miss him altogether. Ten minutes go by before he at last looms up out of the darkness.

'Oh, there you are,' he says obviously. 'I wondered where you had got to. Come and have a look at the music shop over there. I'll buy Anne a new piece for her ukulele.'

We cross to the music shop reluctantly and go inside. We have had no tea and we are anxious to go to the pictures. The first flush of gala spirit has departed. We are beginning to be disgruntled.

The light is bright inside the music shop, however, and it is at least warmer. We wander about among the grand pianos, looking at heaps of music and turning over records in their square paper covers.

'I think I'll buy this,' says Anne at last.

'Yes, do,' says Walter. 'It's a good one. Now you Pauline. You choose one too.'

'Oh, how kind of you,' says Pauline. 'Can I have this?'

'Yes, of course!' Walter turns to the salesman.

'How much is that, please?'

'They are each one and sixpence.'

'It's all right,' says Anne. 'I'll pay for mine.'

'Oh, all right,' says Walter; and Anne has to take out her purse just as she was about to put it back again.

'I'll pay for yours, though, Pauline.'

'Oh, I'd rather buy it myself, thank you.'

'No! No! I'll pay.'

Walter hands over his one and sixpence, and outside the shop he pulls Pauline's hand through his arm. I hear Anne breathing heavily as she follows me across the road.

We go back to the car, Walter unlocks it and we climb inside. We hopefully imagine that the time has now come when we will be taken to a nice hotel where we can have some dinner. But not a bit of it. We sit in the car in silence for a while, and Walter holds Pauline's hand.

At last Anne can bear it no longer.

'Well; where do we go from here?' she says.

'We'll just wait for a bit. My friend said he would meet us here. I don't think he will be very long.'

We sit. The minutes pass and we grow increasingly cross and hungry. It is now half-past six and there is still no sign of Walter's friend. It will soon be too late to go to the pictures at all.

'What on earth is he doing?' says Anne, after ten more minutes have gone by.

'I believe he is having his hair cut,' says Walter. 'Nice lad, you will like old Fred. You just ought to see him playing football.'

At a quarter to seven Anne opens the door of the car, and quietly gets out.

'Look here Walter,' she says, 'I am cold and hungry, and I am tired of waiting. There is a café open over there and I am going to go and get something to eat. If you want to wait for your friend you can. You can come and find me there.'

'I'll come too,' I say hastily.

'So will I,' says Pauline, who has perhaps become a little perturbed by the fast way in which Walter has shown signs of working.

'All right,' says Walter, 'I don't think he will be very long.'

In the café we order ourselves some tea and muffins. They appear to be the most substantial things on the menu, which we see with disappointment, is disgustingly flippant in character. While they are being brought, we retire to the ladies' room, where we take the opportunity of making up our faces in front of mirrors which are actually light enough to enable us to see our reflections. I am appalled when I discover the ravages that a week of neglect has already brought about. My neat eyebrows have sprouted hugely, and I see myself peering up from under a thick growth of vegetation.

Anne and Pauline weigh themselves on a penny weighing machine. They get off it again hastily. In spite of the hardships of the past week, the overwork and the underfeeding, which they have only endured, buoyed up by the hope that their figures at least will have benefited, they find to their disgust that they have each of them put on three pounds.

'I honestly can't imagine why,' says Anne. 'Here am I, weak and worn to a shadow. The machine is probably wrong.'

I look at her burning cheeks blooming with health, and at the clear sparkle of Pauline's lovely eyes. I also look at their plump rotundities, and can well believe that there is nothing at all wrong with the machine.

We drink our tea and eat our muffins. We order a second round. We are well into the middle of a third before the café door opens and

Walter wafts in out of the night. With him is not one friend only, but two.

He brings them over to the table, and solemnly we shake hands. No explanation for the presence of the third male is offered. We begin to see all. Three land girls – three young men. The whole thing has obviously been pre-arranged. This is no casual gathering of the clans.

It is also obvious that the others have been previously warned off Pauline, who from the first is recognised as Walter's property exclusively. I am annexed by a small, dashing individual, the original Fred, and Anne is paired off with the third.

Fred is beautifully made, with slender graceful limbs and a shock of soft tawny hair. He has also a small tawny moustache, and his skin is very white. He comes up to about my shoulder. He moves gracefully on narrow slippered feet, and his smart violet-grey coat is nipped closely in at the waist. I find it hard to credit him with Walter's statement that I just ought to see him playing football. He has more of the appearance of a male ballet dancer, and I feel that he would surely burst into tears if a nasty rough scrum ever muddied his beautiful clothes.

Anne's beau is called Sid. Sid, it seems, is a clerk in an estate office, although he looks much more like the footballer that Fred is supposed to be. He is a dour, heavy-limbed Scot, with a shock of fuzzy hair that stands up on the top of his head like a built-up pompadour. He has no fount of conversation at all and after acknowledging Anne with a slow smile of possession, he sits quietly beside her and gazes at his boots.

Fred talks fast, interspersing his remarks with a series of heavy compliments. He also winks and nudges me in the ribs. He seems to approve of me and tells me so with alarming frankness.

'Some girl!' he says. 'Canny for cuddling, eh! Walter? Little bit of all right you are!'

He smiles disarmingly. He is obviously such a simple soul it would be ridiculous to take offence at him. One would be more offended by the admiration of a child.

'Lovely blue eyes you've got,' he says. 'Do you dance? I'd like fine to take you out dancing.'

Anne's shoe catches me a sharp crack on the ankle, under the table, and I feel the laughter bubbling up within me. I settle down to enjoy myself. I decide that I wouldn't have missed this evening for the world.

The boys order themselves some coffee, and we sit on and on. The hands of the clock above the door move slowly round, and still we sit. Half-past seven strikes, and then a quarter to eight. The dregs of our tea have long grown cold in our cups and the ashtray in the centre of the table becomes piled with the butt ends of cigarettes. Anne has smoked more this evening than she ever has before, and I suspect her of beginning to wish that she hadn't.

At last we make a move. We climb into the car, all six of us. Four of us have to squash into the back. Fred offers to take me on his knee but I thank him kindly and say I will nurse Anne. We park the car in a car park and set out in search of the picture palace. Walter takes Pauline firmly by the arm, and they disappear into the blackout. I have just time mentally to wish her joy when my own arm is seized by Fred, and I too am hurried off into the night.

I almost expect to be seduced there and then, but nothing so interesting occurs. Fred contents himself with pressing my arm tightly against his side, and he leads me carefully along, guiding me with admirable skill, in and out between the Auchterian lamp-posts and sandbags. I begin to see where he got his ability for playing centre-forward.

When we reach the picture palace we find Pauline and Walter are already there. Anne and Sid appear a few yards behind us. The boys each buy themselves a pair of tickets, and we climb the marble staircase till we come to a pair of swing doors. Inside the doors it is pitchy black.

'For God's sake make a stand, and all of us sit together,' whispers Anne.

We are ushered into an empty row, and accordingly the three land girls push in first and sit down firmly in a tight little bunch. This, however, is not in true Auchterian tradition. It is not, it seems, what the boys have been used to and it is not to be permitted. We are made to spread out, and rather than cause a disturbance in the already too interested picture house, we meekly submit.

The film showing is a Wild Western. Anne whispers that we have missed the only picture that we came to see, that she has seen the one showing already, and that we haven't even got in in time for the news. Anne, it seems, is not enjoying her evening.

I have never been to a cinema before where the audience play so large a part. Lusty Scots all, they have paid their bawbees, and they mean to make the most of it. They hoot with laughter on the slightest provocation. Cat calls and whistles of appreciation ring through the hall. They boo the villain whenever the poor man shows his face, and they stamp their feet and shriek with excitement in the final shoot-up. Our escorts have obviously been brought up to this sort of thing and they hoot and stamp and shout with the best. In one excess of enthusiasm, Sid plants his large boot on Anne's painfully blistered feet, and she lets out a howl of anguish.

'Sorry,' says Sid, and so far as I can remember it is his one and only contribution to the general conversation during the course of the evening.

After the film is over and we have stood up for 'God Save The King', we file out again into the night. Once more we are clutched firmly by the arm, and before long we have all foregathered again at the car. The night is bitterly cold. There is frost underfoot, and above our heads the sky is jewelled with stars. Beside the car park a river runs swiftly, impatiently nosing its way between the rocks, and swollen angrily with the recent rain. Walter makes no effort to unlock the car, and for what seems ages, we once again stand and shiver. The boys seem in no hurry to break up the party. They are impervious to the cold, and they repeat over and over again what a pity it is that there are no dances on in Auchterian as they would so like to round off the evening with a hop.

'Well, shall we get in?' I say at last, laying my hand on the handle of the car door. My teeth are chattering so hard I have to hold my tongue well out of harm's way; and the cold air rushes up my silk-clad legs, which are feeling unbelievably cold after the dungarees and gum boots which they have been used to wearing lately.

We part sadly, and with many prolonged goodbyes.

'We must do this again some time,' says Fred, as be bids me good night. 'Got a boy friend, Barbara?'

I assure him hastily that I have.

'I was afraid that you would have,' he says, sighing eloquently, and running his slim hand over his tawny hair. 'Ah, well, there's as good fish in the sea, I always say.'

I feel that this last remark might have been better put, but I am too eager to be away to my warm bed really to care.

Pauline is pulled to one side by Walter, and Anne and I get into the back seat. Tenderly Walter wraps the one and only rug about Pauline, and at last we are ready to be off. On the way home, we see him holding out his hand. Pauline's head droops forward and she seems to be asleep. The hand is ignored. Walter lays it on her knee, but Pauline sleeps on. Anne and I watch developments with interest from the back seat, but as Pauline shows every sign of continuing to snore, Walter's hand reluctantly withdraws. Anne and I feel a new respect for Pauline. She obviously has the situation well under control.

There is hot cocoa waiting in the hall for us when we get back and we wolf it down ravenously.

'I never seem to stop being hungry in this place,' says Pauline sleepily. We are later to learn Pauline never stops feeling hungry in any place. Walter lingers over his cup, no doubt in the hope that Pauline will linger too. She, however, seems to have had enough of his company and she yawns elaborately, and is the first of us to repair to bed. She hears us pass her room, however, as we go up a few minutes later, and she opens her door and sticks out her head.

'Honestly!' she says, 'what a man!'

'Do you think so too?' says Anne. 'We have thought that for a long time.'

'He's terrible! What on earth am I going to do?'

'I don't know I'm sure,' says Anne crossly. 'That is your worry. Ask Barbara here. She has had a lot of experience. Personally, I'm going to bed.'

'What on earth am I going to do, Bee? He is a perfect menace.'

'Who? The woeful Walter? Nonsense. He wouldn't hurt a fly. Tell him you are engaged, and that your fiancé wouldn't like it.'

I little know how this casual comment is to be taken up!

Once we are in bed and Anne is warm again, her sense of humour returns, and we lie for a time going over the events of the evening and shaking with laughter. The bed rocks beneath us, and the tassels on the red velvet canopy dance up and down.

'I've never done so much waiting about in one evening before,' giggles Anne.

'And when Walter said it was because he was getting his hair cut! I didn't know footballers ever had their hair cut.'

'It was specially for our benefit. That's what was so funny.'

'He was away long enough to have it permed.'

'He probably did have it permed! It was corrugated like a piece of old roof. What a party! What a wonderful evening!'

'It was all very well for you,' says Anne. 'You had at least got one that talked. Mine hadn't got as far as that, yet. I'm quite sure that if I'd prodded him he would have blown bubbles like a baby.'

We heave delightedly.

'And tomorrow,' says Anne, 'is Sunday. And nobody is going to get me out of this bed until lunchtime. Not if the house is burned over my head.'

CHAPTER SEVEN
Anne Leaves Us

ON MONDAY MORNING, when the other workers set off for the field, they go without us. Tam keeps us back, and after they have gone he takes us into the granary and fits us up with a large fork each.

He then introduces us to a small girl called Nellie. Nellie has only just left school, and we have noticed her before because she is always about half a drill behind the other shawers when they work in a line across the field. She has still a lot to learn, and we have often felt a sympathetic pity for her. She is just about as slow as we are.

Nellie wears a dirty flowered apron and an old blue dress with a trailing hem. Her nose is in constant need of wiping, and her black Wellington boots have broken toes.

'Nellie will show you where to go,' says Tam. 'It's not a big field, Nellie, you'll get it done by midday.'

We start out. It is a long walk and by the time we arrive, our boots are hurting us painfully. The field seems indeed to be fairly small, sloping upwards in a gradual incline to meet the horizon. The manure is spread out in small heaps (huts, Nellie says they are called), arranged across the field in lines. We each take a line. Pauline and I pull off our jackets and roll up our sleeves. Anne takes off her scarf, and then thinking better of it winds it again more firmly about her throat. We set to work.

At first we are meticulously exact with our spreading. Every forkful of manure is divided and subdivided, so that no two straws are allowed to fall together. As the morning advances however, this care is discarded, and by lunchtime we are simply picking off a forkful of manure and dashing it as hard as we can along the ground, so that it splits into pieces of its own accord.

The manure is newly carted from the farm midden, and it is heavy and sticky with moisture. The pain that we have suffered through our late stooping slips up our backs and transfers itself to our shoulders and arms. They begin to ache unmercifully, and in spite of gloves, the palms of our hands are soon covered with blisters.

Once more our first enthusiasm is dashed and the work becomes increasingly slow.

Nellie continually stops and counts up the huts that are still to be spread if we are to finish the field by lunchtime. While she makes these momentous calculations she rests on the handle of her fork and adds them up on her fingers. As a result she probably wastes more time than any of us, and spends longer in lamenting that we shall never get them spread in time, than she spends in the actual spreading.

'Eh, we'll never get them done,' she keeps on saying gloomily, amply punctuating her words with resounding sniffs. 'Try to keep up with the others, Annie. We'll never get them done.'

After the first half hour, Anne has made up her mind to go home. She says that she is in full agreement with Mr Thompson. This is no job for a woman and she is determined to go in search of kinder and sunnier climes. I try to dissuade her, but she remains unshaken.

'It is all very well for you, Bee,' says Anne. 'You are an absolute stoic. I don't know how you do it, but for me the end has come. Spital Tongues has harboured me for the last night.'

We are just able to reach the crest of the hill by lousing time, and are congratulating ourselves on a task well done when our eyes come up over the level of the skyline. There, below the hill we have climbed, the field stretches away vastly. Hut upon hut of muck march in lines to the horizon, and disappear in a mutual merging point. It is a nasty blow, and it is all we can do to restrain Nellie from shedding tears.

'If only Annie had worked a bit faster!' she moans.

It says much for Anne's self-control that she is able to let this pass without comment.

We limp back to the farm with our pinching feet, and our forks over our shoulders. There are no carts today to help us on our way, and it is a weary trail.

After lunch, Anne seeks out Mr Thompson and breaks the news to him of her impending departure. Contrary to what might have been expected, Mr Thompson is almost pleased. At last his prophecies are coming true.

We watch her start to pack her belongings. When we return at dusk she will be gone, and with her her Balaclava helmet, her maroon siren suit, and her ukulele. No more will we hear her daily prophesying her roaring pass out. The pass out will have become an actuality.

Mary promises to run her to the station in the car. Now that her mind is made up, Anne is repulsively jubilant. 'Ah, well,' she says. 'I expect you two won't be long in following me. You will never be able to stick this out, stoics or no stoics.'

The last we see of her as she waves a cheery goodbye is her craning person as she stretches up to give Spital's Pride a last dose of aspirin. I believe that if she had stayed, out of very shame, Spital's Pride would have put forth a flower.

After Anne's departure, things for a while seem decidedly flat, and we miss her cheery absurdities a lot. We think about her constantly, enviously picturing her wallowing in seas of hot water, and staying in bed every day until lunchtime. Left to ourselves, however, and of necessity living so closely together, Pauline and I become more and more friendly. We bury the axe of contention for good and all, and I find myself liking Pauline increasingly. As I come to know her better, I find her to be a surprisingly simple soul. Her rather overpowering self-assurance that had at first annoyed Anne so much, proves to have been only a cloak for her shyness. She loses too, as we become less guarded with one another, her polished air of sophistication. I find her to be incredibly young for her age and touchingly unsure of herself.

Almost from the first she accepts me as being her senior in general worldly wisdom and experience. She calls me 'Aunty Bee', and she asks me my opinion on many things. At first, I suspect this of being an elaborate leg-pull, but gradually I realise with amazement that she really regards me in this light with all seriousness. If she only knew how little qualified I am to give her advice! I determine however, that she shall never suspect this, and I try my best to live up to an aunt's reputation. Cast as she is into a cruel world, and away for the first time from the friendly shelter of her home, I see that she really is in need of someone on whom to lean. I determine not to let myself appear the broken reed that I am in reality, because I am quite certain that if I fail her, she too will pack up her bags and return to friendlier and more familiar waters.

We discuss at length many things, therefore, and after a time I begin to feel myself quite qualified to take the post of Aunty in a live letter-box. In particular, I have to come to the rescue over the matter of Walter. I find to my amazement, that Pauline is really concerned about him. She has never before had to cope with the advances of an amorous male, and she helplessly resents the attentions that he increasingly bestows on her.

And Walter, as the days pass, certainly becomes a nuisance. He simply lives in our sitting-room and instead of perching on his old roost on the corner of the sofa, he now takes a seat on the arm of Pauline's chair, where he can breathe constantly and passionately down her neck. Pauline seems to be incapable of taking a firm line with him. She brushes him off like an aggravating fly, and then, in the kindness of her heart and attempting to soften the blow, she rolls her eyes at him in apology. Like a see-saw, Walter doesn't know where he is, but after a time he learns to take no notice of the brushings and daily becomes bolder.

I do my best. I tell Pauline what to say to him and how to extract herself with lofty dignity. I tell her to harden her heart and throw him out on his ear. But it is all to no avail. With Walter 'pawing' her, as Pauline puts it, she becomes paralysed with alarm, rather like a hypnotised rabbit. At the critical moment all memory of my advice flies from her and all she can do is to push him feebly away. I even exert myself to try to distract Walter's attention. This is no use either. He never wavers, and like a child that will not be diverted once its mind is made up, he goes right along ignoring my efforts as much as he ignores Pauline's protests.

It is really too bad. After having spent a gruelling and exhausting twelve hours in the fields, it is too much of a good thing to have to come in in the evening, to wrestle with an infatuated suitor. In the end he succeeds in driving us to bed even earlier. At least, we are still allowed the privacy of our bedrooms.

The Thompsons view this infatuation of Walter's with approving smiles. Mary, herself engaged to one of her brother's friends, does all she can to smooth his path for him. Her fiancé, whom she occasionally brings to our sitting-room during the course of the evening, throws out heavy remarks of the 'Lucky dog, Walter. Wish we had pretty land girls,' order, and Mary smiles brightly and knowingly at Pauline.

We continue to spread manure for several days. The huts of muck seem endless, and we have no sooner finished one field than Tam sets us to work on another. At first I find the job novel, and it even has a certain unexpected beauty. With the cold November sun shining down upon the bleached stubble of the fields, stubble that has been scattered with manure, it looks like a cloak of tweed spread out over the shoulders of the farm, and woven out of a cloth of strangely rich and glorious colours. After a while, however, when the first strangeness of the job has worn off, I revert speedily to my first impressions. Once again I see it simply as dug and dying corn.

It is while spreading manure that Pauline and I have our most profound discussions. Out alone in a great stretch of field, with the bare country about us, and the wide sky overhead, we are drawn together in a mutual loneliness so that we exchange confidences in a way that would have been impossible anywhere else. We discuss religion, divorce, and socialism. We also discuss clothes, food, what will be the first meal we will order when the war is over, and our probable future husbands. Love problems being predominant in Pauline's mind, she is eager to know what romantic experiences I have had in the past. I feel that I must at all costs, retain my worldly wise reputation, and, very little wiser than she, I draw deeply on my imagination, and it does not fail me. Pauline swallows it all with an engaging faith, and is suitably impressed by the recounted stories of my skilful handling of certain amorous escapades.

This is a slack week on the farm. The sugar beet is not quite ready and the other workers devote their energies to shawing turnips. For two days Tam allows us a change from our manuring and we go and join them. Although once again we are back stooping, it gives our sore shoulders a rest; and we are glad of the chance of seeing something more of Sally and the others.

They greet us as old friends. They have heard all about Anne's departure, and they too are sorry she has gone.

'Eh! She was a funny one was Annie,' says Sally. 'All those clothes! She could never work in all them things.'

Shawing proves to be a skilled job, and although we all start out in line with the others, try as we may, Pauline and I are soon left far behind. Pauline is at first convinced that this is because the knife she has been given is not a good one, but after trying in turn everyone else's without any better results, she is reluctantly forced to realise that the fault lies not in her knife but in her own lack of skill. On closer examination, we discover that shawing is a little like serving a ball in a game of tennis. Although when watching the others, they appear to hold the turnip by its leaves and then to sever off the root, this proves in fact to be an optical illusion. The naked eye is too slow to be able to follow their flashing knives. In reality the turnip is pulled up and tossed in the air, and the leaves severed off when it is not being held by the hand at all. This is not easy. It needs a steady eye and a fine aim, so that the knife is brought down neatly on the fleshy stalk. It must be neither too high nor too low.

During the course of the morning Pauline complains of thirst, and Sally tells her to 'cut herself a baigie'. This is Greek to Pauline who has never heard of a baigie before. It is, however, only another name for the turnip, and pulling her a young one, Sally shows her how to trim off the skin with her knife and to scrape out a mouthful of the raw inside. I accept a slice as well, but I can work up no enthusiasm for it, and spit it out when Sally's back is turned.

As the work progresses, the field changes behind us from a soft grey green to a striped grey and purple. The dying leaves lie in untidy strips and in our wake is a neat row of small purple swedes. We are filled with an immense satisfaction when at the end of the day we go home, leaving behind us a long strip of shawed baigies. This is the first work on the farm for which we have had to use skill. It is the first time that we have felt ourselves really at one with the professionals like Sally, instead of being classed with little Willie and the other small boys. We feel that we are progressing, and we swell with pride.

The sugar beet crop is to start session on the Monday morning. On the Saturday I have arranged to spend the weekend with some friends. I leave Pauline reluctantly, having loaded her up before I go with good advice. I am rather worried myself over Walter, and I hope that he is in fact as harmless as I imagine.

'He'll almost certainly ask you to go to Auchterian again with him,' I warn Pauline. 'I honestly don't think that you should go by yourself.'

'Oh, I won't, Aunty Bee. I shall tell him I am feeling too tired. All the same, I do wish you weren't going away.'

'Oh, you'll be all right. I'll be back on Sunday, and if necessary I'll horsewhip him for you then.'

'I do hope you won't have to!'

'No, of course, I won't. If things are difficult you can always go to bed.'

'He is a blasted nuisance,' said Pauline bitterly.

I have a wonderful weekend, soaking my weary body in water laden with bath salts, and lying about languidly being waited upon. I am too lazy even to poke the fire. My hostess is gratifyingly impressed by my blistered fingers and my tales of woe, and I derive a great amount of pleasure from being accepted as a martyr.

I return to the farm laden with apples and biscuits, and boxes of chocolate. They at least will make a second front on which we shall be able to fall back when we become too hungry.

I am met at Spital Tongues by a cold and lamplit kitchen, very different from the bright lights that I have left behind me; but surprisingly not unwelcome for all that. There is no sign of Pauline anywhere downstairs, and I eventually run her to earth in her room. As I climb upstairs, I wonder how she has got on with the lavatory door; I wonder if she has had to leave it open or if she has been able to persuade Mary to stand outside for her in my absence.

I open her bedroom door and am greeted by a forlorn figure with a white face.

'Oh, Bee, thank goodness you are back. My dear, you don't know what I have been through!'

We sit on the bed and gradually the story is unfolded. Anywhere else but at Spital Tongues, it would be too fantastic a tale to be believed. Here, however, one feels that nothing is too absurd to happen.

As we had foreseen, Walter had indeed asked Pauline if she would care to spend Saturday evening with him at Auchterian. Pauline had thanked him kindly, but refused.

In a little while, however, Mary had appeared in the sitting room doorway. She was wearing her tweed coat and hat, and was obviously all ready for going out.

'Won't you come with us, Pauline?' said Mary persuasively. 'It must be lonely being here all by yourself.'

Pauline hesitated and was lost. She forgot how Mary's sympathies were all for Walter. All she thought was that if Mary was there, things would be all right.

But she was wrong. What actually happened of course, was that when they got to Auchterian, Mary went off and joined her fiancé, and Pauline and Walter were left alone for the evening.

This time there was no waiting about. They went straight to the pictures, and there they sat for hours, Walter holding the reluctant Pauline's hand. Nothing much happened, however, so long as the picture was showing, for Walter, having paid for his ticket, was content to get his full money's worth and Pauline could wait.

When the show was over, they left. They had arranged to meet Mary and her fiancé in the street outside the picture house. It was by now pitchy black, and there were no stars or moon to light up their way. Neither was there any sign of the sister Mary. She had no doubt been well schooled.

'Ah, well,' said Walter, justifiably satisfied by the way things were going, 'we'll just have to wait. I daresay they won't be very long.'

He pulled Pauline to him and clasped her clumsily to his manly bosom. Pauline pushed him away and dodged into the darkness on the other side of a marble pillar. Walter dodged after her. For several minutes they must have played a breathless chase round and round the mulberry bush. Walter finally cornered Pauline by the ticket office. By this time his fighting blood was up. He clasped her reluctant person firmly, and wedging her wriggling head against his shoulder, he tried to kiss her.

Pauline thought wildly, 'Oh, my God; what on earth would Aunty Bee tell me to do now?'

And suddenly into her brain rushed the words of wisdom that I had once spoken in jest.

'Don't, Walter!' she spluttered. 'Christopher wouldn't like it!'

Walter released her like a hot brick. 'And who is Christopher?' he asked.

'Christopher and I have an understanding!' said Pauline, primly setting her hat straight.

'My God!' said Walter dramatically gnashing his teeth in the night. 'I thought there was something like this.'

Pauline had now regained a little of her self-possession, and once having created Christopher she went on to elaborate him. He was a Harley Street specialist, several years older than she who was the brother of a school friend. They were waiting until she was twenty-one before making their engagement official.

'I've never heard you speak of all this before,' said Walter suspiciously.

'Well, it's meant to be a secret,' said Pauline. 'I wouldn't have told you now if you hadn't been so silly.'

She continued to elaborate Christopher during the rest of their long wait. She gave him black hair, blue eyes, and a lot of money. I believe she was really describing Gary Cooper.

Walter relapsed into gloomy silence. At last he sighed deeply.

'I had meant to bring you to the pictures again next Saturday,' said Walter. 'Now I shall go and get drunk instead.'

With this awful threat ringing in the night, a car drew up by the kerb, and Mary's fiancé got out.

'So sorry to keep you waiting,' he said heartily, shoving Pauline and her ex-suitor together into the back seat. 'But I don't suppose you minded, eh, Walter?'

All the way home the silent couple in the back had to endure a stream of jibes of this heavy brand of humour. Obviously, the two in the front had taken it for granted that with such a wonderful opportunity, Walter could not possibly have failed to ring the bell. It must have been as sickening a journey home for Walter as it was for poor Pauline.

Pauline was utterly exhausted when finally they arrived at the farm, and at last she was able to creep off to bed. She had been badly shaken. Her first experiences with an amorous male had been unfortunate to say the least of it, and she was beginning to think that if this was that thing called 'love' it was not all it was cracked up to be.

On the following day she had to endure silent meals with the family. She was asked to eat with them since she was by herself, and the atmosphere was unbearably strained. Walter had apparently told them of his failure, and the other Thompsons were plunged in gloom.

Apart from meals, Pauline had spent the whole day in her room. 'I've been counting the minutes until you got back,' she said. 'I've never been so glad in my life to see anyone before!'

From that day she makes me promise never again to leave her alone with Walter. I therefore expand my aunty duties and every evening we cling to each other like a couple of leeches. And believe it or not it is still necessary, for in spite of his failure, Walter continues to haunt our sitting-room each evening. He takes up his old perch on the sofa, and sits silent by the hour, carroty hair on end, staring hopefully at Pauline with his large bovine eyes. We find that he even goes so far as to watch her mail as she puts it out on the hall dresser to be posted. In order to support the hypothetical Christopher, therefore, Pauline has to write him long love letters, putting them in an envelope, and sending them to an imaginary address in Harley Street. They are, no doubt, still lying somewhere in the 'unknown' department of His Majesty's post office.

Sugar beet begins in earnest on the Monday morning. We each set off for the field armed with a sharp shawing knife, and the most back-breaking fortnight of all our labours begins. The sugar beet is a long vegetable, rather like a giant carrot, and it is a tough proposition to pull it up out of the ground. Mr Wren has been along the drills already, ploughing up the soil with Dot and Dint, so that the beet have been partially dug up. Even so, many of them have been missed, and to pull them free, we have to kick them loose with the heels of our rubber boots. When our feet are frozen by the frosty earth, this job is most painful.

Each drill of beet has to be gone over twice. First to pull the roots up, beat them together to shake off the soil, and then to lay them down in neat rows ready for being shawed. Then we have to go back again cutting off the limp leaves and tossing the beet into heaps ready to be loaded into carts. The leaves of the beet are crisp with frost, and walking among them in the early morning we are soon wet through. We tie sacks about our waists like the other workers. But even these fail to prevent us getting covered with wet earth. Cutting off the leaves is easy, but to go the whole length of a drill with one's back bent, is gruelling work. It is a great mistake, we find, to attempt to stand up straight in the middle. If one does, it only makes the dull ache an acute agony, and it is harder than ever to continue to bend. It takes us about two hours to shaw a drill of beet, and we grind our teeth and try to tell ourselves that we will not look up again until we have reached the end. Once there, we allow ourselves to collapse, and sinking on to the wet earth we lie stretched full length among the drills. Pauline asks me constantly what the time is. My watch, a miracle of fortitude in itself, goes on ticking away, in spite of the frequent bumps it gets, and in spite of being continually soaked in dew. The days, however, are very, very long. If we had not had a week's training at loading mangolds, I am sure we would have been incapable of standing it. It seems that in spite of us our muscles are at last becoming tougher.

And then we begin loading. The field lies prepared, in wide stripes of green and yellow; our hands are horny from the shawing knife, and stained purple with the bleeding juice of the leaves. We not only use carts to load the beet, but also a tractor with a small wooden truck hitched on behind. This truck is in the nature of an experiment. It has never been tried at Spital Tongues before, and there is a long debate between Tam and Alec, the driver, as to whether or not the tractor is strong enough to pull it. It holds about four tons of beet when the truck is fully loaded.

Alec has a simple job driving the tractor slowly up the field, while we poor labourers slave to keep up to him with our loading. When the wind blows, the dry soil from the beet whirls in a perfect sandstorm about the truck, and those who are loading on the windward side, soon have red and streaming eyes. When the truck is filled it is unhitched from the field tractor, which has large studded wheels, and is hitched to a second tractor, which is rubber-tyred and can pull the truck straight off along the road to the railway station.

I am extremely envious of Alec, who seems to me to be hardly earning his keep, and I long to change places with him and try my hand at tractor driving too. Imagine my joy, then, when a second truck is produced, and Tam keeps them going in a steady exchange. Alec's job now is only that of driving the road tractor. By the time he returns empty from the railway station, there is a full truck waiting for him, and he simply has to hitch it up and then puff off again.

At first, Tam takes over the driving of the field tractor, but after a certain amount of cajolery, my preparatory eye work has its effect, and he allows me to try my hand. It is an easy enough matter, for the field is flat, and all I have to do is steer the tractor straight between the waiting rows of beet. Tam stands behind me on the step and shouts directions, but after a while he gets down and I proudly perform my task alone in all my glory.

I feel like an emperor perched up there on my hard little seat, the mighty iron wheel vibrating beneath my hands; and although I very soon cease to look tidy (or anything like the immaculate beauties who are constantly being photographed on tractors, in the picture papers), I love to feel the wind in my hair, and the welcome warmth of the engine wafting about my frozen body. I think of Anne, and wish that she had stayed. This is just her sort of job, and she could have done it and worn as many clothes as she liked without comment.

Tractor driving also gives me a chance of looking about me. I watch the five Irishmen working with incredible speed in the field next door. They positively seem to gallop up the drill striping the field like a green and yellow peppermint, and they must earn a fabulous amount of money. If Pauline and I had been paid by the piece, we would have been even worse off than we are with our regular weekly wage. One has to cut a staggering amount of beet before one has earned the equivalent of one's keep and board, in addition to about one shilling and sixpence a day, and Pauline and I are still far too slow to make it worth our while. But the five Irishmen know that they have only a few months in which to earn all the money they will need to keep them in luxurious idleness during the summer, and they work as if they are possessed. Tam tells us that they have earned about seventy pounds between them on one field alone.

I can also hear, above the phutting of my tractor, the piggy chorus that is blown over the fields from the sties of a neighbouring farm. This farm is devoted entirely to producing bacon, and whenever the pigs' mealtime comes around, they lift up their voices to such an extent that I can hear them plainly, although they are almost five miles away.

Below the farm, the river curves in its extravagant silver loops down to the sea. I can see the ocean glittering like a naked sword, far on the horizon and sometimes mingling on the wind with the smell of wet heather, I can taste the harsh tang of salt. No wonder the people working all day in this wonderful atmosphere, are so robust and strong. No wonder Pauline and Anne found they had put on three pounds in weight!

When the beet have all been gathered in the first field, Tam waves the horde of workers into the back of my truck. He comes over to me.

'I want you to go into the Twiny Riggs,' he says, pointing to a field some little way off that the Irishmen had already prepared for us. I nod confidently, expecting Tam to come with me on the step. It is therefore something of a shock when I find that he intends going round by the road on his motor bicycle. I have never driven my machine through a gateway, and I wonder anxiously if we will get through. There is no one in the crowded truck who can help me if I get into difficulties, and I cannot help feeling that Tam has been unnecessarily trusting.

We manage to complete our journey, however, leaving the three gateways we have had to go through more or less intact. The new field is steep, with a precipitous hill dropping abruptly down to the station road. At first I fail to see the significance of this hill; I remain unconcerned until the truck at the back of the tractor begins to fill. Then I suddenly find, as we pant upward in low gear, that the front wheels of the tractor are being pulled right off the ground by the weight behind. It is thus completely impossible to steer, and I can only set my tractor in a straight line and hope for the best. Things are no better when we have crested the hill and begin to descend the other side. The hill on this side, is, if anything, even steeper, and beside the road, piled against the hedge at the bottom, is a heap of the workers' bicycles. The truck is still only half-loaded, and it is my job to drive it down this hill, clinging like a fly to a wall, while the loaders throw the beet in behind. It is all very well to drive down the hill. My front wheels are back on the ground now, and the tractor is no longer pawing the air like a startled horse. It is, however, absolutely impossible to stop. I jam on my brake, and slowly but surely the wheels continue to revolve, the teeth bite uselessly into the soft soil. My headlong flight becomes faster and faster. I wish in terror that Tam were here to give me moral support, but there is no sign of him.

'Don't go so fast!' pant the loaders.

'I can't stop!' I yell, panic-stricken.

My words act like magic. With one accord the loaders stop work and look at me in amazement. Suddenly, as they grasp the situation, Sally points to the pile of cycles lying by the hedge at the bottom.

'Eh! The cycles,' she calls, and taking to her heels she leaps down the hill like a stag. The other workers leap after her, and they carry the cycles out of harm's way. This is no doubt a wise move, but it offers me little consolation. I can see no reason for putting the safety of the cycles before my own.

My tractor rolls onward, and the hedge looms ever closer. Just as I seem to hear the twanging of harps and the beat of angelic wings, the hill levels itself out for a few yards, and miraculously we stop. Shakily I dismount. Along the road I can see Alec beetling, on his gaily painted orange steed. Nothing will get me back on mine until I have been assured by a professional that I am not in very great danger. The whole affair has been altogether too like a toboggan ride for my liking.

I now have time to glance at the horses as they cling to the side of the hill with their feet slipping in the soft soil, and their haunches creased and wrinkled by the increasing weight of their loaded carts. Their drivers have had to use chains to act as brakes on the wheels, and even so the poor beasts obviously expect to be pushed flat on their faces at any minute. I have a considerable sympathy for them.

Alec, however, makes light of my fears.

'Oh, you are all right,' he says. 'Your brakes are strong enough. You'll never get up the speed to send you really through the hedge. The only thing that might happen is that this pin may go.' He points to the pin that runs through the shackles and joins the truck to the tractor. 'I've been wondering if it is strong enough. If that goes, you'll have the whole four tons of beet down on top of you.'

With this cheery statement ringing in my ears I say my prayers and climb back into my perilous seat. Laboriously we puff back up the hill, and the work continues. I can never thank my guardian angel enough for bearing my prayer. The day progresses, and the pin continues to hold.

After a time Tam appears, leading a young cart-horse on the end of a rope, a miniature colossus with huge quarters and a wonderful crop of feathers about his mighty hooves. He has wicked little eyes, and peers out of the corners of them like an elephant. His coat is barred with sweat and on his chest are little beads of foam. He arches his tail proudly, and throwing back his head he calls to the other horses as they strain in harness on the side of the hill.

He does not like me or my tractor at all, and tucking his head between his knees, he lashes out angrily. Tam runs out the rope between his hands, and waving his gnarled stick he drives the huge beast about him in circles. It is an example of the mastery of man over the magnitude of matter. Pitting his puny strength against the heaving giant, Tam wrestles with him, digging his feet into the ground and clinging to the rope for all he is worth. His black pomeranian dashes in warily for a snap at the horse's heels, darting out of reach like a toreador before the great warrior can stamp and crush him.

And in the end, when the colt has pitted himself in vain against the determined man who rules him, and has worn himself out, he is suddenly tired, like the baby he really is, and stands shaking and sullen with his proud head drooping. I pass him with my tractor, and although we are quite close, he does no more than twitch his ears at me and flash his eyes in an angry red. Tam approaches him cautiously, and putting up his hand he strokes and caresses the sweat-streaked neck. He croons to him, wooing him like a lover, his hands playing consolingly about the frightened eyes, and rubbing the loose hair from his white star. The colt stops shaking, and at a tweak of the rope he bows his head and follows Tam quietly as he is led away. I cannot help feeling a wave of pity as I watch him go. It is the pity one feels for the wild thing that has been beaten, as it always has been throughout the ages; the pity that one feels for the proud who have been downtrodden, for kings who have lost their crowns.

After tea, Tam comes back again and he takes over my job once more. I am becoming stiff and sore, and I am glad enough to hand over my old boneshaker and to work back the blood into my frozen veins. We are provided, too, with unforeseen light entertainment.

Pauline has worked most of the day on the non-windward side of the truck. Now, she comes over to be with me, and we work in the choking dust with blinded eyes. Pauline pulls down the brim of her black velour hat and attempts to use it as a veil. I myself have adapted my ever useful red scarf to act as a shield. It is thin enough to be almost transparent, and, tied over my face, I can see the truck dimly through a red haze. It serves to keep out the worst of the soil, but the fine brown dust can still work its way through the thin mesh of the cloth and when I take it off at the end of the day, my eyeballs gleam.

'You look exactly like a scarlet bee skep,' says Pauline as I put it in place.

She, however, has less success with her black velour hat. Her eyes are soon streaming, and after miserably wrestling with the dust for a time she resolutely shuts them. She is now working quite blindly. Her first throw fells Sally, who intercepts the beet with her head, and goes down like a log. Pauline is full of contrition.

'I'm awfully sorry, Sally,' she says. 'I'm awfully sorry, really I am.'

Sally kneels in the soil with her head nursed in her arms but Sally is tough, and contenting herself with knocking Pauline's hat down over her eyes, she is soon back at work again.

Pauline's next victim is me. My world reels, and all about me is a scarlet darkness. Fortunately, however, the beet only landed on the back of my neck, and after a yelp of agony, I regain my *savoir-faire*.

'I'm *awfully* sorry, Aunt Bee,' says Pauline.

We work on for a few minutes; Pauline wrestles with the dust in vain, and once again she turns away her head with closed eyes.

Bang! This time it is the steward. It lands on his bald pate and rolls off with a bump on to the iron wing of the tractor. Tam wakes out of his day-dreaming with a howl of pain, and if Pauline could hear the words he uses about her, I feel sure that she would blush. It seems however, that she is completely unaware that she has even hit him, for another two beet fly through the air and find their mark in rapid succession.

Tam stops the tractor. He dismounts slowly, and advances menacingly in Pauline's direction. His ear is covered with mud and a piece of beet leaf is adhering to the back of his coat.

'I'm terribly sorry, Tam, really I am,' gasps Pauline.

They stand and stare at one another silently, Pauline with fear in her large eyes, and Tam searching furiously for the right words. In the end, however, he accepts her apology.

'Girl, you're a menace. You're not safe at all,' he says. 'If you hit me again, I'll trounce you so as you'll not know what's struck you!'

The other workers and I watch this little episode with quaking lips and the laughter big within us; but we dare not show it, and after a savage look about him to see if he is being laughed at, Tam bids us get back to work, and he climbs with dignity back into his seat.

When work is at last done and lousing time has come, Sally is so pleased and so filled with the joys of release that she picks me up and throws me on my face in the mud, out of pure exuberance. There is no one more astonished than Sally when I pick myself up, and catching her about the knees I throw her down too. Pauline takes advantage of Sally's recumbent position, and pushes the black beret down over her eyes. This, however, is not a wise move as Sally promptly leaps to her feet and stuffs Pauline's shirt with a handful of wet leaves. Pauline at least is no boomerang.

CHAPTER EIGHT
Moving On

THE DAYS GO BY and almost before we know it, the last load of sugar beet has been filled and Spital Tongues needs us no more.

During the course of the past week we have received a letter from Anne. She seems to be having a wild round of gaiety after her ten days of country life, and she ends her letter with these words. 'Do write and tell me how much longer you two stoics lasted. Do tell me what Mr Thompson said when, like the ten little boys – "then there were none!"' We feel ridiculously superior when we read this and extremely pleased with ourselves at having stayed our course.

We leave the farm with many goodbyes and a series of agonising handshakes. Tam pats us on the shoulders, and says we haven't done at all badly. We hope we leave him with a higher opinion of us, than the last war land girls. Sally knocks Pauline's hat over her eyes for the last time, and pumps our arms up and down. Mr Wren says with twinkling eyes that he doubts we'll not be sorry to go, and even Evie wistfully makes us promise to send her a Christmas card.

The Thompsons also are nice. Mr Thompson smiles for the first time since we have known him, and says that if he ever needs more land girls he will ask for us to be sent back. We are oddly touched by this, and are more than ever glad that in spite of his forebodings, we have been able to stay until the end. Walter, at the last minute, produces a cardboard box, which he hands to Pauline; and with our luggage once again piled about us, Mary drives us down to the station.

'Goodbye, goodbye,' she says, smiling brightly, as the train draws out.

'Goodbye!' we wave, and feel deeply sorry for her forlorn little figure as we set our own faces toward civilisation, and leave her to her fiancé and her fate at Spital Tongues.

In the train Pauline opens the cardboard box that Walter has given her. Inside, nestling on a bed of dry leaves, is a mangold wurzel.

Pauline begins to giggle weakly and suddenly I have to join her.

We sit back on the plush cushions and laugh until the tears come to our eyes.

The train runs through Spital Tongues and alongside a field where the workers are out. They are shawing turnips again, and as the train passes by they look up and wave their knives in the air. We hang out of the window and wave back. 'Goodbye, goodbye!' we call, but our voices are caught by the wind and carried away. Suddenly one of the workers lowers her knife. When she holds it up again, it has a black dot bobbing on the top – Sally's beret – the last thing that we see of Spital Tongues.

When we reach Carmouth we find our respective parents on the station platform. They greet us joyfully, and seem to be amazed by our apparent robustness.

'But you look so well!' said my mother; and from what I can gather she has been preparing to put me straight to bed, imagining from my letters that I am on the verge of a collapse.

Civilisation has charms that I have never before appreciated, and for the next month I enjoy myself immensely. My life consists of a round of gaiety, lights, music and laughter. I make much of the trials and tribulations that I have so recently endured; but no one really believes me, and after a time, it all seems so long ago that even I begin to forget.

At first the appearance of my hands rather shakes my family and at the imploring of my sister and mother, I treat myself to the luxury of a manicure. When the girl attendant is presented with my broken-nailed, gnarled, and calloused paw, she is visibly shaken. It could indeed be called virgin soil on which to have to work.

Christmas comes and goes, bringing a heavy fall of snow. I settle down happily for a lazy spring for there seems to be little prospect of being 'called to the Colours' again for some time. I ring up Pauline one day and she arranges to have lunch with me in town. We sit at a little table in a busy restaurant and find that suddenly we are absurdly shy of one another. We talk of Spital Tongues and our life there, but it all seems unreal and improbable. Pauline has had her hair waved, and she looks very different from the pink-cheeked, windblown person that I remember. She still continues to call me

Aunty Bee however.

During the course of the next week a large parcel arrives, and proves to be yet another supplement to my land army uniform. Inside the parcel is a smart pair of riding breeches, a mackintosh, two aertex blouses, a green pullover, and a hat. I put on these clothes delightedly, and parading before a mirror, I long for an excuse to wear them. An uneasy picture flashes through my mind, however, of the mud and filth that in the past have run hand in hand with my manual labours, and I look at my riding breeches sorrowfully. I know that one day of farm work will transform them into a sodden, wilting pulp, and regretfully I put them away. I decide that no doubt they have been designed to parade in round Hyde Park, in peace time. I ring up Pauline and find that she too has had a visit from the postman. She is so pleased at her appearance in her new get-up that she has arranged to have her photograph taken. I ask her what she thinks of the new hat. She says she thinks it is rather nice and I ring off. I decide that Pauline has the strangest taste in hats.

The days pass pleasantly and I become increasingly lazy. I begin to take my freedom for granted and I make plans for several weeks ahead for going to stay with various friends. Everyone assures me that no one wants land girls in the winter, and I am quite prepared to believe them. It therefore comes as a complete surprise when lying beside my plate one morning I find an official postcard, telling me to report for duty in three days' time. Three days' time! The fading memory of my recent suffering comes back to me in a rush. I can almost feel my back aching in anticipation! Civilisation suddenly seems more precious to me than it has ever been before. I feel like a condemned person who has only a few hours more to live. I begin to wish I had had the sense to leave the Land Army while there was still time. Now it is too late, and gloomily I ring up Pauline.

I find however, that she too has received her marching orders, and I brighten up considerably. It won't be so bad if she is coming too. Her postcard is slightly more explicit than mine, and we gather that Stoney Hall is a big dairy farm, and that one of us will have to drive the milk van and deliver the milk. Pauline can't drive, so this job will presumably fall to me.

We pack our bags and wait apprehensively for 17th January to come. The snow is still rather deep, lying in drifts in the hills. Stoney Hall seems a remote spot and my father has promised to take us there in his car if he can get through the snow; so when the day comes, we set off hopefully, the car piled to the roof with our belongings.

While waiting we have thought of more and more things that we are likely to need, and by now there is an imposing heap.

We get our first sight of the farm as we crest a hill and the car picks its way cautiously down the bending road beyond. It lies packed snugly together in a hollow of land. Its red corrugated iron hemmels glow in the whiteness of the snow, and blue smoke belches in puffs from a shed in the stackyard. As we draw nearer, we can hear the thumping of an engine, and as we turn into the yard, we see that it is milking time and that the engine in the shed is the mechanical milker.

We are met by a bevy of barking collies and a man steps out of a stable and stares at us. We have the same feeling that we are being closely observed that we experienced on our first day at Spital Tongues. I see lace curtains in the cottage windows pulled aside and eyes peering out at us.

'Could you tell me which is the Smiths' cottage?' I ask the man from the stable.

He answers me in the broad drawl of a dalesman, and he points across the yard to a green painted door.

I cross to the door and knock. A woman opens it and stares at me.

'Are you Mrs Smith?' I ask.

'Yes,' she admits, and calls back into the darkness of the cottage, 'Jim, it's the land girls come!'

I hear a creaking and a scrape of hobnailed boots on the stone flagged floor. A thin man with a small weather-beaten face appears and grins cheerfully. His eyes are very blue, and when he smiles they crinkle up like the eyes of a new-born puppy.

'Pleased to meet you,' he says, and grips my hand. He steps into the yard and catches sight of the rapidly swelling heap of luggage that my father and Pauline are salvaging from the closely packed car. His eyes widen but he says nothing, and going to the car he shakes hands with the others.

'I'll give you a hand,' he says, and picking up two of the cases he staggers off into the cottage. I follow, my arms full of eiderdown

Mrs Smith is waiting in the kitchen, a small child clinging to either hand. 'You'd better bring them straight upstairs,' she says, and she leads me up a narrow staircase to the floor above. She opens the door.

'This is your room.'

Pauline and I are to share a room together. It has a low ceiling and a small dormer window that looks out on to the stackyard. Our beds are single iron affairs that remind me of my schooldays, and a wooden wash basin and dressing-table complete the rest of the furniture. All the woodwork is painted a dismal brown, and I suspect the beds of being hard and narrow.

'Terrible furniture,' says Mrs Smith suddenly. 'You must thank Mr Foster for that. We hadn't got this room furnished. We don't use it in the ordinary way. He gave us this stuff from an old shooting box he has.'

I feel that the average shooter can't have very much taste in interior decoration.

'Oh, it's perfectly all right,' I say, and deposit my armful of bedding on one of the beds. Pauline staggers in at that moment with a slipping mound of stuff. Her face is pink and shiny and her eyes are like saucers.

Mrs Smith takes us downstairs again and shows us her sitting room.

'You can have this room too,' she says. 'We never used to use it except on Sundays.'

We continue to unload our luggage for a while, and by the time it is all installed, everyone is very hot indeed.

'Sure you've nothing more?' says Mr Smith, and somehow I feel that he is laughing at us.

'You can have tea as soon as you are ready,' says Mrs Smith. 'It's set in the kitchen.'

Tea proves to be a magnificent spread. There are masses of newly made scones and cakes; and a plate of cream-filled Swiss roll. Pauline and I have seen nothing like it for months and we fall upon it with delight. It is, however, a somewhat silent meal for we are still rather shy of the Smiths and they of us. The two children sit in high chairs on the hearthrug, and we can feel their curious eyes boring into our backs. Mrs Smith tells us that they are twins. They are a robust pair with plump pink legs and beautiful blue eyes. They have soft curly hair and we learned that they are called Jack and Marian.

After tea we go upstairs to unpack. Our luggage overflows in the little room, and soon it has the appearance of being piled up in banks about the walls.

Eventually we relax and we sink exhausted in front of the roaring sitting-room fire.

'This is a definite improvement on Spital Tongues,' I say, as bright flames lick up the chimney. 'A nice fire and a huge tea.'

'Yes, it was a lovely tea,' says Pauline. 'I like the Smiths too.'

The daylight begins to fade, and I switch on my small portable wireless. Mrs Smith comes in and draws the velvet curtains over the window. This is not a very effective blackout, as there is a wide strip of light down either side of the frame.

'It doesn't really matter on this side of the house,' explains Mrs Smith. 'The windows only look into the stackyard, and the wardens never come round that way.'

I can't help feeling that this attitude is typically British!

The cottage consists of five rooms with a long scullery and a small bathroom made out of an old washhouse. Downstairs there is the kitchen and the sitting-room. Upstairs there is the Smiths' bedroom, the twins' bedroom, and ours.

The sitting-room is pleasantly furnished with grey velvet chairs and a long sofa. These, however, do not really interest us as we nearly always sit on the floor. There is also a piano (given to Marian by an aunt) and a small square mahogany table. On the table we soon accumulate a perfect mountain of things. Daily the stack mounts as our stay progresses, and like the tower of Pisa it topples skyward at an ever-increasing angle. When it comes to the point when gravity is too much for it, it falls down and we build it up again slightly more securely.

The door opens and Mrs Smith thrusts in her head. 'Would you like a bath, Miss Whitton?' she says, 'the water is hot if you want one.'

We are amazed at this sign of civilisation in a cottage one third the size of Spital Tongues, and we accept eagerly. The bathroom has a bath with a peeling bottom, and a damp smell that mingles pleasantly with carbolic. The bath is rather short so that I am forced to sit with my knees tucked under my chin. The water is scalding, however, and I get out with a scarlet stern. To get to the bathroom we have to go through the kitchen. The Smiths are sitting in their battered chairs beside the kitchen fire. Mr Smith is smoking a long black pipe and he has run his hand through his hair until it stands up perpendicularly on his head. Mrs Smith has her feet thrust into carpet slippers, and in her lap is a bundle of darning.

There is a silver collie curled up on the rug by the fender, and she lifts her tail and thumps it as we pause to say good night. Mr Smith asks us what farm jobs we have had to do so far, and we tell him proudly of our exploits at Spital Tongues. Even he doesn't seem quite to believe us. He tells us that he will call us next morning at half-past six. The early milking is all done by the dairy people, and all I will have to do is to load up my van with the crates of milk and then drive it away. If I am gone from the farm by seven he says it will be soon enough. For the first week, until I have learned the secrets of the milk round, Mr Smith will send the boy whose job I am taking over round with me.

'But what I'm going to do with you Miss Gardener,' he says to Pauline, 'I'm blest if I know. It's a problem, mind, I'm telling you!'

We say good night, and climb the narrow little stairs to our room.

'I can't get over having electric light,' says Pauline. 'And telephone! Did you see it on the window-sill in the kitchen?'

It is bitterly cold in our room after the warmth of the kitchen, and we pull off our clothes and are soon in bed. The light switch is over on the far side of the room by the door, and we decide to take the switching of it off in strict turns as it is a miserable pad back to bed with bare feet on the cold linoleum.

At first I cannot sleep. I had forgotten the quiet of a country night after the noise of my month in town. Down beneath our window is the byre, and we can hear the stamp and rattle of the chained cows as they move about in their stalls. My bed is quite as hard and narrow as I had foreseen, and for a while I toss miserably from side to side. By the creakings on the other side of the room, I guess that Pauline is doing the same.

CHAPTER NINE
Charlie and the Customers

IT SEEMS NO TIME, however, before we are suddenly awoken by a hefty banging on the door. It is pitch dark in the room, and although I am awake in an instant, I cannot at first remember where I am. I put out my hand to switch on the lamp that stands beside my bed at home; than as my knuckles bump against the hard side of a chest of drawers, I suddenly remember.

'Thank you!' I call, and I hear the stamp of Mr Smith's boots as he goes downstairs.

'What's the matter?' says Pauline.

'Wake up, you lout. We've been called.'

I find the light and switch it on. My clothes are in a pile on the chair and I struggle into them. I am not at all sure what one wears for delivering milk, but I suppose that it will be a cold job and I dress accordingly. Round my head I tie my dear old scarlet scarf. It has been washed since we left Spital Tongues, and it is a recognisable red again.

Downstairs in the kitchen, Mr Smith is making himself a pot of tea.

'Like a cup?' he asks and he digs out a box of biscuits from the shelf of a cupboard. The tea is scalding hot, and I feel it all the way into my inside as it goes down. Mr Smith turns on the wireless. He likes a good volume of noise, and we are nearly blasted out of the kitchen as a result. We stand drinking our tea and listen uncomprehendingly to the news in Norwegian.

'Funny way these chaps talk,' says Mr Smith wonderingly.

We go outside, leaving the wireless blazing away into the empty kitchen. Pauline tells me later that she was slowly dressing in the room overhead, when a perfect cloud of dust was whirled into the air by the first shock of the noise.

The farm is seething with activity. The mechanical milker is hard at work and whining away like a sewing machine. A girl in a white overall is bottling milk in the dairy, and there is a stack of full crates waiting to be loaded into the van. The van is a small green affair, and on the side is painted a picture of a benevolent white cow standing knee deep in a field of daisies. A young man is already building the crates into the back. This is Charlie; Mr Smith introduces me to him and Charlie grins, his hands full of crates.

'Good morning, my dear!' he says agreeably.

Charlie has the most incredible hair. It is blond and wavy, and its owner is obviously very proud of it. It smells strongly of violets, and is combed back carefully in its many kinks until it stands up almost in a point. Charlie wears a large green burberry. I am sure that never has a mackintosh had more capes and peaks, even in the times of the Dandies. It billows out about his small person like a ballet dress and is tied tightly about the waist with a belt.

I get into the van, and Charlie closes the doors behind. There is only a seat for the driver and I have to perch myself on the floor on a smelly little cushion. However, Charlie has given me a very smart money pouch to hang about me, so I am comforted. He also hands me a bunch of books, filled with completely indecipherable hieroglyphics. These, it seems, are my accounts.

Charlie gets into the driving seat and presses the self-starter. The engine whines feebly and stops.

'Look at that!' says Charlie in exasperation, and he gets out the starting handle. He swings it round frantically without rousing so much as a cough. 'Darn it!' says Charlie.

He goes round to the back and begins unloading all the milk crates again. Then he gives a shout. Apparently this performance is quite a usual one, for almost at once a little crowd of people appear from nowhere, and the van is shoved out of the garage and across the yard.

Charlie climbs back into the driver's seat and attempts to start the engine by putting it in gear. This fails too, and the van advances out of the yard and down the road in a series of jerks. At this point Mr Smith appears with Pauline. She looks as sleepy as I feel.

'What, not gone yet?' says Mr Smith, and sets his shoulder to the back of the van.

A small hill runs down past the farm, and we push the van to the bottom without any success. Gideon, the horseman, is then despatched back to the farm to bring a cart to haul us back up the hill again. While we are waiting, Mr Smith and Charlie peer into the engine and fiddle ineffectually with the van's intestines.

After half an hour has gone by, the van is at last started; but not until it has been pushed down the hill and hauled back up again many times, and we are all feeling very warm.

We take it back to the yard and the crates are once again loaded. By this time, milking has stopped, and wonderful smells of cooking breakfasts are being wafted out of the cottage doors. I am ravenously hungry after all our exertions, but we have already dallied too long. Leaping into the driving seat, Charlie drives away like a madman. We rocket down the road. I cling desperately to the swaying van, and my springless seat leaves my tail and hits it again repeatedly. We shoot round a corner, the milk bottles banging in the back with a noise like a machine gun, and the crates rattling together, so that I am almost deafened.

'Have to be careful round this bend,' says Charlie, accelerating at it on the wrong side of the road. 'Nasty in the winter when the wet leaves are about.'

I long to point out that wet leaves and snow have much the same skidding tendencies, but we fly round it on two wheels.

We turn into the high road, and dash on in to Wallbrugh. Wallbrugh is a small market town, and stopping the van beside a public house, we see another van already parked waiting for us. Instead of a white cow knee deep in daisies, this van has a brown cow; and when its driver dismounts, I see that he is a taller, broader edition of Mr Smith. It proves to be his brother.

'So you've got company today, Charlie,' says Mr Smith's brother.

It appears that the milk in his van is a halfpenny cheaper than our milk, for ours is supposed to be tuberculin tested. We swop several crates, therefore, exchange the local gossip, and go on our way.

'He comes from "Glittering Stones",' Charlie explains as we rocket along. 'Mr Foster owns that farm too. Runs them together sort of thing.'

I crane eagerly from my lowly seat and attempt to take stock of just where we are going. I am sure that I shall never be able to remember the intricate network of roads, or the various houses at which we stop and deliver milk. And all these houses, it seems, get different quantities.

'However do you remember which houses get what?' I ask, as Charlie confidently selects two pints and a half, and I follow him up a gravel drive.

'Oh, you just get to know,' he says.

This is not very helpful. I am convinced I shall never get to know if I go on delivering milk all my life. I therefore determine to concentrate on learning which are the houses we visit, and to make out a list of what they each get. It is for this reason that my account books take on a somewhat novel appearance. Often I have no idea what the name of my customer may be, remembering her only by the place where I leave her bottles of milk. Thus, I write her down in my book as 'Mrs Waterbutt', 'Mrs Greenpailing', or 'Mrs Steps'. Mr Smith is vastly amused by this method of doing things, and when he goes over my accounts with me once a month he always does it with roars of delight.

Going on a milk round with Charlie presents me with an excellent illustration of the deceitfulness of the male. At every house we come to he appears to be an enormous favourite with the maid. He knows every one by her Christian name, and several times I am witness to a sly pinch on a neat round behind. Each obviously thinks that she and she only, is the one interest of Charlie's young life. If she only knew, her Romeo bas a perfect repertoire of Juliets!

One house that we go to is in a very poor part of Wallbrugh. We leave a half pint at the top of a dark flight of stairs, and at the sound of our steps the door opens and a harassed woman, with a child in her arms, greets us good morning. Through the door I glimpse a shabby room of pathetic poverty. It comes as such a change after the neat, trim little houses that we have been visiting it is like a douche of cold water in the face. At the woman's skirts is a plump little boy with a shock of curly hair. His face is covered with dirt, and his nose is badly in need of wiping. He stoops to pick up the bottle of milk, but his mother, afraid, no doubt, that he will break it, snatches it away from him. He opens his mouth and yells. His eyes remain completely dry, but shriek upon shriek rends the air.

'You bloody old bitch!' he says; and as his mother shoves him back into the room and closes the door, we hear him shrieking a flood of filthy abuse at her. He cannot be older than five.

'They are a poor lot,' says Charlie, as we climb back into the van. 'She always pays up to the last minute, though. More than some of the toffs do.'

We leave the town and drive out again into the country. At every house where we stop Charlie carries in the milk with a cheerful, 'Good morning, my dear,' and a smiling face. I am already drooping wearily. I am cold and hungry, and my head has begun to ache with the rattling of the milk bottles. I wonder how Charlie can keep saying, 'Good morning, my dear,' as if each time is the first.

At one farm, there is a man employed whom Charlie warns me solemnly against. It seems that he is a homicide who has already attempted to kill two women of whom he disapproved.

'Never cross him,' says Charlie. 'Always agree with anything he says and you'll be all right.'

At this moment the stable door opens and the man steps out. He is certainly a fearsome-looking creature, with an idiot's head and a tongue that hangs out almost to his chin. I have no desire to end my young life yet, and I determine never to leave my van unless I am well armed with a large quart bottle of milk. If the worst comes to the worst, I decide that I can always hit him over the head with that. It may surprise him if it does nothing else.

Another point on the milk round where I am likely to meet sudden death proves to be the level crossing. It is a primitive affair without gates as the road is seldom used. The line curves away from me in a steep cutting and I can only see a few yards of it on either side. Before it is safe to cross, therefore, I have to switch off my engine and listen to hear if anything is coming. If I hear no sound of a train, I run over to the other side where I can turn the van and come back up again. If I hear a train I wait until it has gone by. On windy days it is almost impossible to hear the trains until they are right on to you, and Charlie tells me cheerfully that he has several times got over the line with only a few seconds to spare. He also tells me that he once lost a crate which fell out on the line because he had not fastened the doors properly.

'Made a proper mess, my dear,' he says.

Charlie's lodgings are a few miles away from the farm and we stop there while he has his breakfast. By this time we have almost finished the first round. The full crates in the van are much depleted, and instead of chubby little bottles with gleaming cheeks and silver tops, we have taken in a ragamuffin crew of old 'empties', their faces dirty and their sides streaked with milky water. The first time Charlie told me to 'bring back the empties' after setting down my full bottles, I did not realise that milk bottles have subtle designs and distinctions. I only saw a whole crowd of empty bottles standing at the back door of the house, and filling my arms with them indiscriminately I staggered back to the van. Charlie greeted them with horror.

'*They* don't belong to us!' he said, holding out a couple of pints with bloated mumpy necks. 'They belong to Wicklow's dairies. You don't want to take them up.'

And so I learn that often a house has milk delivered daily by three or four different milkmen, each with their own sort of milk in their own sort of bottles, and seemingly with no sense of rivalry between them.

Charlie disappears into his lodgings, and then hurries out again.

'My landlady says would you like to come in for a cup of tea?'

I greet the proposal joyfully. My feet are terribly cold, and I have been beating them on the floor of the van, and sitting on my hands in an effort to get warm.

As I perch in a chair before a blazing kitchen fire, and accept a cup of tea from the hospitable hands of Charlie's landlady, I cannot help reflecting on the novelty of my position. I wonder if in my grandmother's day I should have been considered compromised by having breakfast with a strange milkman whom I had never seen before.

Charlie tucks in with relish to a steaming plate of eggs and bacon. The smell is most enticing, and I feel very like a Bisto kid, as I sniff it in appreciation. I long for my own breakfast, and tentatively ask

Charlie how long it will be before we get back.

'Not long now,' he assures me. 'We've only got another ten miles or so to go.'

I feel much better when we do start off again, and the milk bottles do not seem to jangle quite so loudly in my head. My hot cup of tea lies comfortingly in my middle, and my face and hands are glowing from the heat of the fire.

One of our next ports of call is in the Bluehill Yard. The Bluehill Yard is a group of houses built on a hill about a cobbled square. As we drive the van in through the gateway a flock of hens scatter wildly in all directions with raucous squawkings and several tail feathers missing. In the corner of the yard is a cottage. Outside the cottage is a coalhouse, and peering out of the coalhouse with bright black eyes is the oldest old woman I have ever seen. She is bent double, and hacking away at a log with a little hatchet. Her gnarled hands are so wasted that I almost expect them to dissolve into dust at any minute, and her little face is wrinkled up like a prune. She is Granny Royd.

The whole of the time I am to do the milk round, I am never to see Granny Royd outside her coalhouse. Every single morning when I drive my van in to the square, there she is hacking away at a log with her little axe. I become so used to seeing her there that I believe that if she had ever been missing from her shed I would have been as astonished as if the little figures in the weather barometer that I used to have as a child had stepped down off their stand to go out shopping.

Granny Royd has a sister almost as old as herself, and it is she who has the running of the house. Although she looks as if she has been washed up with the Flood, she is an active little person. She goes out gathering sticks each day, and with her grey hair blowing in a long tangle about her shoulders, she looks as if any minute she may leap on to a broomstick and fly away. I pass her in my van one day, walking in the middle of the read, and dragging a vast branch behind her like a tough little pony. I have to stop the van and help her to lift it on to the grass verge before I can get by. She is stone deaf, but as her weekly bill is always the same, we have no difficulty in dealing with each other.

In the opposite corner of the Bluehill Yard, live the Willsons. Mrs Willson keeps her false teeth in a tea caddy on the mantelpiece. She tells me that she 'bought them secondhand by post, so that they have never been a very good fit', and she only wears them on Sundays. She also keeps her money in the same tea caddy, and when she comes to the door to pay me, we have to wrestle with the coppers that will slip down in among the teeth.

Back at the farm once more, Charlie unloads the empty crates and fills up again with a fresh supply. It is now almost eleven and I have had no breakfast. I catch a fleeting glimpse of Pauline as she disappears round the stackyard in the charge of Gideon and a horse, and I see that she is indeed wearing her land army hat.

Breakfast is laid for me in the kitchen, and Mrs Smith has cooked a delicious heap of bacon and potatoes. My stomach is rattling with rage at being neglected so long, and I bolt down my breakfast at a revolting speed. I just get it finished by the time Charlie is knocking at the door wanting to know if I am ready.

The second milk round is much nearer at hand. Most of our customers are people working on Mr Foster's estate, and they all eye me with a maximum of curiosity. We end up at last at the big Hall. I have by this time learned how to carry nine milk bottles at a time without letting any drop, and I follow Charlie into the big kitchen with my arms full. The kitchen at the Hall is a world of its own. There is Mrs Harrison, the cook, a motherly soul who rules her staff with a rod of iron; there is Mr Blenkinsop, the long and drooping butler with a neck like Mr Chamberlain, and a heart of gold; there is Nancy the kitchen maid, Wallace the chauffeur, McAdams the gardener, and Billy the gardener's boy. All of them I am to come to know well, but this first morning their guarded scrutiny is almost more than I can bear.

I am weary indeed when at last the morning's work is finished, and I stand with Charlie in the dairy counting up the takings of the day. My blue mackintosh, fortunately a proved antique before I started, is covered with rust stains from the crates, and streaked with milk from the dirty bottles. My head is swimming with trying to remember pints and gills and how much they all cost. I watch

Charlie blankly as he adds further incomprehensible hieroglyphics to the columns in the account books. I decide that I shall certainly never probe their mysteries with his help alone, and I determine to get Mr Smith to explain them to me with all possible speed.

During lunch, at which both the land girls eat hugely (but I slightly less so, for memories of my late breakfast still linger with me), the Smiths lose some of their shyness, and we like them increasingly. Mrs Smith eats nothing, but perches on a chair and watches her dishes being rapidly cleared. It becomes a mystery, as the days pass, when Mrs Smith does eat. We certainly never see her.

Pauline has spent the morning in leading loads of straw with Gideon. Little pieces of straw are still adhering to her person, and her round childish face is already red with the cold, fresh air. She tells me that Gideon is an incomprehensible person, owing to his dalesman's drawl and the loss of all his front teeth. This lack of teeth with the people in the country seems to be more or less universal. They lose their own teeth at an early age, and few of them bother or can afford to buy any false ones.

The only other thing that Pauline has learned about Gideon is that he is a great admirer of Nelson Eddy. Nelson Eddy is one of the few film stars that Pauline does not admire. On her dressing-table upstairs she has photographs of Gary Cooper, Charles Boyer, and Melvyn Douglas. Mrs Smith goes for many days under the impression that these are photographs of Miss Gardener's boy friends, and she is quite disappointed when she finds that they are not.

After lunch Pauline and I are introduced to Mr Weir. Mr Weir is a Scotsman, and he is delighted with us when he discovers that we have so recently come from Scotland. Mr Weir is a character. We spend the afternoon loading manure from the farm midden to a stack in the field. Mr Weir falls for Pauline at once, and immediately, with a Scot's eye, sees her possibilities as a source of amusement. The Scots are excellent at inventing their own form of humour and Mr Weir dispenses with formality from the start. He calls me Barbara and Pauline, Tubby. He also knocks Pauline's land army hat down over her eyes.

He is embarrassingly free of all forms of embarrassment. While loading manure into a cart one is apt to come across odds and ends which are best passed by without comment. Mr Weir has none of this nonsense. He picks up the discarded caul of a calf on his fork and holds it out for our inspection.

'Now that is bad!' he says disapprovingly. 'They ought not to toss them on to the manure. They infect it, and it infects the ground. It'll give the cows contagious abortion.'

Pauline, always easily embarrassed, blushes furiously.

Mr Weir also goes into lurid details of his sister who is suffering from cancer.

'Had to have her breast removed,' he says with relish. 'Left one, it was. Stuffed full of tubes as a pincushion.'

The job progresses at a leisurely pace, and there is none of the agonising hurry that we have been used to suffering. Mr Weir makes up his mind to lead five loads of manure before lousing time, and he intends to lead neither more nor less. He talks cheerfully while he works, and we learn a lot about him. He tells us he served in India during the last war, and he stops work and clicks his tongue in a strange assortment of sounds that he assures us is Indian. Now he is married and has a small son and daughter.

When lousing time comes we have just led the last load of manure down to the stack, and we ride back with him in the empty cart.

'Well, that's that!' says Mr Weir as we help him unhitch his horse. 'Look slippy, Tubby. Loosen that chain. That's it. You'll be a man before your mother.'

In the scullery we kick off our boots on to the floor and pad through into the sitting-room. Mrs Smith follows us with tea. She sniffs.

'Pow! What a smell. Do you mind taking off them things? You'll smell the house out.'

Upstairs we change. Pauline puts on a bright scarlet jersey and a pair of blue trousers. When we return downstairs Mrs Smith shies like a startled horse, and nearly drops the teapot.

'Good heavens!' she says frankly.

Mrs Smith is always frank. She never makes the slightest effort to disguise her opinion, and it is most refreshing.

The tea is as sumptuous a spread as the one we had the day before. We sit on the floor with plates on our knees and consume a large quantity of new scones. Pauline swells almost visibly. Although half my size, she has twice my appetite, and it is no wonder her figure becomes increasingly round.

The evening passes happily. We sit by the fire and listen to the wireless and talk. We dissect the world and rebuild it to its advantage. We discuss young men and laugh once more over Walter and his mangold wurzel.

'Trust me to get someone like that,' says Pauline bitterly. 'The first time anyone shows any interest in me and it has to be Walter!'

'Never mind,' I say, slipping back easily into my auntly character. 'You are young yet.'

CHAPTER TEN
Delivering the Goods

THE DAYS PASS and gradually I learn my new job. I learn how to load my van so that the crates need the minimum amount of shifting; I learn how much milk each customer gets. I also find that each customer expects you to remember her particular wants, even if you forget everyone else's. I have to know each one's family history; I have to know that Mrs Bird's daughter is 'in service'; that her day off is Tuesday, and that she spends the afternoon with her mother. Her favourite pudding is rice, and therefore Mrs Bird likes to have an extra gill of milk every Tuesday morning. Woe betide me if I forget! Frequently I am given an order for extra milk several weeks ahead, 'Just so as you'll have it for me,' as my customers say. Whether they expect me to have to work the cows up so as to prepare them for this extra strain to be imposed upon them, I do not know. Perhaps my customers visualise me sitting in the field playing persuasively to the cows on a paper comb.

It is not long, either, before I find that my customers are divided into two groups. There are those that I like, and those that I dislike intensely. Often I have never even seen the latter. They arouse my hatred by leaving their empty bottles in a filthy unwashed state, so that I get covered in sour milk carrying them in my arms. They infuriate me by signifying that they want an extra pint by leaving their coppers in the bottom of an empty bottle, floating on a pool of filthy water; which runs out over my glove as I shake the money into my hand. They have gates that will not open easily; dogs that daily pursue me, snapping at my seat when my arms are already fully occupied with slipping pints. Some of them pay late, running up their account so that my books become impossibly involved. Some of them never have any change, and I have to wrestle with my money bag, seeking in the clumsy pouches with frozen fingers. I hate them one and all! But there are also my favourites. There is kind Mrs Wallace, who always makes the postman and myself a cup of tea. There is Mrs Ferguson who sometimes slips an egg warmly into my hand; and Mrs Bruce, whose empty bottles are as clean and shiny as a new pin.

At some of the houses I soon find I have a circle of friends. My particular admirers are gardeners, and for some reason we always get on well. I begin to be as deceitful as Charlie and, rolling my eyes, I try to make every gardener think that my daily visit to his estate (with the chance of seeing him, of course), is indeed the one bright spot of my day. It pays me well, for I am showered throughout the year with a perfect fan mail of vegetables. Little bunches of primroses are surreptitiously pushed into my hand, or perhaps a paper bag with a pound of their employer's tomatoes.

Mr Foster's under-gardener Billy, is my especial victim. He is a nice lad and we get on famously. Whenever I park my van in the backyard of the hall, he is certain to be somewhere about.

His admiration is flattering, and we even get to the stage of exchanging photographs. I still have his somewhere. He asks me repeatedly to go to the local village hop with him, but here I hedge, for I suspect that, once having gone, the situation afterwards might become rather difficult.

I find that I am frequently showered with invitations of one sort or another. I am asked out repeatedly by policemen, railway porters, chauffeurs, and fellow milkmen, and I begin to think it must be the effect of my new land army pullover.

When my milk round is finished, I join Pauline in the fields. She, poor soul, hasn't nearly as amusing a time as I have and she is bitterly jealous of my conquests, even if they are only under-gardeners – or so she says! She longs to learn to drive so that she can take turns at going out with me in the van. This attitude I encourage. At present I find I am terribly tired, for unless Mr Smith will occasionally take my van for me on the Sunday, I can never get a full day off.

We approach Mr Smith on the subject and he applauds the idea. I think that, to be honest, he is finding it difficult to keep Pauline fully employed. It is a slack time on the farm and there is really no job for her to do.

With a red 'L' tied on the back and front of the van, we therefore set out.

After the first morning I vow that never again will I promise to teach anyone to drive. Pauline has never so much as held a steering wheel before, and the experience of sitting beside her, as we rocket wildly down the road, is harrowing in the extreme. She has a disconcerting habit of being too nonchalant about the whole proceeding. She slaps herself into top gear with an agonising series of jolts, and then zooms along cheerfully with her foot flat on the accelerator. Only I realise what is likely to happen if we meet with a sudden crisis. Pauline never has a qualm. It never occurs to her that a child may run over the road or a car suddenly stop in front of her. She roars along humming happily to herself and carelessly pointing out things of interest in the passing scenery. For one whole morning I devote my entire lesson to showing her how to stop. Pauline thinks it is a silly game, but I am so grim and determined that she is quite frightened of me and submits meekly to my orders. After this, I feel slightly happier.

We have a nasty moment one day, however. A large lorry with a long tree trunk sticking out behind, reaches a narrow bridge at the same moment that we do. I earnestly say my prayers. I have no means of stopping the van, for the handbrake is over on Pauline's side.

'Stop!' I implore Pauline, but Pauline is too frightened to find her brake. The little van with the white cow on its side, rushes on, and the driver of the lorry blows his horn frantically. I grasp the wheel and we mount the pavement. Breathlessly we squeeze by. There isn't an inch to spare, and we leave our mirror behind on the side of the lorry.

'Stop, Pauline!' I demand. We stop. I am white and shaken and Pauline's face is red. She opens her eyes very wide, peering anxiously up from beneath her ridiculous hat.

'I'm terribly sorry, Aunty Bee. Really I am!' she says.

She is an apt pupil, however, and after six weeks have gone by I tell Mr Smith that I think she is ready for her test. He gives us the afternoon off, and we drive into Wallbrugh where we have arranged to meet the examiner. Pauline is paralysed with terror and is quite certain that she won't pass. I hand her over to the examiner, and surrender him my smelly little cushion on the floor of the van.

They start off without mishap and I watch them out of sight. It is cold waiting for their return, and I go into the station waiting-room which is nearby and which has a blazing fire.

Sitting around the fire are two taxi drivers. They remind me very much of Anne, for they wear a staggering quantity of clothes. I can see a series of sleeves protruding from their wrists, and round their necks are thick woollen mufflers.

We begin talking. One of the taxi drivers is a stout man, and he is smoking a short clay pipe with a silver covering on top. He contributes little to the conversation, but when appealed to by his mate, he nods and says an occasional 'Aye!'

The other taxi driver is talkative. It seems that he has led a charmed life, for, like a cat, he has been in the jaws of death many times. He fought in the last war, and he pulls out of his pocket a piece of shrapnel that he tells me was dug out of his chest. He insists on showing me his scars. He gets up slowly and unwinding the woollen muffler, he takes off one jacket after the other and lays them carefully on the waiting-room table. Like a dismembered globe artichoke the discarded layers make an imposing heap. He unbuttons his shirt and his woollen vest, and exhibits a red weal that runs in a gash above his heart.

'One inch lower and I would have been a goner, eh Jack?'

Jack nods and says, 'Aye.'

'Had a real lucky life I've had,' says the taxi driver, buttoning himself up again and heaving his way with my help back into his jackets.

'Went down on the *City of Glasgow* once. Swam about for hours clinging to a piece of drift. Perishingly cold it was.'

He huddles over the fire as if shivering from the very memory.

'Then I was buried,' he says. 'Up to my blooming neck, by a ruddy shell. Whizz – bang! We hear it coming and we all duck. Blew to pieces the whole ruddy fatigue. Should have been killed too, by rights, eh Jack?'

Jack nods and says, 'Aye!'

'Been at this job long?' asks the taxi driver, looking at my land army clothes.

'Not very long.'

'I thought not. Come from the town, don't yeh?'

'Yes.'

'I thought so. You can't fool me. Do you know how I knew?' asks the taxi driver. 'I knowed by your voice,' he says, prodding my knee triumphantly with his finger. 'You've had education, I can see that. Been to a secondary school, I shouldn't wonder!'

'Well, yes.'

'You can't fool me; eh Jack?' said the taxi driver.

At this moment I hear the excited padding of rubber boots on the platform outside, and Pauline bursts in with a beaming face. She flings her arms about my neck.

'I've passed, Aunty Bee!' she shrieks. 'The nicest little man! I wasn't a bit frightened; well, not after the first few minutes.'

I thump her enthusiastically and we prepare to go.

'So long,' says the taxi driver.

'Pleased to meet you I'm sure, eh Jack?'

Jack nods, 'Aye' he says, and waving goodbye we leave them to their fire.

Joyfully, Pauline wrenches the 'L's' off the front and back of the van.

'You'll let me drive home, won't you Aunty Bee?' she begs.

We roar home at an agonising speed, and I very much wish that she was back under my charge again so that I could have a little to say in the matter.

The Smiths are delighted at Pauline's success. By this time they, and we, are the best of friends. They tease us unmercifully and refuse to regard us as anything more than a big joke. As a matter of fact this is the general attitude of the entire farm. Mr Weir's nickname for Pauline has stuck, and except for the Smiths, who continue to call us Miss Gardener and Miss Whitton to the bitter end, we are known respectively as Tubby and the Straight Banana. Tubby, however, is the favourite scapegoat of the farm, and whenever she is seen she is certain to be followed by someone whistling the tune of 'Roll out the barrel'. She is the most teasable person I have ever known. Her very appearance asks for it, with her absurd hat, which she wears perched on the back of her head; her shirt tails which constantly work out of her trousers, and her fine hair which hangs in a shaggy fringe about her face. She has the biggest eyes I have ever seen, and she opens them very wide with an air of curious innocence.

Mr Smith pulls her leg unmercifully, and stuffs her up with nonsense, which she accepts with an engaging faith. One day at lunch he speaks of the vet coming to castrate the young bulls.

'What does castrate mean?' asks Pauline with wide open eyes.

'Well, what do you think it means?' asks Mr Smith.

'Well, I've always thought it had something to do with castor sugar. I thought you fed the bullocks on sugar beet to keep them small.'

Mr Smith looks at her incredulously and then bellows with laughter.

'Well, don't you?' asks Pauline.

When Mr Smith can speak he explains kindly and slowly. 'When the vet comes to castrate the cattle, Miss Gardener, he comes to separate the bullocks from the bull.'

'Sort of "cast" them into groups,' says Pauline intelligently. 'I see.'

Mr Smith bellows again. His little blue eyes swim with tears, and he shakes his head helplessly and gives it up.

'Eh, I don't know, Miss Gardener. You're some comic, mind, I'm telling you!'

Pauline helps herself to more shepherd's pie, and continues her investigation.

'But what is the difference between the bulls and the bullocks?' she asks.

'Well, one have teeth in the top of their heads, and the other have teeth in the bottom.'

'Oh, I see. And the vet comes to see which is which?'

Mr Smith continues to chuckle and to shake his head, muttering, 'Castrate castor sugar!' over to himself. 'That's a good one that is,' he says.

To celebrate Pauline's success at driving, we invite the Smiths to come into Wallbrugh that evening to go to the pictures. I have by this time persuaded my father to let me buy a small car, so that I can get over to my home on my free weekends. This car is very American. She has the character of a competent stenographer with shiny horn-rimmed spectacles and an Eton crop. Her name is Priscilla, and she is very smart and black and business-like.

Mr Smith says that he will stay at home and put the twins to bed if Mrs Smith will go. After a good deal of persuading she agrees, and to make up the four we ask Mrs Weir to come along too.

We make a wonderful evening of it. Mrs Smith enjoys the pictures hugely, criticising the love scenes with a keen eye. 'The silly fellow!' she, says scornfully in a loud ringing voice. 'Why can't he kiss her and be done with it!' At the most tensely sentimental pieces she shrieks with laughter. I can feel her shaking in the chair next to me, and I begin to laugh in sympathy. At any minute I expect us to be flung out by an indignant management.

After the picture is finished, we repair to a 'pie and pea' shop that Mrs Smith knows of. Pauline and I are passionately devoted to pies and peas, and Mrs Smith gives them to us for a treat every Friday for tea. The 'pie and pea' shop is really a bakery. We buy our pies and peas from the shop below, and then carry them on piping hot plates up to the rest room above, where we sit at little tables and eat.

I amuse the company by doing an imitation of some of my customers, and they shriek with delight. The party goes with a swing, and I enjoy myself immensely; far more than I used to enjoy cocktail parties in the old days. But then I always thought cocktail parties were overrated.

After the last pea has been chased round the plate, and been captured and disposed of, we go back to the car. We buy ourselves large ice-cream cornets from a corner café, and sit in the dark primness of Priscilla, sucking them with relish. Mrs Smith says she can sense Priscilla disapproving. We drive home. The evening has been a success, and we are all determined to have another again soon.

When we get back, however, we find that Mr Smith has had a miserable evening coping with the twins. For a long time after we left they had lain in bed shouting for their mother. Jack had dropped off to sleep at last out of exhaustion, but Marian continued to weep and demand drinks of water. When the water was produced, however, she refused to take it and pushed it crossly away.

'What's the matter Marian!' demanded Mr Smith sternly. 'Marian, what is the matter?' Manlike, he did not realise that Marian didn't know what was the matter, that she was only tired out and wanted to be left alone to sleep. They had continued to confront one another, Mr Smith demanding with what he hoped was the air of a stern father, what the matter was, and Marian's wails growing ever louder. In the end she succeeded in waking up Jack, and as we enter the cottage door, their two voices are rising furiously to a climax. Mrs Smith tosses down her gloves and bag on the kitchen table, and rushes upstairs to the rescue. Mr Smith descends looking sheepish.

'Little beggars!' he says. 'That's the last time I take on them for the evening. Proper spoilt, that's what they are. Mind I'm telling you.'

It is enormous fun having Pauline to go with me on the milk round, the only fly in the ointment being that she now wants to share my job of driving. Mr Smith says that he can only spare her to go with me for a few weeks, however, so I behave nicely, and give her her turn at the wheel. With her help we complete the round at a very much faster speed. Alone, on a Saturday, when I have to collect the money, it is sometimes as late as three o'clock before I am finished. With Pauline to help me (even if her money sense is not strong, and she constantly gives the customers wrong change), we romp round in fine style and get finished in no time. Before long Pauline begins to collect a circle of admirers too. The grocer's man spends hours hanging over the side of her door, gazing into her eyes and tapping the end of her nose with his pencil. We find these little attentions help to keep up our self-esteem!

On a Saturday we sometimes have a small boy in the van. He is the son of Mr Weir, and he is a great admirer of that children's paper called *The Dandy*. *The Dandy* is published on a Saturday, and with his Saturday's sixpence clutched hotly in his hand, we agree to take Tommie as a passenger as far as Wallbrugh, where the paper can be procured. But Tommie is only allowed to come with us on the strict understanding that he earns his passage. We make him deliver milk for us, and while he scurries round with his arms full of bottles, we sit in the van and pore over *The Dandy*. We adore the doings of 'Keyhole Kate' and shudder at the powers of the 'Man with Iron Hands'. The tone of the paper is very much more bloodthirsty than those I read when I was young, and I am amazed at the toughness of modern juveniles. Perhaps their early education at the pictures is partly responsible.

Sometimes now, when I want a weekend off, Pauline does the round for me. On these occasions, however, I always return on the Monday; to be met by a stream of abuse from my customers, for although Pauline is very willing, she never seems to be able to get everything quite right. Either she delivers the wrong quantity of milk, or she simply falls into a daydream and forgets to give a customer any milk at all. Many have had to chase her furiously down the road. On several occasions she has delivered a pint of cream instead of a pint of milk; and although we never have complaints on this score, there is always an irate householder somewhere else who has got the pint of milk instead of a pint of cream.

We sing lustily at the top of our voices as we go on our way, and soon, we and our van become quite well known. We always wave to everyone we see; men working on the road, hedgers and ditchers, white line painters and fellow milk deliverers. This is good policy, as wherever we go we sow the seeds of friendship. Then when we get a puncture or our van refuses to start, there is invariably a friend in need somewhere close at hand.

My milk van is often the sole link between some of the outlying cottages and civilisation. We have a regular bunch of daily papers which we agree to deliver, and for which a Wallbrugh paper shop pays us one shilling and ten pence per week as commission!

The staff at the Hall become our firm friends and, in time, even Mr Blenkinsop loses some of his melancholy and slips us an occasional apple that he has snaffled from the dining room sideboard. Mrs Harris, the cook, opens her heart of gold to us. We arrive at her kitchen when our ebb of life is at its lowest. We are weary and hungry, and the succulent smells of her cooking are more than we can bear. Our eyes become rounder and rounder, and we discover that if we hover long enough in the vicinity of her larder, Mrs Harris will invariably take pity on us and cut us a slice of her apple pie, or even offer us a sausage roll!

'I've never seen anything like you land lassies,' she says. 'You are a perfect couple of Dr Barnardo's. Ever open doors, that's what you are!'

CHAPTER ELEVEN
Green Geese

WE ARE VERY SAD when the work on the farm becomes such that Mr Smith can spare Pauline no longer. I go my solitary rounds once more and Pauline returns to her field labours. She is very cross when this happens, and she complains bitterly to Mr Smith that I have got the nicest job and that it isn't fair.

Mr Smith is a kindly soul, and as a measure of recompense he promises to allow Pauline to drive the tractor. It is a great day when she is at last allowed to squeeze herself into the saddle. She is breathless with excitement, and her shirt hangs out of her trousers even more than usual, under the stress of her emotion. Mr Smith takes her into one of the meadows and lets her harrow up the dead grass. For the first few corners Pauline is so enthusiastic she makes her turns far too sharply, and she cobbles up the wire teeth of the harrow in a hopeless tangle. After a while, however, she settles down and learns to drive solemnly and sedately round and round. She finds that, as with a lawn mower, she leaves behind her stripes of differently coloured grass. This delights her and for a time she amuses herself by drawing pretty patterns until Mr Smith notices what she is doing and descends indignantly to stop her.

'You daft lass! You can't tell which bits you've done that way' he points out.

'Oh, I see,' said Pauline. 'This is such fun Mr Smith!'

She sets off again, this time with better results. She must indeed be enjoying herself, for she even works on late instead of coming in to tea. It is an unheard of thing for Pauline to miss a meal!

Lately, Pauline's appetite has increased at an alarming rate. I have never seen anyone eat as much as she does, but, as she says, the fresh air makes her hungry. She has second helpings of both dishes at lunch as a matter of course, and if she is working near the cottage and can persuade Mrs Smith to give her anything between meals, she does. One day after an especially large lunch, Mrs Smith carries the remains of her pie through into the scullery. Pauline goes to put on her boots, and seeing the pie, she is unable to resist it. Mrs Smith catches her as she is licking out the last of the dish.

'Miss Gardener!' gasps Mrs Smith.

Pauline gives a guilty look in her direction and speeds out into the farmyard. She looks exactly like a puppy that has been caught stealing and expects to be whipped, and Mrs Smith and I laugh helplessly.

'Well, I never!' says Mrs Smith as she puts the empty pie dish under the scullery tap. 'Take the food out of the mouths of the poor dogs, now, will you?'

As well as driving the tractor whenever it is needed (and the job is not too skilful), Pauline is allowed to work with a horse and cart. She is passionately fond of animals and she adopts one of the horses on the farm as her especial pet. Bett is a fat creature with a pretty head and cunning little eyes. She has Pauline taped from the first day they confront one another and she sucks up to her unscrupulously. Pauline is flattered by the whinnies that greet her from the wily Bett, and every evening she takes her sugar and goes and talks to her in her stall. Bett is more interested in the sugar than in the talking, but for the sake of the one she puts up with the other with a good grace and allows Pauline to sit by the hour in her manger.

If ever there are any mangolds to be led for the sheep, or loads of hay from the stack to the stable, Pauline hitches up Bett and the two of them set out. Bett knows just how weak and kind-hearted Pauline is and, being female herself, she knows just how best to exploit her. Sometimes after considerable difficulty, Pauline will back her into the required position beneath the haystack. Bett waits until Pauline has climbed up into the hay, and then, impervious to her indignant reproaches, she ambles off and away until she can pull herself mouthfuls of hay from the side of the stack. These she munches appreciatively and watches Pauline wearily descending the ladder to push her back once again into position. Bett would never dream of behaving in this way with anyone else. She has learned long ago that it does not really pay a horse to misbehave. But with Pauline it is different, and except for evoking a reproachful, 'Now, Betty darling, you must be a good girl,' she knows that no form of unpleasant retribution will descend on her. Sometimes they go through this performance for ages before I or little Tommie, or one of the men appear to hold Bett's head.

'I don't know what's come over Betty today,' says Pauline invariably. 'She's usually such an angel.'

As the year advances, lambs begin to be born, and Pauline is given the job of going round with Mr Smith to feed the sheep. They set off with sacks of crushed meal upon their shoulders, and the grey collie Tinker dancing about their heels. Tinker is an excellent sheep dog. She is a graceful creature with wise eyes and infinite patience. She will crawl inch by inch for yards, on her belly, if her charges are nervous or apt to be wild; and she seems to sense an order almost before it is given. She has the most engaging habit of dragging herself up to you on her seat, and I have never seen any dog laugh as she does. Her lips wrinkle up in a positive grin of welcome when she sees you coming, and her little teeth flash in a broad smile. But Tinker doesn't like cows! If she sees a cow she tucks her tail between her legs and makes off as fast as she knows how. She obviously regards herself as exclusively a sheep dog, and although she lives on a dairy farm, she regards cattle as vulgar, dangerous animals, of which a wise dog fights shy. Mr Smith has therefore, a second dog, a black collie called Rip, whose job it is to see after the cattle. He is a fine strapping masculine sort of dog, and he snarls and snaps at the cows' heels until even the fat old grandmas are persuaded to get a move on. He and Tinker set up more than a working acquaintanceship, and before many months have passed, Tinker is invariably found to be once again in the family way. Her puppies are pretty little things, and she makes her home at the end of a long tunnel which she digs in the side of the haystack. She only keeps them there for a short while, however, and after a few days a safer and roomier home has to be found for them. She chooses an old derelict lavatory at Stoney Hall for this purpose. It is an earth closet that has long been out of use, and one evening Mr Smith traces her to it and finds her family of four warmly tucked up in the open seat.

One evening Mr Smith is busy and he asks me to go with Pauline to help her feed his sheep. Pauline is delighted to be able to tell me what to do for a change, and she sees to it that I carry the biggest sack of corn. The sheep are penned in a muddy corner of a field, and their hungry bleats are plaintive in the cold evening. They are penned off by a piece of wire netting nailed to stakes driven into the ground. The wire is waist high, and we find it a problem to get over this while at the same time carrying our heavy sacks of meal. In the end we have to help one another, and together we swing the sacks over and into the mud on the other side. Once there, we hitch out sacks back on to our shoulders and stagger off for the distant wooden troughs. The sheep bleat more anxiously as they see us coming and they begin to approach us cautiously on their stiff peglike legs.

The ground has been churned up to a complete quagmire, and with our heavy sacks to bear us down, we are soon ankle deep in the soggy mud. Suddenly I step right out of my rubber boot and leave it behind me. I am carried on by my weighty sack and I step with my stockinged foot into the mire. Somehow I lose my other boot, and I am left standing up to the ankles in mud, with my two empty boots leaning drunkenly in the mud behind me. I giggle helplessly. Pauline giggles helplessly.

'All right, Aunty Bee. Don't try to move. I'll get them for you.'

She staggers toward my empty boots, but before she knows it, suck! – she leaves one of hers behind her too! We shriek with laughter. The sheep feeding becomes a riot! We rescue our boots and reel off to the wooden troughs. We pour out the meal, spilling a shameful amount of it on to the mud. The sheep nudge about us, coughing and bleating, and shoving one another eagerly.

'Now we count them,' says Pauline. 'We count them over three times. Just to make sure.'

The first time we get a hundred and four. The second time we get them to a hundred and two, and the third time to ninety-seven.

'How on earth can anyone count them when they keep moving about like this?' I gasp weakly.

'Come on, now, Aunty Bee, count them again. One of the numbers must be right.'

We count them again, and this time we make ninety-three.

'There is hanky panky going on somewhere,' says Pauline. 'There must be, Aunty Bee.'

'How do you manage to count them usually?' I ask.

'Well, Mr Smith generally does it. It always looked so easy, I never tried.'

'Let's, give it up. I expect they are all here anyway.'

'I don't think we ought to,' said Pauline doubtfully, but she nevertheless follows me over to the cutter and we begin slicing turnips.

We take it in turns to turn the handle of the cutter for it is heavy. It is hard work, and the turnips pour out of the cutter into the bassinette below in a perfect torrent. When the bassinette is full we carry it over to the troughs and empty it. On each journey we lose one or other of our rubber boots, and finally we give up trying to continue the job in them and take them off altogether. Pauline's big toe sticks out through her land army sock. This is another characteristic of Pauline's. She never by any chance thinks of washing her socks or darning them, and as her land army career progresses, her toes and heels become more and more in evidence and the amount of intact stocking daily decreases. It is bitterly cold squelching round shoeless in the mud, but we find that to keep on putting back our boots makes them impossibly dirty inside.

'We must look priceless plodding round like this among the sheep,' giggles Pauline. 'Oh, if my mother could see me now!'

The one who is not turning the handle has the job of keeping the cutter supplied with a steady stream of turnips. It is an easy job forking them from the turnip pit up into the cutter, and it is very pleasing to be able to stand back lazily and watch one's red-faced companion breathlessly doing the hard work. On this occasion however, it seems to be my turn at the handle more often than it is Pauline's. When I eventually comment on this, Pauline points out that this is quite fair really, because she has to do this every night whereas I don't; which is, of course, true. The turnips are frozen in the pit, and as she prizes them loose with her fork they roll in a sudden liberated cascade about her feet. Their juice is solidified by the frost, so that they look as if they are coated with fine amber, and it makes them hard and more difficult to cut.

When we are eventually finished, we pick up our muddy boots and our empty meal sacks and make our way back to the farm. We are still bubbling with laughter, and we link our arms about each other's neck and begin to sing and stagger in a state of seeming high intoxication. We punctuate our repertoire amply with hiccoughs, and as we turn the corner and enter the yard, who should we see but Mr Foster.

We blush scarlet and hastily assume a more natural position. We smile brightly and say 'good evening', but we are painfully aware of our stocking-clad feet, and of Pauline's big toe, which is still visible even though amply covered with mud.

'Oh, Aunty Bee, what must he think of me now?' whispers Pauline as we scurry for shelter into the stable. 'I seem fated to put my foot in it.'

I am quaking with laughter. All too vividly I remember Pauline's first encounter with Mr Foster. It happened when she had only been at Stoney Hall a week. She was washing her hair in the scullery sink when suddenly she heard a knock at the back door. Mrs Smith had just gone out to get some sticks and Pauline thought that it was she who was knocking, unable to open the door because her hands were full. It really was quite a natural conclusion to draw. It was just bad luck that it happened to be Mr Foster instead.

When Pauline opened the door to him her hair was hanging down over her face in a dripping mass. She had no jersey on, and her round person was thinly clad in her winter woolly vest. For an awful minute they gaped at one another; then Mr Foster regained control.

'My God!' he said, and turning on his heels he rushed off into the stackyard.

What Pauline felt must remain unrecorded. Sufficient to say that it took her many many weeks to recover, and to this day she can never meet Mr Foster without blushing.

One of the jobs that Mr Smith finds for us to do is picking stones. We are sent off daily to some vast plateau, each with a battered bucket, and told that we are to gather all the stones we can see and build them into heaps. This is boring in the extreme. We feel after we have been stone-gathering for one day that we have exhausted all its possibilities. After gathering them constantly for three weeks, we begin to feel like pieces of old Gorgonzola with the whiskers growing, out of sheer stagnation. We make up stories which we tell each other to pass the time; but even one's imagination grows sterile after a few days. Occasionally we take a few minutes off and sit for a rest on our upturned buckets. They make comfortable seats in an inverted position, and we sit in the sun and think how pleasant it would be never to have to do any work again.

One of Pauline's jobs, while I had the fun of taking the milk van out, was the dreary monotonous one of cutting thistles. She cut these endlessly. If Mr Smith did not know what to do with Pauline, he gave her a gee-ball and told her to go out and cut thistles. She became so fed up with cutting thistles that it positively began to prey on her mind. One day I found her sleepily peering out of the window to see if it was raining, at five o'clock in the morning. If it was fine there was a chance that she might be given some other job to do; but cutting thistles can be done in all weathers, and if it rained, it was certain that that was what would be her lot. She became quite good at it in the end, and she swirled her gee-ball with quite a professional sweep. The gee-ball is a sort of sickle with a long handle. This implement was Pauline's constant companion for many days. She even began to take a certain amount of pride in her thistle cutting. She might not be able to plough or milk, or manage a horse, but at cutting thistles no one could surely find fault with her! But one afternoon Mr Foster was walking round the farm with Mr Smith, and the two stood and watched Pauline for a while over the wall. She was unaware of their gaze, for she was lost in one of her day-dreams, and it was only when Mr Smith repeated to her what Mr Foster had said that she knew about it.

'Huh!' Mr Foster had observed in disgust. 'How many thistles does she cut? One a minute?'

When Pauline heard this sacrilege about her thistle-cutting ability, she was speechless.

We do not escape our full share of manure spreading, even after leaving Spital Tongues. Mr Smith sends us out to a big sloping field where the hateful little huts march in rows, and wait for us. We set to work. On the other side of the field Gideon is working with his horses ploughing up the manured stubble into bleeding strips of wet earth. There is a steam of sweat hanging over the horses in the cold air. They seem to be an immense power to pull so small a thing as a plough, and in Gideon's steady hands the furrows curl over in beautiful exactitude and with seemingly incredible ease.

Pauline can hardly spread her manure for watching her beloved Bert; and she glues her eyes on Gideon to see that he does not treat her roughly. In the end she can contain herself no longer, and she sticks her fork in the middle of a hut of manure and goes across to see how Bert is getting on. Bert makes a quick examination of Pauline's pockets and, finding them empty of sugar, she loses interest.

'Will you let me try and plough, Gideon?' asks Pauline eagerly.

'All right,' says Gideon good-naturedly. 'But keep it straight, mind; and don't let it get too deep.'

Pauline, with elaborate care, winds the rope reins about her hands and grasps the handles of the plough. 'Get up, Betty!' she says.

The great horses plunge forward. They move much faster than Pauline has anticipated, and although she succeeds in retaining her grasp of the plough, her feet are left very far behind. Her stern sticks out at an incredible angle as she proceeds up the furrow. She has the appearance of being pulled along by the plough rather than of driving it, and Gideon and I laugh at her retreating back until our eyes stream.

'Eh, she's a funny one is Tubby,' says Gideon; and follows her up the field to get her out of the tangle that she manages to knot her horses into when trying to turn them at the top.

Pauline, however, is well satisfied with her performance, and returns with a flushed face, tucking in the tail of her shirt.

'I ploughed, Aunty Bee!' she says delightedly. 'A whole furrow, all by myself.'

The next day she has a chance to try her hand at another sort of ploughing. Gideon and his horses are replaced by Charlie and the tractor, and of course nothing will do but that she must try her hand at this too. Pauline loves to feel that she is in command of the powerful, even though she may be very far from being in command in point of fact.

Charlie is a great admirer of Pauline's, however, especially when she opens her large eyes very wide and says, 'Charlie, darling, do be an angel and let me try!'

What defence has anyone against that? For several furrows, Pauline rides in proud glory, and Charlie stands beside her so that nothing can go very far wrong. Occasionally, the shears of the tractor catch on a boulder and the safety catch opens, dropping the plough and allowing the tractor to proceed alone. This device saves the metal from becoming bent. Whenever this happens, Charlie grinds the tractor into reverse gear. They reverse and pick up the plough, and where the boulder was they stick a stake in the ground to mark the spot. Later on Mr Weir and Gideon will come along with a cart, dig up the boulder and carry it away. Pauline is very puzzled by these boulders. She cannot understand how it is that year after year a field can be ploughed up and still new boulders appear, boulders that were seemingly not there at all the year before. One day at lunch, Pauline tackles Mr Smith on this subject. His eyes twinkle and as usual Pauline swallows everything that he tells her.

'Well, you see, Miss Gardener,' says Mr Smith solemnly, 'stones grow, same as vegetables. Every year they get a little bigger. Mind, it takes a long time, but one day even a little pebble will be a big stone.'

'Do they really?' says Pauline, uncertain if her leg is being pulled or not. 'I've never heard that before.'

'Oh, but they do. It's right enough. You plant a stone in the garden here and dig it up before you go. You'll find it a lot bigger maybe, if the war is long enough.'

His manner is so sincere that poor Pauline is completely taken in.

'Do you know, Aunty Bee,' she tells me later. 'Mr Smith says stones grow. I never knew that before, did you?'

'Don't you think he was teasing you? It doesn't sound likely to me.'

'Oh, do you think he was?' said Pauline sadly. 'Why do I never know when people are being serious! It isn't fair, really it isn't!'

The tractor driving progresses favourably, and apparently the friendship between Pauline and Charlie progresses too. In the end

Charlie pays more attention to Pauline than to where he is going, for suddenly there is a grinding crash, and looking round, I see Pauline and the tractor disappearing rapidly through the hedge.

Pauline immediately loses interest in the whole proceedings. Her urge to drive the tractor leaves her, and after apologising anxiously to Charlie, she beats a hasty retreat back to the manure, and leaves him to salvage his tractor as best he can.

'Oh, dear!' sighs Pauline as she listlessly hurls a lump of manure off her fork. 'Why does everything go wrong the minute I touch it? It isn't fair, really it isn't!'

We eagerly await lousing time to come, however, for tonight we are being taken out on the spree, and with that ahead, no amount of ditched tractors can depress us for long.

Pauline has many cousins, one of whom is also a friend of mine. He has managed to take a night off from the Army to come and take us into town, and we have been looking forward to it eagerly all the week. It is now over a month since we put our hands back to the plough, and we are beginning to feel the need of a little light entertainment.

When lousing time comes therefore, we hurry back to the farm, and plunging our bodies into the bath, we attempt vainly to remove the lingering odour of manure. I am just at my most abandoned wallowing when a knock comes at the front door, and Pauline's cousin arrives. John has a habit of arriving when I am in my bath, so he is used to having to wait for me. Mrs Smith therefore, has ample time to study him, and I hope anxiously that he will pass the test. I put considerable store by Mrs Smith's opinion, and if she disapproved of my friends, I really believe that I should have to reconsider them in a new light. I have indeed tried to pretend that it is not me whom John is coming to see but his cousin Pauline. When I first put this suggestion into general circulation, Pauline could hardly forbear to let is pass undenied. She feels bitterly towards John, because he too can never resist teasing her. I admit that his pet name for her is somewhat cruelly chosen. It must be maddening to be introduced to all his friends as Emma, the Portable Balloon Ballast Company.

John, however, spoils my carefully laid camouflage by asking

Mrs Smith for me instead of for Pauline. Mrs Smith shows him into the sitting-room with gleaming eyes, and banging on the bathroom door she calls, 'Hurry up, Miss Whitton. Your young man is here.'

We settle ourselves joyfully in John's powerful car and are rushed luxuriously into Carmouth. It is delightful to relax after a day's labours, and to hand one's destiny over into the capable hands of a youthful admirer. John disapproves heartily of my land activities and he makes a sympathetic audience to whom I pour out all our woes. Tonight, however, he is not feeling very well. He has a temperature and suspects that he is getting 'flu. When I hear this, I suggest that he ought not to have come.

'I simply dared not ring up and cancel it, Bee, after I had promised,' he says.

'I should think not!' says his hard-hearted cousin from the back seat.

John takes us to dine at a restaurant in Carmouth. Here we eat hugely and at great expense; especially Pauline, who is delighted that her cousin will have to foot the bill. Our faces are flaming like a couple of radiators, after a day's exposure in the fresh air, and we find it is quite impossible to keep any powder on our noses.

After dinner John takes us to a play. The theatre is delightfully gay and civilised after the somewhat cramped quarters of our local picture house at Wallbrugh, and Pauline and I sigh with contentment, and settle back to enjoy the show. The unusually soft seats, however, combined with our large dinner and the fresh air that we have been inhaling all day, soon have their effect. Before the first act is over, I am yawning, and to my annoyance I miss a good half of a most excellent play simply because I fall asleep. Poor John too, is in a doped condition. His temperature rises steadily and I begin to be really concerned about him.

After the show is over we go back to find his car. He puts me into the front seat, and it is now my turn to be wrapped with the one and only rug. Pauline is just preparing to climb into the back when John finds that his tyre is flat. This is a frightful blow. I offer my assistance, but he firmly will not hear of my moving, saying that he can manage perfectly well with the help of Pauline. Poor Pauline is yanked out of the back seat protesting bitterly at the injustice.

'Let Aunty Bee come and help too!' she moans. 'She's just as young as I am. It's not fair, really it's not.'

'Shut up,' says her cousin rudely. 'Don't be such a lazy little beast. It won't do you any harm to work some of that fat off!'

'Well, let Aunty Bee come too! If I've got to suffer so should she.'

'Shut up and hold this torch,' said John menacingly. 'If you don't be quiet I'll never bring you out to dinner again. You aren't old enough.'

I cannot help smiling sleepily into the night. Quivering with rage under this final insult, Pauline holds the torch for John and hands him nuts as he wrestles with the offending wheel.

'It's not fair, really it's not,' I hear her muttering.

On the way home the moon comes up and the drive is unbelievably lovely. In spite of the dipped lights, John can see the road plainly and the trees are pinned against the sky like pieces of black lace. Pauline, worn out by her enforced labours, goes to sleep crossly in the back seat, and my head sinks happily on to John's shoulder. The night is still and quiet, and I am filled with peaceful content. I could go on driving like this until the end of the world.

When we turn into the stable yard, I see a streak of light appear in the cottage window of the dairy family, and I know that the farm espionage system is at work. I know that a full bulletin of my comings and goings will be in circulation next morning; but in one thing anyway I determine to disappoint them. I open the car door and we get out. We say good night.

'Good night, Bee,' says John. 'Good night Emma you little beast. See you again soon.'

As we go up to bed we hear the soft purring of his car as he turns it in the yard, and points its nose once more to civilisation. We go into the bathroom to wash, and find the floor is covered with large black beetles. We surrender it to them with one accord. Washing can wait until the morning.

CHAPTER TWELVE
Pauline in Spring

THRESHING ON THE FARM is an important day for everyone. All hands are needed to feed the greedy threshing machine, and even the dairy people (who ordinarily are held aloof from all common or garden farm labour) permit themselves graciously to be drawn into it. For days beforehand Pauline and Gideon have been leading loads of corn from the stacks in the yard and packing it into the loft in the granary. This is a pleasant job, and when my milk round is finished I am sometimes allowed to go and help them. Pauline and I crouch with bent backs under the corrugated iron roof of the hayshed. We fork down the sheaves to the waiting cart below, where Gideon builds them into a neat load. It is cramped at first, working beneath the tightly packed roof, for there is only a small hole left in the side of the stack where we are able to stand. Occasionally, the handles of our forks hit the iron with a savage ring. For some reason, no matter which sheaf one selects as one's next victim, it always turns out to be another part of the one you are already standing on. It is sure to be completely fast and immobile and one wrestles with it without result. I really don't know why this should be, but anyone who has forked sheaves will tell you that it is so.

We hang our coats on an iron rafter and become steadily hotter in the cramped space among the corn. As the carts are loaded, however, we gradually make more room for ourselves, and as Gideon comes up we go down. Very soon we are able to talk to him.

'Seen any films lately, Gideon?' says Pauline, carelessly tossing him a sheaf when he is not looking; so that it catches him unawares on the back of his neck.

The atmosphere is thick with dust, and there are a million rustlings in the dry corn husks at our feet. The sunlight strikes in at us in a horizontal line, and picking out the whirling grains of dust, it moulds them into a solidly revolving column. There is something timeless about a hayshed. Up there in the half-light with the scent of mustiness in my nose, and the warm body of dead corn under, over, and all about me, I feel as if I could step outside and find I had wandered into almost any century. A sparrow scrabbles loudly on the iron roof, and very distantly I hear the mournful lowing of a cow.

'There is an awfully good one at the Odeon at present,' says Pauline, wrestling to find a sheaf that she is not standing on. '"Crash Pilot"; Aunty Bee and I saw it last night.'

When threshing day arrives everyone hurries through his work so as to be able to get started early. Each man has his own job. Mr Smith cuts the strings of the sheaves and feeds the mouth of the tractor with their dismembered contents. Pauline and Mr Weir keep him supplied from the stack of corn in the granary loft. Gideon and Bob, the dairyman, stand at the spout where the threshed grain pours out, waiting for the sacks to fill so that they can tie them up and carry them away. Little Tommie Weir acts as chaff boy, and it is his job to keep the sifting heap of chaff that oozes out in a perpetual yellow stream, scraped out and cleared away from the thresher. Peter and Reg, the two sons of the dairyman, stand with me at the side of the thresher. It is our job to cart away the threshed bundles of straw and build them into a stack in the hayshed outside. This is probably one of the dirtiest jobs there is on the farm, and by the end of the day my red scarf is thickly coated in a velvet dust.

Everyone works like a machine. There must be no hitch, for if one person gets behind with his job, it holds up the whole proceedings. There is a pleasant atmosphere of comradeship however. We are all working in unison for a common cause, and threshing day has the atmosphere of being something out of the ordinary run of things and rather an occasion. Mr Smith slashes his strings with a cheerful exactness and is quite impervious to stray mice that frequently run up his trousers. Mr Weir and Pauline are occasionally able to kill these mice as they scuttle out of the corn to seek safety in the hollow walls. Mr Smith keeps the mutilated dead bodies beside him in a neat pile; then when the occasion arises and I have my back turned to him, he will suddenly bombard me with an absolute rain of them from his lofty platform. I don't like dead mice. The louder I scream, the more he likes it. Pauline likes it too. It is not often that she sees anyone else being teased, and she finds the sight refreshing.

Our first threshing day at Stoney Hall falls on a wet afternoon. Pauline and I are for once early, and we arrive at the granary before Mr Smith is ready to begin. The thresher has not yet been started, and Mr Weir is wandering intelligently about poking an oil can into different parts of its inside.

'Hullo you two!' says Mr Weir, squirting a jet of oil automatically in Pauline's direction. 'And how is my little Tubb today?'

'Nearly dead, but otherwise all right,' says Pauline removing the oil from her cheek with an already indescribable handkerchief.

'Will you come to the pictures with me tonight, Tubby?'

'Rather, where shall I meet you?'

'Now that's not right!' says Mr Weir reproachfully. 'You shouldn't appear so eager. It's not nice'

'I like that!' says Pauline. 'I wouldn't go to the pictures now if you were to ask me on your bended knees!'

'I won't do that Tubb. Never fear. A man doesn't have to go to the pictures for his entertainment when you are around.'

He makes a playful dive for her hat, but Pauline leaps aside. She over-balances however, and sits down hard on a heap of straw. Mr Weir makes another dive for her hat. Pauline, imagining that he is going to tickle her, emits a shrill scream.

'Don't,' she implores. 'I'll do anything! I'll be good! I promise I'll be good! But whatever you do don't tickle me!'

Mr Weir, who hadn't thought of this himself, wonders why it had never occurred to him to do so, and promptly tickles her. She rolls in the straw and shrieks for him to stop. I take pity on her.

'Look out,' I say, 'here's Mr Foster!'

It is not Mr Foster, but my warning has the desired effect and Mr Weir withdraws hastily. Pauline straightens herself, puts on her hat, tucks in her shirt and gets to her feet with a scarlet face.

'Why is it always I who get teased in this place?' she says bitterly. 'Aunty Bee – oh no! Never anyone but me. It's not fair, really it's not!'

The thresher is started. The great belts whine into activity and the iron teeth masticate eagerly, hungry for their fodder of straw. The thresher is always a wonder to me. I never can fathom its intricate pulley and hooks, and it always astonishes me that anything looking so clumsy and Heath Robinson, should really do what this machine does.

Today, however, the thresher is misbehaving. It is lazy, for it spits out bundle after bundle of straw all loose instead of being neatly tied up with a girdle of knotted string. Whenever this happens, Reg puts up his fork and bangs on Mr Smith's platform to tell him to stop work. The engines are halted. Everyone relaxes except Mr Smith and Mr Weir, who climb about the thresher's intestines, threading strings through slots, and reminding one of a giant sewing machine. We watch their efforts detachedly, squatting on the straw, or leaning on our forks and talking idly. There is a sudden scuffle up in the loft and Pauline descends to join us, feet first down the shaky ladder. Her shirt has, as usual, worked its way out of her trousers and her face is very pink and shiny.

'Would you like to swop jobs for a bit, Aunty Bee?' she says. 'Mr Smith works at such a rate, he is a perfect menace. I haven't worked so hard since we left Spital Tongues.'

I consent gladly, for I spent a day threshing during my month's training, and I am well aware that Pauline's job is in fact the easiest of the lot. We change places, and when the thresher is under way once more, I work up in the loft beside Mr Weir. Mr Smith certainly keeps us busy, and he takes an infinite delight in rushing through his sheaves so that for a few minutes he is empty-handed, and he can grin at us, wrestling to work free a sheaf for him, and tell us to hurry up.

'Come on! Come on! Come on!' he says. 'You're holding up the whole party. I've never seen such a slow couple in my life.'

We pay him out for this by tossing him a perfect shower of sheaves, far more than he can manage. They mount up around him in a golden barricade, until only his small red face with his agitated hair, can be seen above it.

'All right,' he says at last, 'keep your hair on! Give a body time to turn round.'

It is not very long before the string again breaks, and Reg's fork bangs for us to stop work. Pauline's face immediately appears up the ladder.

'I think I like my own job best, Aunty Bee,' she says.

When the threshing is finally done the great machine whines to a stop, and sighing gently, it subsides and allows the dust to settle once more upon it in a thick white blanket. The atmosphere gradually clears. The dust stops puffing like a cloud of smoke out of the doorway into the stackyard, and Mr Weir and Pauline sweep up the floor of the loft with a couple of hairless brooms. Mr Smith closes his knife and puts it away. He casually searches his trousers for any stray mice that happen to be lodged there, and dropping them on the floor, he kills them with his boot.

I shall never forget one day. We had spent the morning threshing and at midday we knocked off for lunch. Mr Smith is very interested in politics. We were in the middle of a heated discussion about the policy of the 'Eye-tally-anns' as he calls them, when he suddenly bent forward and gazed earnestly into our faces.

'I'll tell you what,' said Mr Smith. 'I've got a mouse!' He went out into the scullery, plunged his hand down his trousers, and sure enough there the mouse was! He tossed it out into the yard as casually as if it were a beetle, and going back to his lunch, he took up the discussion where he had left off. Pauline and I were speechless. The thought of finding a mouse in our own trousers sent chills of horror up our spines. I am quite sure that if such a thing ever happened to me, my clothes would come off in a heap no matter where I was. I should expose my nakedness any day rather than endure the suspicion of a mouse in my pants.

The day after threshing is over, Pauline is given her beloved Bett and a cart, and told to clear away the heap of chaff, and empty it on the floor of the hemmel among the bullocks. Pauline would enjoy this job if it were not for the unwelcome presence of young Jack Smith. Jack Smith can be a tiresome small boy when he chooses, and this is a day when he does. When he discovers the heap of chaff it presents him with a wonderful new world in which to play, and he is not slow in realising its possibilities. He attaches himself to Pauline like a leech, and whenever she is likely to find him most in the way, there he is sure to be. He shows a lively interest in the whole proceedings.

'What are you doing there, eh?' he says.

'I'm loading the chaff into the cart, Jack,' says Pauline.

'What are you doing there, eh?'

'I said I'm loading the chaff into the cart, Jack.'

'What are you doing there, eh?' demands Jack again.

Pauline does not answer. Jack begins to dance up and down in the chaff, and he repeats his question over and over again. He knows quite well that he is annoying Pauline almost beyond endurance, but the devil of mischief is big in him and he is driven on.

'What are you doing there, eh? What are you doing there, eh, Miss Gardener?'

Pauline suppresses her longing to commit murder, and works stoically on. He continues his chant the whole time she is filling her cart. He continues it as he accompanies her to the hemmel, and he sings it all the way back again.

Pauline assures me later that he must have asked her what she was doing there, eh? quite a hundred times before her control finally snapped.

'Jack!' she said menacingly. 'If you say that again I'll fling you head first into the yard.'

'What are you doing there, eh?' says Jack.

Pauline makes a dive for him and catches him by the seat of his pants and by his collar. She will stand a lot, but here at least she can take a firm line. She shakes him like a rabbit, and tosses him right into the middle of the heap of chaff.

Jack is very much more astonished than hurt, but when he picks himself up he is red in the face with rage. He yells. He feels as injured as Bett would feel if the much put-upon Pauline were suddenly to turn upon her.

'I'll tell my mum!' he shrieks furiously. 'You – you land clapper!'

Mrs Smith's reception of him is, however, disappointing. She is more amused by the retribution that has descended on him than sympathetic, and she tells him that Miss Gardener was probably quite justified.

'That land clapper!' he says. 'That land clapper!'

'Jack!' says Mrs Smith aghast, 'wherever did you hear that?'

Jack explains that this is the name that the dairy people have for us.

'Land clapper!' he storms.

Marian is sitting demurely on the hearth playing with a ball, and Marian is our friend. She cannot let this pass.

'They are not land clappers, Jack!' she says severely. 'They're the land army!'

'They're land clappers.'

'They're not, Jack! They're the land army.'

'They're land clappers.'

With division thus threatened in the home, Mrs Smith hastily causes a diversion by offering them both a slice of bread and jam. They subside satisfied, but all is not forgotten. For many days, whenever a bone of contention rises between them, they revert to their old argument. Long after they have forgotten what they mean, they continue heatedly to insist respectively that we are land clappers, or that we are the land army.

Marian is an attractive small girl and she is a great friend of ours. She early organised Pauline into giving her pick-a-backs up to bed at night, and she has always felt more tolerant towards us than Jack. One morning at midday we were sitting round the table having our lunch. The day was hot and I was wearing a minimum of clothing. My jumper was a thin one with little holes in it, and Marian sat in her high chair studying it intently for a long time. Suddenly she leaned over to her mother and said in a loud confidential whisper:

'Mummy! Miss Whitton hasn't got a vest on!' She was shocked profoundly.

Lunchtime with the Smiths was always a hilarious affair. Mr Smith would tease Pauline unmercifully, and if she had done anything wrong, he would take the opportunity of pointing it out to her. Pauline was always very contrite on these occasions.

'I'm awfully sorry, Mr Smith, really I am,' she would say.

Sometimes when the tirade that descended on her was particularly heavy, or the brick that she dropped was an especially large one, she would hang her head and cover it over with her table napkin.

She continued to eat however, carrying the food uncertainly to her mouth and disposing of it under the shield of her clumsy veil.

'Stay like that, Miss Gardener!' said Mrs Smith encouragingly one day. 'It's a great improvement to you. It saves us seeing your face.'

Pauline emerged in speechless indignation.

'Mrs Smith!' she said. 'Is that kind! Is that fair! Just for that I'll pour water down your neck!'

'You wouldn't dare,' said Mrs Smith. 'I'll break a plate over your head if you do.'

Pauline turned to face her, glass in hand. Whether or not it was an accident I do not know, but the water certainly got spilt down Mrs Smith.

Like a flash, Mrs Smith whipped up a plate and rapped Pauline smartly over the head. No one was more astonished than Mrs Smith when the plate broke in two, unless it was Pauline. We laughed helplessly. I must say that I have never seen anyone take a teasing better than our dear Tubby.

There are dozens of children at Stoney Hall. I have never seen so many all about the same age anywhere else. There are Jack and Marian, Mr Weir's Tommie and his small sister, Gideon's baby, and three all under ten from the prolific parents of the dairy family. There is also a little tough aged two from the molecatcher's cottage down the road. His name is Cecil.

Cecil is the Mussolini of the entire farm. I have very seldom found it in me to be able to hate a child, but during my stay at Stoney Hall I come very near to hating Cecil. He has black curly hair and a sullen pugnacious little face. The other children go in mortal terror of him. I do not blame them. I am frightened of him myself, and he is wont to bite them and try to gouge out their eyes with his finger. Cecil invariably has a dirty face. He wears small Wellington boots, and in his heart I don't believe there is a spark of human kindness. Tough is not in it! One day he emerges from the byre when I am waiting up on the hay shed for Mr Weir to find the ladder to let me down. Cecil does not see me there, and when he comes out of the byre he frowns furiously and looks about him.

'Wonder where those kids have got to!' he says. He stumps off in search of them. He must be the youngest of the 'kids' by a good two years.

When Cecil is about, the wretched animals have a miserable time. He has no fear of them at all, and he would as readily punch a horse on the nose as kick the behind of a dog. But the kittens have the worst time of all, and many a dripping little wretch I have had to rescue from an early grave in the horse trough.

Cecil could hardly walk before he wanted to try his hand at forking hay. It is an incredible sight to see him, aged two years, staggering across the yard with a hayfork over his shoulder and on the end a heap of hay, very little smaller than the ones Pauline and I are wont to lift.

Children begin to play a rather prominent part in my farm existence. There are a number of them on my milk round, with whom I come into daily contact, and some of them I begin to dislike almost as much as I dislike Cecil. There is a young lady called Iris, for instance. Iris has flaxen hair cut in a heavy fringe over her brow. Every day when I drive my van up to the row of cottages where she lives, Iris is waiting for me. In one of the cottages lives a pleasant woman called Sally. Sally is a post girl, so she is very seldom at home when I arrive with the milk. I am never certain how much milk she wants, as she gets a gill extra some days, but on these occasions she usually leaves a message with one of the other cottagers. One day, when I am confronted with Iris, she dances in front of me. 'Sally wants a pint, Sally wants a pint,' she sings. So decided is she that I presume Sally has entrusted her with the message. I leave Sally a pint.

Next day, it is the same – 'Sally wants a pint, Sally wants a pint,' sings Iris.

Sally gets another pint.

This goes on until pay day at the end of the week. Sally pays on a Sunday as that is her day off, and when I go for her money she demands to know why I have persistently left her a pint all the week when she has not asked for it.

'Well, the little girl said that you wanted it,' I say.

'That little limb of mischief!' says Sally. 'Don't you believe a word she says! And do you know what? She has begun drinking my milk now. When I get back at night I find my bottle half empty on the step. I think you had better put it in my washhouse where she can't get at it.'

After this, I take no further notice of Iris's assurance that, 'Sally wants a pint.'

'No she doesn't Iris,' I say. 'You know quite well that Sally doesn't want a pint.'

'Oh, but Sally *does* want a pint,' Iris persists.

Another of Iris's dear little traits is to insist on 'pushing me off' when I start away in my van again. This not only leaves a mass of sticky fingerprints on the back of my van, but one day it very nearly proves fatal. This particular morning when I drive off I am followed down the road by a shrieking and gesticulating mother. Thinking I have forgotten her milk I stop, but it seems that it is not her milk that she is worried about, but Iris, who is discovered clinging to the handle of the back door of the van, and whom I am cheerfully carrying away. Her mother is cross. She blames me, which I feel is hard. I feel that Iris wouldn't be much loss to anyone anyhow, but I suppose I cannot expect her mother to feel the same.

It is growing warmer as the year advances and the nights are becoming shorter. I no longer leave the farm in darkness, and for this I am rather sad as I can no longer witness the coming of the winter dawn. I had no idea before I went on the land how lovely the sky could be before the sun is up, for in ordinary circumstances I am tucked away warmly in my bed. However, having to get up early, anyhow, I learn to look forward to the dawn with considerable pleasure. The dark inkiness of the winter sky grows gradually lighter; softly the bands of cloud separate and become streaked with glorious colours of primrose yellow and white. There is nothing so clean and refreshing as a winter's sky on a cold fine morning. It is like douching one's face in a mountain stream, or standing naked before an open window.

As the sun grows warmer, the seeds that have been sown the year before begin to appear, and all about the ploughed fields hovers a faint promise of coming green. The corn blades melt free from the soil and stand singly among the clods of bare earth. The turnips spread their oval leaves and turn their backs in a silver sea as the wind fans them.

Pauline and I are given hoes, and we set off with the others to thin the turnips out. This is a highly skilled job, and at first we are hopelessly clumsy at it. We are not only clumsy, but also slow. The other workers, hoeing up their drills in line, soon leave us far behind. Everyone on the farm is out today, for, as with the sugar beet, turnip hoeing is paid by the piece and a lot of extra money can be earned. Even the dairy family and little Tommie Weir take a drill; even old Mr Weir bends his back with the best of us. He is Tommie's grandfather and has long been pensioned off; but like the flies he has woken up out of his winter sleep with the coming of the sun.

Hoeing turnips is the first really hard job that we have done since we left Spital Tongues. It is back-breaking and extremely sore on unused muscles. By now, however, Pauline's and my arms are as hard and firmly developed as those of a couple of elderly charladies. I shudder frequently when I think of what I shall look like if I ever again wear evening dress.

Hoeing turnips is not as easy as it looks. One has to pull up all the plants except one at six-inch intervals. Of course, what happens with the novice is that one pulls up all the plants leaving none standing at all. This is particularly likely to happen when Mr Foster appears and walks over to see how we are getting on. Our muscles contract nervously in our anxiety to prove to him once and for all, our praiseworthy skill. He watches silently. The hoe pulls out a line of seedlings. It carefully sorts out the one that is to be left standing, hovers for a moment, and then with invariable maliciousness it descends and wrenches it out too leaving a bare foot of earth with no seedlings standing at all. One can almost hear what Mr Foster is thinking as he walks away.

We have long since given up trying to keep up with the other workers. They work in a straight line up the field with Mr Smith at their head and little Tommie several yards behind. Old Mr Weir however, is just about our mark. Old Mr Weir has the same ideas as his son about not being hurried. He works slowly and leisurely, his old back bent and his horny hands shaking with age as they clutch his hoe. He looks as if he might have been gardener of the Garden of Eden.

Pauline and I, by working flat out, can just about keep up with him. Even so, he shows much more enthusiasm for the job than we do, and with the vision of an extra ounce of tobacco looming ever nearer, he toddles up his drill with never a pause. I try to side-track him by suggesting that it must be about time that he stopped and had a smoke, but he is a fly old bird, and only chuckles and works on.

The sun grows hotter and hotter. The field is completely treeless, and we develop an unquenchable thirst. Mrs Smith puts us up a bottle of water to take with us, and Pauline is perpetually drawn hedgewards to take a swig. The heat beats up from the dry earth, and the sun beats down on our bowed heads. I have discarded my heavy land army overalls for an old cotton dress, and Pauline is decked out in a very natty pair of shorts. These shorts cause a sensation when she first appears in them, but Pauline is impervious to scorn, and with the obstinacy that she has all along shown over her hat, she persists in wearing them. Only when Mr Foster turns up does she show any sign of embarrassment.

In spite of our few garments, however, the sweat is soon dripping liberally from us. Often, as I move, it runs down my legs and scatters in drops about my feet. I cannot believe, as I long for a little wind, that I used to shiver in my van so short a time ago.

At half-past three, the other workers knock off for tea. We, however, are to work on until five, when we will stop for good, half an hour before the others do. It is difficult to realise, however, when we see the row of contented workers squatting in the cool of the hedge, that we are really benefiting by this arrangement. They are maddeningly content to sit back and watch our labours, and we have to bear the sight of a pantomime of men drinking tea with unnecessarily loud relish, while all the time they are laughing at us and watching our discomfort out of the corners of their eyes. But once our lousing time has come we get our revenge. We knock off work with ostentatious gladness. We call to each other in loud voices about what we hope to have for tea; and make plans for spending the rest of the day sitting on a rock with our feet in the cool river. Now it is the others' turn to turn a deaf ear, and we go home comforted in the knowledge that at least it is we who have laughed last.

The river winds in the valley below the farm, and is amply banked with proud and lofty trees. In among their trunks are hundreds of wild raspberries, and later on in the year we will vie with the children on the farm, as to who can eat the most. They were planted there long ago, as pheasant food by a past owner of the Hall.

Pauline and I eat a huge tea, and then lazily make our way down to the river. It is wonderfully peaceful there, and we take off our shoes and wade out to a rock where we sit with our feet dangling in the water. The water is clear, and peering down into its peaty depths we can see caddis worms, dragging their clumsy houses about on the sandy bottom. They frequently lose their balance and roll helplessly over and over. There is also a crowd of little fish. They eye us uncertainly for a time, but after we have stayed very still for several minutes, they lose their fear and come and nibble curiously at our toes. We must appear as strange things to them, but it is a pleasant feeling to have them nibbling and bumping their fishy noses against our bare legs.

Pauline is delighted with them but in the end she cannot control her chuckles, and the little fish take fright and rush away.

'Oh, they've gone,' I say reproachfully. 'You frightened them.'

'I couldn't help it, really I couldn't. They were tickling, Aunty Bee.'

The stones are warm beneath us, and we pluck off little strands of moss and toss them out into the current. They spin and whirl and we watch them until they are out of sight. Above the river a host of gnats swirl and rise in an ever moving cloud, and suddenly the smooth surface of the water is broken and ringed by a rising trout. A man with a rod passes on the opposite bank and looks at us as resentfully as we look at him.

The light fades quietly, and the banked trees become an ever darker green. A bat flashes in a curving arc out over the river and circles about for a while snapping at the gnats; and then vanishes. We sit on in complete contentment. We are united by the still of the evening more closely than we are during the heat of the day. I watch Pauline affectionately as she hangs over the water and plunges her brown arm deeply into its frozen heart. Her fine hair hangs in disorder about her face, and it reminds me of the days, not so long ago, when I had felt so bitterly towards her. Now such a feeling seems absurd. I carry with me the ever-increasing pleasure of her companionship, her dear foolishness, her warm humour and her kindness of heart. I love her for her hat, her unruly shirt and her holey stockings; for her innocence and simplicity and for her great good humour.

'Aunty Bee,' says Pauline, cupping her dripping hands under her chin and gazing up the slowly flowing river, 'how old were you when you were first kissed?'

'That is my secret, Tubby.'

'No, but really Aunty Bee; do you think anyone would ever want to kiss me? Do you know that I shall be nineteen in a few months? I must be the only girl in England who has got to that age and never been kissed once.'

'Well, Walter wanted to, didn't he?'

'Walter! It would be Walter, wouldn't it! Trust my luck!'

'Oh, don't be silly. Of course you will be kissed! You'll probably be married a long time before I am.'

Pauline sighs heavily and shakes her head. 'No one will ever want me,' she says. 'It's all very well for you. You are different.'

'Oh, nonsense Tubby! You just wait and see. One day you will be walking down the street and the sun will be shining and the sky will be wide and blue. And someone nice will see you walking, and he'll fall in love with you. And he'll stop and buy you a bunch of flowers from a passing coster barrow! What's your favourite flower, Tubby?'

'Daffodils.'

'Well then, he'll buy you some daffodils; and it will be springtime, and everyone knows that anything can happen in the spring.'

'And what then?'

'Oh, he follows you and he finds out where you live, and he

rings the bell of the house and just dumps the flowers down on the doorstep. Only with them is, of course, a note.'

'What does it say?'

'It tells you of his lost heart and begs you to meet him for dinner at a lobster café in Soho.'

'And do I go?'

'Well, you know better than I!'

'Oh, of course, I go! And there he is, the tallest handsomest man I've ever seen, looking exactly like Gary Cooper –'

'And you order lobsters – '

'And listen to the music, and it's all too wonderful for words!'

'You see? What did I tell you?'

Pauline subsides and the light dies out of her eyes.

'Oh, but that's just a story Aunty, Bee. It won't really happen.'

'Yes it will, you just wait! I'm psychic about these things. The gipsy never lies.'

'Nice Aunty Bee! Tell me some more.'

And so we sit on. The day fades and a little wind shuffles the surface of the river. It becomes cold, and when we at last get up and go back to the farm we are stiff and cramped with sitting.

Inside the cottage the Smiths are drowsing before their kitchen fire. Tinker is at their feet, and on Mrs Smith's knee is her pile of darning. The wireless is playing. It has never been turned off since Mr Smith turned it on when we first got up this morning. All day Mrs Smith does her housework to its accompaniment. It is a ceaseless background to her life.

'Well, where have you been?' says Mr Smith.

'We've been nibbled by trout,' says Pauline impressively. 'I've hardly any toes left.'

'You ought not to be so fat!' says Mr Smith. 'Anyone would be tempted to take a bite out of you.'

Pauline hurls herself on him and they rock in crazy battle about the kitchen.

Tinker watches them warily with a disapproving eye, and when they approach too near her and her tail seems in danger, she leaps for cover beneath the kitchen table. Mr Smith calls to her softly, sucking the air cunningly between his teeth, 'Tink, Tink, Tink,' he says.

Tink heaves a sigh and goes into reluctant action. If her master is in danger, Tinker supposes she must surrender safety and go to his aid. She leaps up and snaps her teeth at the seat of Pauline's baggy shorts. She growls menacingly. Pauline gives a yell. She swings round and lets go of Mr Smith. Tink, face to face with the enemy, retreats hastily again under the table.

'Tinker!' says Pauline reproachfully, 'I thought you were my friend!'

She turns back to Mr Smith and they begin to wrestle again furiously.

'Jim!' protests Mrs Smith as her darning basket is upset and all her reels of cotton roll about the floor. 'For shame!' she says. 'You are nothing more than a couple of children.'

'Tink, Tink, Tink!' says Mr Smith.

Tink sighs unhappily and launches herself reluctantly into another attack. She is really not at all sure that this sort of thing comes under the duties of a sheep dog.

'Ouch!' says Pauline. The fight stops abruptly and Mr Smith laughs mockingly at her discomfort.

'Fatty!' he taunts.

Pauline draws herself up with what she hopes is imposing dignity.

'Mr Smith,' she says. 'I'd have you know that in a few months' time I shall be nineteen. Kindly try to treat me with more respect.'

'Says she, waving her wooden leg,' murmurs Mrs Smith in an audible aside.

Pauline's dignity collapses like a burst balloon, and she joins us as we laugh helplessly.

'No, but honestly Aunty Bee,' she says as we stamp up to bed. 'Setting a dog on me is the last straw! Really it is!'

CHAPTER THIRTEEN
Hay in Summer

IT IS DURING the early summer that I first make the acquaintance of Dicky. Dicky is a lonely officer in charge of a group of soldiers who are billeted in an old derelict hall. One day he rings up Mr Smith and asks him if I will deliver them a daily quota of milk. Mr Smith promises that I will. When I hear this, I sigh, for my accounts weekly become more complicated, and I know that dealing with the Army is apt to be an involved proceeding.

Each Monday afternoon I am allowed to stay in so that I can set my books in order. I settle myself on the floor of the sitting room with the books spread around me in a circle and a box of chocolates handy to revive me. I have three different prices to cope with, for as well as having both tuberculin tested and the cheaper 'Grade A' milk, I also have the estate people to account for, and they get their milk at half the normal price. There is also the added complication of the times when people like to pay their accounts. Some of them pay weekly, others every fortnight, and some once a month or quarterly. Woe betide me if I ask them to pay before their time has fallen due! They regard it as a personal insult.

After many weeks, during which I nearly contract brain fever, I am just beginning to sort myself out when the Government produce an assortment of Government grants. I now find that some of my customers get their milk for nothing, while others get one free pint in two. And all these grants have to be signed and reclaimed by me from the local Milk Board.

In any case, I have always been hopeless at arithmetic. In spite of much time and money which has been spent on my education, my mind still becomes blank when I am confronted with figures, and I have to do every sum with the aid of my fingers. In time, however I hit on a system which serves me very well. I make myself a 'Sinking Fund'.

My 'Sinking Fund' consists of a small tin box, in which I put any extra money that I find I have at the end of the week, and which I cannot account for in my books. Some weeks I find I am short, and then I delve into my 'Sinking Fund' and make up the money from its contents. On the whole, things more or less even themselves out. I find that at the end of my stay at Stoney Hall, when I hand over my books to my successor, there is only five shillings unaccounted for as a residue from all the months that I have wrestled with them. This five shillings I enter into my books under 'extras', and I close my tin box for the last time. I am well satisfied, for my books are at least left in no worse confusion than when I found them.

When my accounts are finished on Monday afternoon, I have to drive my van to the Hall, where I can wash it with the hose in the stable-yard. I always enjoy this job. Apart from anything else, it gives me an excellent chance of keeping up with the social gossip of the Foster household. And Billy manages to spend the greater part of his afternoon in attentively watching me soak myself with the hose.

I find that washing a van is a very wet job indeed. Invariably by the end of the afternoon I have succeeded in transferring a greater part of its mud to my own person. The hose at the Hall has an unpleasant will of its own. The water belches through it at an uneven pressure, and it has a habit of suddenly twisting itself round and spitting an unexpected jet into my face. This is particularly so when I am washing under the mud-guards. It not only spits out sideways, but runs down my sleeves and soaks me to the waist. However, on the whole, I enjoy myself immensely, and the beautiful white cow on the van's side is my especial joy and pride. I wash her and sponge her face with infinite care, and she comes up, as Billy says, 'A fair treat!'

The stable-yard is an excellent point of vantage from which to watch the comings and goings of the inhabitants of the Hall. It is the hub of their universe. I watch the little Fosters arriving at the stable for their daily ride, and I view them enviously and with critical eye as they set their feet in the stirrups and ride away. I watch Mrs Harrison and Nancy, the kitchen-maid, filling up Mrs Foster's mobile canteen with urns of tea and trays of cakes, and I smile at Mrs Foster as she climbs in and drives away.

Taking the milk to Dicky's soldiers proves to be a most enjoyable proceeding. They go up the class rapidly, and it is not long before they rank high in my list of favourite customers. Every morning my van sweeps past the sentry with a cheerful toot on the horn, and I stop it with a flourish in the yard. The Company Office looks out on to the yard, and as soon as I arrive there is a clatter of boots on the wooden stairs, and a sergeant and a corporal or two hurry over to help me lift out my big metal churn. This I am quite capable of doing myself, but I foster the illusion that it is too heavy for me. This suits everybody, and the whole proceeding develops into a daily ceremony. We become very matey, and after the churn has been disposed of, we stand and chat and pass the time of day. There is always competition as to which gentleman can be the most gallant, and I begin to feel my self-esteem rising by leaps and bounds. I am popularity itself! The sergeant is my special admirer, and we are just getting on really intimate terms when Dicky appears, and the sergeant has to retire with a disjointed nose.

My first meeting with Dicky is purely accidental. He stops in the yard and we talk for a few minutes before I go on my way. I catch the sergeant eyeing him coldly however. The next morning when I arrive, there is no cheerful clatter of boots on the office stairs. Instead, Dicky emerges from the doorway and we earnestly discuss the pros and cons of recovering the milk account from the N.A.A.F.I.

And so it goes on. The next day Dicky appears again. This time he says he has come to examine the empty churn which his cook has put out for me to take back. He says that he wants to see if it is quite clean, but he becomes so interested in our light chatter that he quite forgets to look. I am amused.

Dicky, it appears, is extremely lonely. He is barred by superior rank from spending his evenings with his men, and he is the only officer for miles around. He is very sorry for himself, and touchingly eager for my company. He is also very handsome. He asks me to go out to dinner with him and I accept.

I spend the afternoon before this invitation, in hoeing turnips, but the work is no longer so arduous, for I am able to look forward to an amusing evening. Poor Pauline hears of it with gnashing teeth, and she registers ostentatious envy. She sighs deeply and shakes her head.

'Always you, Aunty Bee,' she says. 'Why can't I ever be asked out anywhere?'

She is very curious to know all about Dicky, and she examines me closely on the subject of his appearance. She seems to be disappointed when she hears he has no squint. She says she could forgive me and let me have him if only he had a squint.

'Well, anyway,' she says finally, 'I bet you find he bores you stiff, Aunty Bee. We are sure to find he is a butcher or a sausage maker in civvy street!'

In spite of her forebodings, however, when lousing time comes I wash the day's grime from my person and put on my going-out clothes in a happy frame of mind. Dicky calls for me in his car, and I am assured that apart from my irretrievably damaged hands, my appearance does not disgrace him. Pauline is rather downcast by the arrival of Dicky's car, for to her, a young man in a car spells the beginning of romance. I see her woebegone face watching me out of the window as I climb into the front seat beside him. She makes me feel hateful, and I wish that she could come too.

As we drive out there are faces at nearly every window of the farm, and I know that Dicky is causing something in the nature of a major sensation. Country people are fundamentally matchmakers, and after the evening I spent with John, the whole farm unanimously decided that it was only a matter of time before he and I became engaged. Dicky is something they had not foreseen, and from the first my faithlessness to the innocent John is looked upon with disapproval.

When I get back that night I find Pauline in bed but awake. She sits up and, as I undress, she fires at me a volley of questions.

'Well, was he a sausage maker?' she demands.

'Not quite; he makes films.'

'He what?'

'Makes films.'

I pull my dress over my head. There is a silence and then Pauline recovers her voice.

'You mean he is a film star, Aunty Bee?'

'No, but he knows all about them. He's a script writer.'

Pauline moans and turns her face to the wall.

'This is the end,' she says. 'There is a limit to human endurance and this is it.'

'What is the matter now?'

'Well, really! That you who don't care a fig about films, should have a script writer who knows all about the stars, as a boyfriend! And little Pauline, who would give her soul to hear about them all, hasn't even met him! I ask you, Aunty Bee! It is the end, really it is!'

I sit myself on her bed and brush out my hair.

'Pauline, I'm sorry, honestly I am, but I knew you would want to meet Dicky and I have told him all about you. I'll ask him if he has a boy-friend whom he could bring along one night and then you could come too and we could have a party. You'd like that, wouldn't you?'

Pauline flings her arms about my neck.

'Aunty Bee,' she says, 'you are an angel, really you are!'

After a hot three weeks the turnip hoeing is finished, and the feathery plumes of hay are long enough for cutting. One morning Gideon sets out with his horses, and all day long the grassy sea falls in waves before the blades of his jagged knife. He mows the field in an ever decreasing square. The cut grass fades in the sun as it falls, and turns to striped rows of brown and silver. Gideon works all morning and by the afternoon the hay is dry enough to be turned.

We set out with our long-handled forks, and Mr Smith shows us how to walk down the strips of hay, twisting it over with our forks into long ringlets, and turning it from silver to a damp olive green. It is a pleasing job. I enjoy seeing the surface of the field ruffle behind me as the sea is ruffled in the wake of a wind. High overhead a lark is singing, its tiny body suspended interminably in heaven. It seems to sing because it is as necessary for it to do so as it is for it to breathe. In the middle of the field, Gideon is still working with his two horses, his monotonous voice calling encouragement, or shouting an order, as his clumsy machine clicks back and forward at the corners.

At tea-time Mrs Smith appears, a bag in either hand, and Jack and Marian dancing at her heels. She has brought us a packet of bread and scones and some lemonade in a bottle. We sit in the shade of a dyke with Gideon. The two horses stand plucking at the prickly hedge with velvet mouths, and swishing their tails at the flies with a regular motion.

Next day the first field of hay is finished and Gideon and his team go on to pioneer another. Behind him he leaves the broken spears of a vanquished army, their brave plumes broken, and their white bones bleaching in the sun. A host of dying marguerites and clover flowers load the air with the heavy scent of their mortality, and the already laden bees are completely intoxicated.

Everyone works in the field today. There is a holiday atmosphere in the air, for the hay is a carefree harvest, unburdened by the harder work that the corn crop entails. Also, it marks the first real coming of summer. The men work with their jackets off and their braces straining over their damp shirts. Beneath their limp caps they have white cotton handkerchiefs to stop the sweat from running into their eyes, and to shade the backs of their necks from the burning sun.

Each night as we undress for bed, Pauline and I examine ourselves to see how our sunburn is progressing. Pauline's arms and legs are tanned as brown as a berry, and in the front her fine hair is bleached almost white. Her skin turns to a beautiful honey gold in the summer, and I envy her, for I am one of those tiresome fair-skinned people who burn bright scarlet and then begin to peel. This gives Pauline great satisfaction.

Today the strips of hay that we turned yesterday, are dry and crisply green. Pauline is given Bett and is allowed to rake. As she drives up the field she rakes the hay into lines that the rest of us can build into little kyles. Then Mr Smith arrives with his motorbogie. In the front of the bogie are fastened wooden prongs, and gathering up the kyles on these, he sweeps them into a collection of big heaps. Out of these heaps we will make the pikes. I find there is a distinct art in building hay pikes. They must be symmetrical at the base and gradually taper to a rounded point at the top. They can very easily become lop-sided, and this is bad, for when the time comes to cart them to the stack, they are awkward to load on to the bogies and often overbalance at the gates.

At first Pauline and I succeed in making only very odd-shaped pikes, and we are delighted when finally we produce a fairly recognisable one. We stick a twig on the top with a piece of paper on it bearing the words 'A Nous la Victoire' scrawled in pencil.

When tea-time comes we all stop work, and have our tea in circles at the bottom of the pikes. I decide that there is nothing quite so peacefully English as having tea out in a hayfield. The sharp blades of the grass spear a pattern on my bare legs, and the soft pike of hay behind me breathes a drowsy scent, and fills me with a most delightful summer enchantment. Mr Smith is in no hurry to begin work again. The light will last late, and he sees no sense in rushing. There will be plenty of time to put up the last pikes before sunset. The men light their pipes, and the women, who have come to the fields with their husbands' teas sit back and watch their children tumbling in the piles of hay.

The country is spread out at our feet in all colours of green and golden brown, and looks like a giant patchwork quilt. Here and there where other farms have begun their hay harvest too, the fields have a pimpled appearance as the little pikes rise in a series of scattered dots. A train ambles leisurely down the single line leaving behind it a white tress of smoke. A black bee, heavy with honey, blunders like a ball of sooty thistledown into the hay beside me, clings for a moment, and then zooms away again high into the sky. Strapped to its legs are little scarlet honey-bags, and with its dark striped body, it is a thing of amazing beauty.

My sandwiches finished and my bottle empty, I twist over on to my stomach. The talk and laughter of the others seems far away, and as I gaze down into the grass stems I feel I have grown suddenly very small. I see an ant, huge as a lion, peering into my face with curious eyes. It climbs the trunk of a grass stem, loses footing, and climbs again laboriously. It is busy and intent with its task. The strange moon that is my face, has been adjusted satisfactorily to its universe and it has become used to it. Hurrying with the egged body of a Siamese twin, it goes on unheedingly about the business of living.

'Who are you going out with tonight, Miss Gardener?' Mr Smith's voice comes as from a great distance.

'Ah!' says Pauline mysteriously. 'That would be telling.'

'Come and look at the moon with me, Tubby,' says Mr Weir.

'Meet me in the cowshed after dark!'

'You know what they say, Tubby,' says Gideon. 'If you can't be good be careful. Don't you trust him a yard. Old 'uns are always worst.'

'Do you know the one about the bishop and the goat, Tubby?'

'No, what?' says Pauline eagerly.

'Don't know, I'm sure' says Mr Weir maddeningly. 'I've never heard it either.'

'Golly! My hands are blistered,' says Pauline after a while, picking with her nail at her horny palms.

'My feet are something cruel,' says Mr Weir. 'I get bad feet in the summer, Tubby. The smell is something awful. Mrs Weir won't let me take my socks off. I always go to bed in them in the summer.'

With this startling revelation we commence work again.

Piking the hay with Gideon, I am suddenly aware of a squeaking at my feet.

'What on earth is that?' I say, peering down at the grass.

'Mice,' says Gideon. 'See them?'

He points, and suddenly I see a neatly woven ball of grass deeply concealed in the roots. The knife of the mower must have missed it by inches, and only the thick tufts in which it is hidden have saved it from destruction. Gently, I part the grass and peer inside the ball. It is a nest of mice, very soft, naked and with blind eyes and little hooked paws of dirty pink. They squirm and twist in a grey ball, squeaking and sensing my presence, although they are still too young to see.

'Let me kill them,' says Gideon raising his boot.

I stop him however, for although I do not like mice, the thought of death coming to them out of the darkness, pulping their soft bodies into the earth before they have even seen the day, appals me.

Gideon laughs at me. 'You are soft,' he says. 'Them's vermin. Do a lot of damage, they do.'

'Never mind, Gideon. Leave them alone. I'll never speak to you again if you kill them!'

This awful threat has its effect, and Gideon leaves them alone.

The next day there is a wind blowing, and as we arrive at the hayfield, we see the little loose wisps caught up and curled like ringlets out over the grass. It proves difficult to keep the hay in place long enough to build the pikes, and after a while Mr Smith hits on the idea of using me as a sort of paperweight. This affords everyone a lot of amusement. My dress is pink. It has a full skirt, and as the increasing height of the pike carries me higher the wind rushes round my legs and blows up my dress like a balloon. A sudden gust lifts my skirt and blows it over my head, exposing a pair of pink cotton pants and a considerable amount of my person. There are howls of delight.

'Ee! You are rude, Aunty Bee,' says Mr Weir. 'You're making me blush. Keep your skirts down, do!'

'Good as a pantomime, eh Gideon?' says Mr Smith. 'First-rate principal boy you'd make, Miss Whitton. I'd come miles to see you in a few spangles, mind, I'm telling you!'

I refuse to be embarrassed but my discomfort persists all the afternoon. I am lent out from pike to pike, and everywhere I go I am like an umbrella that has been blown inside out.

Almost before we know it the days pass and the pikes are dry enough for stacking. Mr Smith and Mr Weir spend a busy afternoon in overhauling the bogies, greasing and cleaning them of the grime and dust they have accumulated since they were last needed. Pauline implores Mr Smith to let her have one of the bogies to work with her beloved Bett. Mr Smith agrees, but after the first day he is forced to exchange Bett for a more sober and less imaginative horse who will display less cunning. On her first morning, owing to Bett, Pauline takes an hour to lead one pike. Bett, with hay all about her, flatly refuses to stand still, and while Pauline is wrestling to put the chain round the bottom of the pike, Bett cheerfully ambles off to eat her fill elsewhere. In the end, even Pauline's patience is exhausted. Yet, although she surrenders Bett gladly enough for a more biddable beast, she does it vowing to the end that she does not know what has come over Bett, for generally she is such an angel!

While Pauline is working with her bogie, my job is on the stack back at the farm. I love this, for from my lofty perch I can see the farm spread out beneath me, and the coming and going of everyone. The bogies creep like beetles about the face of the distant fields. Mr Smith and I work at the top of the stack, stamping it down and beating it even under the red corrugated iron roof of the hayshed.

At last the stack has grown too high for the men to fork the hay up to us easily, and Mr Smith announces that we will now erect the derrick. The derrick proves to be a thing that looks like a disintegrated iron maypole. It is packed in the rafters of the granary where it lives during the year when it is not needed; and when I see its lofty position, I wonder how Mr Smith proposes to get it down. He seems quite confident, however, and begins to erect a series of pulleys, by which it is to be lowered slowly to the ground. Everything goes well until Mr Weir, who has been perched as a potential lever in the rafters, loses his footing. He succeeds, however, in falling on the right side of the rafter, and clinging grimly to his rope, he counterbalances the end of the derrick to which it is attached, thus preventing it from coming crashing down on top of us. It is an incredible sight to see him dangling there. His feet kick wildly, and a stream of most sanguinary language pours down on our heads. Gideon, with great presence of mind, and at great danger to himself, catches the feet and sets them on his own shoulders, Mr Weir recovers himself slowly, but for some reason he is considerably annoyed.

Once the derrick is down there still remains the problem of how it is to be erected. Although setting up the derrick is a yearly occurrence, Mr Smith soon discovers that he hasn't got the slightest idea which of its bolts go where. Like a baffled jigsaw puzzler he persists in vowing that he is quite sure there must be some pieces missing. Mr Weir is certain that if only he can have a go, everything will be solved. It takes him half an hour and a lacerated thumb to teach him better.

In the end, it is old Grandpa Weir who makes a suggestion which gives us the key. After that the whole thing seems simple enough. With much straining of sinews, and 'mind I'm telling you's' from Mr Smith, the derrick is eventually set up. It is only when we step back to admire our handiwork that it occurs to us that there is still something wrong.

'Well, I'm b--' says Mr Smith, whose control of language is fast snapping, 'the flaming top is on upside down.'

Down comes the derrick once more. This time Mr Weir is quite sure that he has a wonderful grasp of its workings. Mr Smith has lost heart and he agrees to listen. He might have known what would happen. The bottom half of the derrick is carefully and correctly set in place, and Mr Weir is left with no means of getting on the top half. Down it comes again.

Mr Smith is determined. Having set his mind to the erection of the derrick he will not be defeated, and finally, by taking the binder to pieces to improvise some spare parts, the Heath Robinson contraption is at last set up. By now it is tea-time, and with sighs of content at a hard task overcome, we sink down in the hay at the top of the stack.

A haystack makes a pleasant bed, in spite of myriad spears of dry grass that prick our skins to a dull red rash. There are soft grey moths that every now and then, as we move about, spin out of the hay, fluttering in the still air like burnt paper. The blue swallows dart in a flight of shot arrows all about the red iron roof above us.

From my lofty perch I can watch Reg going with Rip to the meadow to bring home the cows for the afternoon milking. Presently the sleepy beasts amble along the road with nodding heads, dry hooves kicking up a trail of dust in their wake. Long chains of saliva swing and drip from their mouths into the white road at their feet, and their great bags swing like pendulums to the rhythm of their leisurely walk. Even Rip is subdued, and quiet with the heat. He trots behind them with his tongue lolling and his proud brush trailing in the dust. Today he has no energy for snapping at their heels.

Reg shuts the gate of the meadow and walks after his dog. He belongs to a strange family. I am never able quite to make the dairy people out. They are a separate unit from the rest of us, keeping themselves to themselves, and seldom even speaking to us unless they need. Nevertheless, they regard our actions with considerable interest. Everything we do is noted by them, and they have invented the most complex system of espionage to watch our activities. Nothing and no one can go anywhere without being observed. An eye watches the yard seemingly all day, from the cover of a lace curtained window. In the wooden walls of the dairy is a line of holes that have been bored with a hot poker. Through these we are constantly observed without the observers themselves being seen. The effect is most sinister.

After three weeks of ceaseless toil the last pike is built into the stack. The farm pauses again for a few days rest, and in the shorn grass of the fields only the grey pock marks are left, showing where the drying pikes have stood.

One day after lunch, Mr Smith pushes back his chair and beckons to me.

'I've a nice job for you today, Miss Whitton,' he says. 'Come out to the stable for a minute.'

'What is it?' I say, following him outside.

'I've two calves to go into the mart. You'll have to take them to Wallbrugh in your van.'

'What!'

Mr Smith grins at the horror in my voice, and as we go into the stable he hastens to reassure me.

'It's perfectly all right, woman! Nothing to be afraid of. You'll just have to register them, that is all.'

'But how do I do that?'

'Oh, ask one of the lads there. They'll show you the office.'

Lying in the stable are two calves. They are tied up in sacks, and their heads are sticking mournfully out of the top.

'Moo!' says one of them doubtfully, and I am inclined to agree with it.

We lift them into the back of the van, however, and I back it out of the garage and set off. As I near Wallbrugh I become more and more unhappy about my mission. My instructions seem slender in the extreme, and I feel sure that there must be more in taking calves to market than I have been told.

When I arrive at the mart it is already in full swing. It is a seething mass of men and animals, both in and out of pens. There are sheep in lorries, cows in calf, pigs in pokes, and collie dogs in every stage of hysteria. The large trucks are backed up against the loading docks, and frightened beasts are being persuaded up the wooden gangways by shouting and gesticulating men. Some of these men have the most startling methods of persuasion. They bow out their cheeks and blubber their lips like Red Indians. Many of them are scarlet in the face and they emit shrill noises in varying and penetrating keys. Around the iron rails of the pens there are lines of farmers, poking pigs with walking-sticks and staring lovingly at their own possessions, or critically at their neighbours.

I feel very green and foolish among all this expert activity as I modestly back my van in among the giant trucks. I open the back doors, and the calves and I look at each other with dislike. I have no idea what I am expected to do with them. I toy with the temptation to push them in someone else's pen and then quickly drive away, but I remember in time the tradition of my Land Army uniform, and regretfully discard the idea.

I look helplessly about me at the many chequered and britchered figures, and I presume that they must be 'the lads' referred to by Mr Smith. I am just wondering which of them I dare ask for advice when I hear a voice from behind me.

'Can I help you, miss?' says the voice.

I swing round and see a burly red-faced individual in a white mackintosh. I recognise him as a fellow milk deliverer to whom I have often waved as I passed him in my van. Yet another friend in need!

'Oh, please do!' I say. 'I've got to cope with these calves, and I haven't the smallest idea what to do with them.'

'Oh, so they've given you a change of job! I've often seen you with the milk, and thought how much of it I should drink if you brought it to me.'

'That's really very gallant; but I enjoy my milk round; except the accounts, which I find a bit trying.'

'Ah,' says my new friend. 'Now that is where I'm all right. I'm my own master, so it doesn't matter if I do get them a few shillings wrong.'

'You're lucky, but what about my calves? What do I do with them?'

'I believe they've got to be registered. Come along and we'll find the office.'

I look doubtfully at my two calves and wonder if I can leave them, or if we have to bring them along too.

'It's all right,' says my guide. 'No one will touch them. We'll come and get them afterwards.'

He takes me down an alley between the crowded pens of bleating sheep. At the end there is a round wooden building, rather like a huge solidified roundabout. We go inside.

Through an open door I catch a glimpse of a sort of arena, a circle of cement banked about with tiers of wooden benches. The benches are crowded with farmers, most of them with catalogues in their hands. They are all peering intently at an alarming-looking bull which is being led reluctantly round the room at a most uncomfortable angle with a stick through the ring in its nose.

My friend, however, gives me little time to look about me. He hustles me into a second room where there is a long bureau at one end and which reminds me of a post office. This room, too, is crowded with farmers, and we have to shoulder our way through tweed-clad forms to the other end.

'There you are,' says my friend. 'Just give the particulars to the man there. He'll give you a couple of labels.'

I gather up my courage and fix one of the men behind the bureau with an eye like the ancient mariner.

'I've got two calves,' I announce. 'I want to register them.'

The man looks at me and I can see that he hates me on sight. 'Right-o!' he says. He bangs a large and imposing ledger down in front of him in which he prepares to write my full particulars. I almost expect to hear him warn me that anything I say may be taken down and used in evidence against me.

I am the only woman in the room, and I am uncomfortably aware of the interest I am arousing. I am increasingly grateful for the moral support of my fellow-milkman, but even he cannot prevent me from feeling a little like a prize heifer myself.

I begin answering questions as to my calves' ownership and place of residence. I am rather at a loss, however, when the unpleasant man behind the counter asks me what colour they are. I rack my brains. To me they are just calves, but in the end I hope for the best, and say that I think they are both brown and white.

'Red and white,' says the man reprovingly.

I am stung. 'They certainly aren't red,' I say tartly. 'They are brown.'

The man looks at me pityingly. 'Don't you know nothing?' he says. 'Red is brown – same thing, see?'

I am silenced.

'Sex!' says the man, consulting his ledger.

'I beg your pardon?'

'I said sex,' says the man. 'Sex of calves. What sort are they?'

Silently I curse Mr Smith with all my heart. How could he let me come all innocent and unprimed into this den of thieves! He must have known that I should have to face this awful inquisition. He must have known that I wouldn't have the slightest idea what sex his wretched calves were. I am absolutely at a loss.

I become conscious of an ominous silence all about me. Several of the farmers have stopped talking and are looking at me with amused eyes and laughter hovering about their lips. I have obviously been accepted as the funny act of the party. Any minute now they are expecting to have to hold on to their chairs and split their sides with mirth.

'You mean he or she?' say I, playing for time.

'Yes, that's right,' says the man showing signs of approaching exasperation.

'Do you know,' I say in a conversational way, 'I haven't the slightest idea. You see, I never really looked at them in that light. They are both tied up in sacks.'

This is their cue. A ripple of laughter spreads round the room. My words are caught up and passed from mouth to mouth, and the laughter rises to a roar.

'Eh, these wummon!' I hear someone say, and I am furiously conscious of a blush that is spreading upward from my neck.

'Well, I must say!' says the loathsome man in a ringing voice. 'How do you expect me to register calves if I don't know their sex. Or don't you think it matters?'

I murmur that I shouldn't have thought it would at that age. This remark is greeted as another pearl, and the room again wipes the tears from its eyes. Old members explain to new-comers what it is all about, and heads crane and peer in my direction.

'You go and take them out of their sacks, my girl, and find out their sex. If you don't know how at your age, God help you!'

This witticism brings down the house, and scarlet in the face I push my way out into the fresh air. I am furious with Mr Smith, and can hardly wait to tell him what I think of him. My friend has followed me outside, and I notice crossly that he is also smiling.

'I'm terribly sorry,' he says, however. 'I'd no idea Mr Smith hadn't told you all the answers or I would have primed you up before we started.'

'Just wait till I see Mr Smith!'

'Never mind; you made their day for them, and we'll soon find out. Come along.'

We find the calves still lying placidly where we left them, and we ascertain that they are both he's.

'That really is all,' says my friend as we go back to the office. 'There is nothing else he can possibly ask you.'

'Ah!' says the man when I have fought my way back to the bureau. 'Belinda blue eyes back again. Well! Are you any wiser?'

'They are both he's,' I say with dignity.

'Oh!' says the man. I suppose you mean bull-calves. Right! There you are, numbers 18 and 19, and don't go and lose your labels. And don't waste any more of my time.'

Once more we return to the van, and we tie the two labels round the necks of the calves.

'What do I do now?' I say.

'Oh that's all right,' says my friend. 'You leave them to me. I've got to hang about here anyhow, so I'll see to them for you.'

'Will you really? That's terribly sweet of you.'

'No it's not; only next time I pass you in your van, don't go sweeping by. Don't be in such a hurry. Stop and have a chat.'

'Yes, of course. What is your name?'

'Glen Douglas,' says he, helping me into my driving seat and carefully closing the door.

'You are called Barbara, aren't you? Oh, it's amazing the way these things get around! Do you like books?'

'Yes, very much.'

'Good. Next time I see you I'll lend you one I've just finished. I'd like to know what you think of it.'

'Thank you,' I say, somewhat taken aback by this glimpse of a literary farmer.

I cannot resist a question. 'It's not by Jeffrey Farnol, is it?'

'No, why?'

'Nor a bound copy of John Bull?'

'Good heavens no!'

'Then I'd like to read it. I didn't know farmers ever read anything else. Thanks for the help. Goodbye.'

Musing on my new acquaintance, I drive back to the farm. In spite of the red face and the white mackintosh, I decide I rather like him.

When I get back I search out Mr Smith and give him an indignantly graphic description of my discomfiture at the mart. I get no satisfaction from him at all, and when I demand why it was that he did not send me forewarned, he only giggles and says he wanted to see what I would do. What Stoney Hall would do for amusement without its land girls, I really do not know!

It is still quite early in the afternoon, and Mr Smith tells me that my next job will be to help Pauline, who is working in the hayfields clearing up the mouldy hay from the pike bottoms. He is going that way himself to have a look at the sheep, so we walk up to the field together.

Pauline greets us joyfully and waves her hands.

'Come on Aunty Bee,' she says. 'The nicest job – too easy! Keep your bottoms clean, that's all. Mr Smith says that nothing else matters so long as you keep your bottoms clean.'

This startling statement, of course, refers to the pikes, but Pauline sees nothing odd in the way she has put it. I dare not catch Mr Smith's eye, as I know that the laughter that is big in both of us will then become uncontrollable. I solemnly set to work, and under Pauline's repeated entreaty to keep my bottoms clean, I gather up the old musty bay and fork it up on to the bogie.

Mr Smith leaves us and goes on to see after his sheep.

'Well,' says Pauline. 'How did you get on at the mart?'

'My dear, it was simply frightful! All most embarrassing. I had to go and register the calves in a room like a sort of post office.'

'How did you know what to do? I should have been terrified.'

'Well, a farmer whom I've seen on my milk round took me under his wing. He was rather sweet.'

'Aunty Bee!' says Pauline pushing her hayfork savagely into the soil and leaving it standing upright and quivering like herself, 'come clean! Who was it this time? What a girl! Did he ask you out?'

'No, of course not, Tubby. Nothing so exciting. We only talked about books and things'

'Books!' says Pauline setting viciously to work again. 'You only talked about books! I've never heard of such intimacy, Aunty Bee! When I meet a young man I can never get him further than the weather.'

CHAPTER FOURTEEN
Battle of the Bees

BUT PAULINE IS WRONG. At the end of the week Mr Smith gives her the weekend off and she goes home. She finds an invitation waiting there for her from two maiden aunts. They invite her to spend Saturday with them, and on the Saturday evening to join a party they are taking to a dance at the University. Pauline does not expect very much from this invitation. She has met parties arranged by maiden aunts before and she knows that most of the young men invited are generally too 'nice' to display any interest in anyone other than the maiden aunts. However, she has nothing better to do, so she goes.

The party proves to be quite as awful as she has suspected. It consists of a doctor and his wife, the curate, an embryo archaeologist and Major and Mrs Blenkinsop. Mrs Blenkinsop does not dance, so Pauline has been presumably invited as a partner for the Major.

During the course of the evening, however, Pauline suddenly becomes aware of a sensation that she has felt before. It reminds her of Walter, and looking about her, she finds that the embryonic archaeologist is fixing her with warm and moonstruck eyes.

He asks her repeatedly to dance. He dances very badly indeed, but she is so delighted at finding something masculine, and at least fairly youthful, showing an interest in her, that she stifles her cries of pain and smiles up into his face as persistently as she is able.

It seems that the embryonic archaeologist is a university student whose name is Sebastian. He has a rather large adam's apple, and he talks almost entirely about his mother. But Pauline resolutely ignores these things, and decides that his eyes are quite nice; or would be if they were not set quite so near together.

She goes down with a swing and the evening is an unqualified success. By the end of the night he has promised to take her to the pictures the following weekend, if she can persuade Mr Smith to let her off. Pauline promises joyfully to fix Mr Smith, and they part with a warm but damp shake of the hand.

Pauline is full of Sebastian when she gets back to the farm. She tells us that he is 'nothing to look at all, but he's really rather sweet' and Mrs Smith and I nearly burst with curiosity. Pauline's young man becomes the chief topic of conversation during the next week. The whole farm bids her Godspeed when the weekend comes and earnestly hopes she will enjoy herself with him at the pictures.

She comes back bubbling with excitement. It appears that Sebastian behaved beautifully during the film; and after her experience with Walter it is 'so nice to have a real friend who does not continually want to be messing me about.'

'He really is rather sweet,' Pauline tells me. 'And it is exciting to feel that someone is taking an interest in me at last.'

She announces her final triumph on the Monday morning: Sebastian has shown great interest in where Pauline is working, and he has promised, as she will not be able to get into town for the weekend, to come up to Stoney Hall by bus to see her there instead.

We tease her unmercifully all week, but for once Pauline does not care.

'Better take him down by the river, Miss Gardener,' says Mr Smith. 'That is where all the lovers go, you know.'

'Oh, but we're not lovers, Mr Smith. Just friends.'

'That's what they all say. But mind, I'm coming along behind you on the tractor. I'm going to trail you wherever you go.'

'Oh, Mr Smith, you couldn't be so mean!'

'Oh, but I am. I'm not letting some lad take you off into the blue without keeping an eye on you both. And where I can't take the tractor, I'll have Miss Whitton here stalking you through the undergrowth.'

'That's right, Jim,' says Mrs Smith, 'and if ever you see anything you blow your warden's whistle!'

When the Saturday comes, excitement on the farm is at fever pitch. I have unfortunately arranged to go home this weekend, but I am strongly tempted to stay so that I may see the wonderful Sebastian for myself. Pauline begins getting ready for him hours before he could possibly arrive, and as I drive away I see her excited face, in all its warpaint, at the sitting-room window as she waves me goodbye.

All the time I am at home I wonder how Pauline and her young man are getting on. I know it means so much to her, and I do most earnestly hope that all goes well. When I drive back to the farm on the Sunday, I can hardly wait to put my car away, before I hear what has happened. Pauline is in the sitting-room. I open the door and burst in, eager for news.

'He never came, Aunty Bee! The little twirp never came! Here I sat for hours and hours waiting and all dressed up ready, and in the end he didn't come at all.'

'Pauline!' I gasp appalled. 'But whatever happened?'

'Absolutely nothing. That's what made me so mad. If he'd broken his neck or caught mumps I could have forgiven him, but he'd simply forgotten. The little beast!'

'But what did you do, Tubby? Did you ring him up?'

'Yes, of course. After waiting ages. And he talked for hours, but didn't even mention coming up. And in the end I said hadn't he meant to come this Saturday, and he said, "Oh did I say I would? I'm so sorry, I'd forgotten" – Forgotten!'

'Well, what did you say?'

'I didn't say anything. I just slammed down the receiver. That's the end of Sebastian. I'll never speak to him again as long as I live.'

'Oh, Tubby, I'm so terribly sorry, and he seemed so nice.'

'He didn't! He was a hateful little creature with an adam's apple and little ratty eyes. I don't know why I ever thought I liked him! But if anyone here dares tease me about it I'll burst into tears, really I will.'

Fortunately everyone else joins poor Tubby in her disappointment, and the general inclination of Stoney Hall is to wring Master Sebastian's neck for him.

After this setback, Pauline is rather tender on the subject of young men for some time.

My own friendship with Dicky progresses by leaps and bounds. I like him increasingly, for he is a kind-hearted, understanding sort of friend, whose sympathy and affectionate undemonstrativeness is just what I need after a hard day's toil. He frequently rings me up and asks me to go to a picture with him, or to have dinner in Wallbrugh. I am always glad to go, for he does not mind if by nine o'clock I am so sleepy that I can hardly keep my eyes open. With my early morning start ahead of me, I insist on being in bed by ten o'clock.

The weekend after Sebastian's failure to turn up, it is my turn to stay to do the milk round. Pauline arranges to spend the weekend at home, and I promise to meet her on the Sunday evening in Priscilla at Wallbrugh Station.

Dicky is very downcast when he hears that I have promised to go home on Sunday as soon as I have finished my milk round. He is to have the day off, and he says he hoped I would go on a picnic with him. I cannot disappoint the family, but with sudden inspiration I ask Dicky if he would like to come home with me. Dicky says he would. When we arrive home, my family are glad to see us but behave somewhat characteristically. My mother says, 'Goodness, how you smell, child! Go and have a bath, do.' My father pounces on Dicky and sweeps him into the garden to be interrogated. While showing him the delphiniums and roses, he questions him closely as to his antecedents and intentions; and then having decided that both are honourable, he thaws and becomes quite friendly. The day passes pleasantly, and when we leave again in the evening, we are laden with fruit and flowers and bundles of clean laundry. It is a beautiful evening and the hills are soft and distant and gently shadowed. The broom is out in a golden mass, and the little new bracken fronds are uncurling in a million shepherd's crooks. No doubt the scent of broom combines with the fading light to make my Dicky feel sentimental, for we have not gone very far before he shyly puts out his hand and covers mine as it lies upon the steering wheel.

I am not at all sure that I want this. Ours has been such a perfect friendship, unencumbered so far by the more cloying sentimental emotions. I am seeing so much of him that I foresee that an amorous Dicky might very soon become tiresome; and I ponder, as I drive with his hand on mine, as to what line I will be best advised to take.

I offer to drop him off at Stoney Hall, from where he can walk to his billet, but he begs to be allowed to come on with me into Wallbrugh to meet Pauline. Foolishly I consent. The dusk is fading to the long shadows of night, and as I drive along I have to switch on my lights. Pauline is returning on the last train, and as we stop in the station yard, I sincerely hope that it will not be late.

I push Dicky out of the car and ask him to find out what time the train is due. He goes unwillingly and with obvious reluctance. I see a decidedly sentimental gleam in his eye, and am filled with foreboding. He is not gone long before he hurries back joyfully. The wretched train is late he tells me gleefully It won't be in for half an hour.

'What a nuisance,' I say, and out of the corner of my eye I see that Dicky is preparing to draw me close within the circle of his arm. Suddenly I am struck with an idea.

'I know,' I say brightly, 'let's go and get an ice cream while we wait. They have very good ones round the corner, and I don't expect they are shut yet.'

'All right,' says Dicky, but his tone is unenthusiastic. We get out of the car and go round to the café. The café is brightly lit and filled with a cheerful collection of people. I eat my ice slowly, and spend much time in criticising the various people about us. I then order a second.

I manage to while away a good quarter of an hour. Dicky is stamping with impatience, and when I am at last finished, he fairly rushes me outside. We go back to the car.

'Just see what time the train will be coming in Dicky, there's a lamb,' I say.

Dicky hurtles into the station and is back almost before I know it.

'It will be in in a quarter of a hour,' he says and gets determinedly into the car beside me.

The twilight of a summer night is all about us, and in Priscilla it is almost dark. There are still fifteen minutes to go, and I know that to expect Dicky to sit silently beside me all that time is asking too much of anyone. I am hardly surprised therefore when he gently turns my face to his and kisses me.

I smile at him in the darkness and pat his cheek. This is all very well, but I have no desire to have Dicky sitting kissing me solidly for a quarter of an hour. A diversion must be produced from somewhere. Suddenly I remember the fruit on the back seat that we have brought back with us from home.

'Nice Dicky,' I say. 'Have a grape?'

'No thank you,' says Dicky, taken aback.

I, however, am not to be diverted any more than he is. I lean over the back of my seat and find the large bunch of hothouse grapes that are in the basket among the strawberries.

'Are you sure you won't have one, Dicky?' I say, pulling one off and popping it in my mouth.

'No thank you, darling,' says Dicky.

After his first astonishment at my food-before-all policy, Dicky decides to go right ahead and ignore it. He thinks no doubt that it is just one more of women's idiosyncrasies. He devotes his attention to my ear and salutes it passionately. I continue to eat grapes. I wind down the window beside me and toss out the stones. Dicky, attempting to kiss me again, is forestalled by a sticky mouthful and he is forced to return to my ear.

We sit on. The minutes pass. I eat grapes and Dicky tells me that I have the most angelic blue eyes he has ever seen. He works himself up to a climax. He assures me I have a neck like a swan's, eyes like a dove's, and lips like cherries. He breathes heavily and whispers into my ear passionately. When he comes up for air I am still eating grapes.

'Are you still eating those confounded things,' says Dicky indignantly. 'Honestly, I've never known such a girl. Where the hell are you getting them from?'

When the train comes in, I greet Pauline joyfully. My bunch of grapes are almost done, and I am just contemplating having to turn my attention to raspberries.

It is only a few days after this episode that Bridget arrives. Bridget is my pony. She has been living on the fat of the land ever since I went into uniform, and I have always nurtured the hope that one day I might be able to have her with me on the farm, to ride in the evenings.

It is a great moment when she arrives, peering anxiously over the top of her wagon. The whole farm turns out to see her as she stalks down her wooden runway, and she has to suffer much feeling of her legs and opening of her mouth by everyone who thinks he knows anything at all about horses. The general opinion about her is that she is too fat. With this I am in entire agreement. Bridget carries her stomach like a hammock, and like a hammock it swings from side to side when she walks.

I have managed to engage for her accommodation a pleasant pasture with a sunny outlook and a shady tree under which she can stand. I tear her away from her admirers and, leading her off down the road, I turn her loose.

And then begins, as Pauline puts it, 'The battle of the Bees'. I have, it seems, chosen Bridget's domicile too well. She approves of it so heartily that when I go down to try to catch her the next evening, although she will come over and take a mouthful of corn, she will not let me get near enough to her to put on her halter. We circle round one another warily. She watches every move I make, and she knows just how near to me she dare come without being in danger of being caught. She is quite polite to me; she nods. She even passes a few remarks on the weather and the beauty of the evening, but she makes it quite plain that that is as far as she is prepared to go.

I try subterfuge. I turn my back and I shake my tin of corn enticingly. I pretend that I haven't the slightest interest in Bridget or her whereabouts, and that catching her is the last thing that I am trying to do. Bridget stands and watches me politely and with interest. She obviously thinks I am as mad as a hatter, but she is not taken in in the very slightest.

Pauline is sitting on the fence at the bottom of the field, watching from a distance. She is vastly amused and occasionally shouts encouragement in a way that I find particularly exasperating. Only a cat that will not be played with has the power of making you feel as silly as a horse that will not be caught.

'Come and help me drive her into a corner,' I call at last.

Pauline swings herself off the fence and advances through the buttercups. We spread out and wave our arms. Bridget tosses her head and canters off to the far end of the meadow. We walk after her. She allows us almost to reach her before she swings round and canters blithely back again. Wearily we turn and retrace our steps. The field is big and we are very few. After a while, even Bridget grows tired of the game and simply canters round and round us in circles, with her tail arched over her back, and making noises at us through her nose that we can only interpret as an intended raspberry. We become very warm indeed, and Pauline ceases to be amused.

'What a horse, Aunty Bee!' she pants. 'Do you do this every time?'

'No,' I gasp. 'I can't think what's come over her. She is usually such an angel.'

We become crosser every moment and begin to feel more and more silly.

'I don't think we'll get her tonight,' I say at last. 'Her blood's up now. We'll have to try again tomorrow. I'll try to think up some strategy in the meanwhile. "Cunning to catch cunning", you know!'

During the next day I lay my plans carefully, and when I set out in the evening my hopes are high. I know Bridget of old and I know that if I can only surprise her, the lady is mine. Since last year she has grown a mane. It is long and blackly flowing, and hangs in a heavy curtain to her shoulders. I think that in this mane lies the secret.

When I appear with my little pan of oats, Bridget seems quite pleased to see me. She evidently bears me no malice for my dishonourable intentions of the evening before, and she waddles forward hospitably enough graciously making me free of her lush paddock. She pokes her nose forward for a mouthful of oats, and only takes the precaution of keeping her eye warily on the rope that I have in my hand. She does not notice my other hand that steals up and locks itself in her long mane.

When she suddenly becomes conscious that I have in some unsporting manner attached myself to her, she is very surprised. She snorts and goes rapidly into reverse gear, but I cling on grimly, and after a bewildered blink or two, Bridget shrugs her shoulders and lets me put the rope about her neck. Round two is to me.

Pauline, who has prepared herself for a further exhibition of horseplay, is quite disappointed. However, we saddle and bridle Bridget, and lead her out on to the road. She is so fat that I am forced almost to do the splits as I sit astride her. Pauline has borrowed Mr Smith's bicycle, and Bridget and I clip along as fast as we can behind as she zig-zags off in a cloud of dust.

But the next evening Bridget remembers. When she comes up for her tin of corn, she stands as far away from me as she can, and cranes her nose until the tip of her lips only can just reach the grain. All the time she watches me warily, and at the slightest movement of my hands she backs away. I can get no nearer. She is as cunning as a cat, and I have to confess myself once again defeated. I try everything, but all to no avail! Round three goes, without any doubt, to Bridget.

The next day I get a halter made by a saddler in Wallbrugh. I do not like halters, for I have heard of so many horses who have been strangled by them, but better a catchable horse in a halter than a useless one without. It only remains to catch Bridget first, to put it on her.

I do this finally, with a bean mash. We all have our weaknesses and Bridget's is undoubtedly bean mash. She cannot resist it, and it proves her downfall. While she eats I slip the rope about her neck.

Once the halter is on however, things are only a little better. It does not take Bridget long to learn that it is now not safe to come near me at all, and she simply ignores me, and will no longer be seduced by my rattling the corn tin. Once or twice I succeed in catching her by suddenly emitting a shrill squeal and throwing myself flat on my face in the middle of the field. This performance invariably arouses her curiosity, and she begins to crop round my recumbent person in ever narrowing circles. If I have the patience to stay there long enough, she begins to get really worried. She hopes that I haven't chosen her field to commit suicide in, or to have a heart attack. These things are bad for a horse's reputation, and they carry with them a nasty smell of scandal. She draws very close, and peers down at me anxiously. She sniffs me and decides that if I am dead I can't have been dead for long.

Very gently I lift my head. I begin talking in comforting dovelike tones. I thank her for her justifiable concern, but assure her that I have in fact only been taking a nap. Bridget is relieved. She begins to feel silly. She begins to remember she has been taken in this way before, but she smiles apologetically and explains that after all a horse does like just to make certain. I stroke her reassuringly. She forgets that I am still trying to catch her, and she doe s not notice my hand fixing itself firmly to the noseband of her halter. When she does notice it is too late.

Pauline, who has been watching these girlish capers from the hedge is convulsed with mirth. She tells me I have no idea how silly I look lying flat on my face in the middle of a field, with a horse walking round and round me only a few feet away. I am too flushed with the laurels of victory to care how silly I look.

One day when we go to the field to take Bridget for a ride we find that she is entertaining. She has the company of an old bullock, and she has obviously fallen for the animal in a big way. When we attempt to catch her she charges round us in a circle and then trots back to the bullock to tell him what a clever horse she is. The bullock, however, has the character of an old Anglo-Indian Colonel. He is past the days when his heart was set all a-flutter by the judicious display of a trim ankle, and he is obviously finding these gambollings of a foolish filly extremely tiresome. In the end he can stand it no longer. He puts down his great head and makes a run at Bridget. There is no mistaking his meaning, and she moves hastily out of his way. She is wounded by this display of cruelty on the part of her hero, but after watching him as he walks off, she makes up her mind to forgive and forget, and follows him. He hastens his step crossly and makes for a gap in the hedge. Across this gap is a strand of wire, but it is high enough up for him to be able to duck his head and shoulder his way underneath it. He goes back to his own field, and joining the rest of the bullocks he no doubt forgets all about her.

Bridget is amazed when she sees her beloved disappearing seemingly through the hedge. Then as the possibilities of the thing catch up with her, she becomes interested. Where he can go she can surely go too. She sees a sudden vista of new and unexploded worlds spreading out before her. She dashes up to the gap in the hedge but, alas, she is brought up with a jerk by the strand of wire. Poor Bridget, this is an awful blow! She is too big to be able, like the bullock, to worm her way under it. She peers over the wire and sees him placidly eating, well out of her reach. She is furiously angry. She lays her ears back along her head and blows out her nose. She gives that bullock the biggest raspberry he has probably ever had.

One day, a command invitation comes to us to go and have tea with the Fosters in the Hall. We are rather shaken by this, for apart from telling Mrs Foster that 'Yes, we are quite comfortable, thank you', we have never spoken to any of them. Long before we go poor Pauline, who is always shy when confronted with strangers, begins to suffer agonies. She says that she knows she will develop hiccoughs in the middle of tea because she always does when she is nervous.

On the great day, we are out all the afternoon cutting hedges; or rather Mr Weir cuts the hedges and Pauline and I rake up the thorns and clear them off the road. This would be a pleasant enough job if it were not for the green fly and midges that come out of the hedge whenever Mr Weir shakes it and settle on us in clouds. We are soon covered in bites, and we can feel the hateful little things crawling about all over us inside our clothes.

When we come to wash our faces for the party, they are blotched and swollen with bites, but having made ourselves nice clean girls we put on our going out clothes and set off for the Hall.

We know, of course, a considerable amount about the Fosters from their kitchen staff. Taking around milk gives one a pass into the kitchen world that is undisputed, and I have all along been accepted by my customers' servants as one of themselves. I have, as a result, been able to revel in backstair gossip to a staggering extent, and I know of the existence of a quantity of skeletons that are kept in seemingly respectable and unsuspected family cupboards. Occasionally, after having first learned all about them from their servants, I have actually met some of my customers face to face. It is odd to meet them as the stranger they think me, when very probably I know a great deal more about them than they would like.

When we arrive at the Hall, it is well after five, and we are very hungry indeed. We are both extremely nervous and somehow it feels all wrong to be let in as visitors at the front door, instead of walking in with the milk at the back as we are used to doing.

Mr Blenkinsop opens the door to us, but it is a strange Mr Blenkinsop, and from his aloof manner as he politely asks our names, you would never guess that he is the same butler who has often given us a stolen apple, and a friendly slap on the stern. Only as he opens the sitting-room door and we are ushered in, do I glimpse the ghost of a wink that hovers in the corner of his eye.

The whole family is assembled there to meet us. There are Mr and Mrs Foster and their two daughters and three small sons; there is also Nannie, a dour Scot who is universally disapproved of by the kitchen (Mrs Harrison always refers to her as 'her and her trays').

The sitting-room is a large room with many arches. Before we can notice anything else a bevy of snapping terriers hurl themselves upon us, in a seeming mass attempt to put us to flight. With me, at least, the attempt is nearly successful.

The terriers are called off eventually by a variety of youthful Fosters, for whose bravery and prompt action I am deeply grateful.

'I'm so sorry,' says Mrs Foster, directing a well-aimed kick at the seat of a still belligerent canine. 'Be quiet, Fairy! Do come and sit down.'

We come and sit down. Tea is set out on two little tables by the fire and I see Pauline's hungry eyes making a comprehensive summary of the food thereon. Pauline's appetite is still enormous.

'Shall we have tea at once?' says Mrs Foster. 'I'm sure you must be hungry after your day's work. What have you been doing?'

She fixes Pauline with a kindly eye, and Pauline, who has just chosen that minute to blow her nose, blushes bright scarlet.

'Cutting hedges,' she manages to get out. 'The midges were awful.'

'Nannie doesn't let us say awful,' suddenly announces the youngest Foster. 'She says it's not a nice word.'

Pauline looks at me miserably, and the blush that was preparing to go changes its mind and stays for the rest of the afternoon.

At this minute tea is brought in by the aloof Blenkinsop, followed by Nancy carrying two boiled eggs on a silver salver. It seems that these eggs are for us. None are supplied for anyone else. We greatly appreciate this difference paid to us as hard labourers who have earned our teas, but if Mrs Foster only knew it, we would so very much rather not have the eggs. It means that while we draw our chairs up to the table and begin to eat, the rest of the party stand by with popping eyes and watch us at work.

Pauline is fond of eggs, but when she has them boiled she makes the stipulation that they must be hard boiled. She will have nothing to do with them if they are in that soft and runny condition when they slop out of the shell and trickle in a sticky mess down her chin. At least, ordinarily, she will have nothing to do with them. Today she has no choice. The spoons that Blenkinsop has given us are small silver affairs not very much larger than salt spoons. The eggs prove to be very soft and very runny indeed, and we take a long time to eat them. While we are busy, the family watch us closely and presently I hear a penetrating whisper from the youngest Foster, announcing to Nannie that 'the lady's got some egg on her chin!' Pauline, poor soul, hears this too. She quickly drops her spoon, clutches her napkin, and sweeps it up to her mouth. As she does so, the corner of it catches the half empty egg and flicks it over. It rolls along the table and rapidly approaches Nannie, leaving behind it a trail of yellow. I know that the scarlet Pauline would like to sink through the floor. I understand only too well the misery she is suffering, and I very nearly develop hiccoughs out of pure sympathy.

'I'm terribly sorry, Mrs Foster. I'm terribly sorry, Nannie, really I am,' says Pauline.

After this the party goes from bad to worse. Pauline is utterly demoralised, and although Mrs Foster is extraordinarily kind and assures her that it does not matter at all about the egg, she never really recovers. Mr Foster lapses into a gloomy silence.

Pauline's next mishap occurs over the strawberry cake. The strawberry cake is a large sponge cake lined with cream and stuffed with crushed strawberries. It is extraordinarily good and Pauline accepts a large helping. It is also a very difficult cake to eat. If it is cut into pieces the filling oozes out on to the plate and is wasted. If it is not cut, the filling oozes on to the cheeks and chin of the eater. It is probable that portions of it will also break off and drop into one's lap. Pauline does not foresee all this until too late. By the time she has finished tea, the tablecloth around her plate is scattered with drops and splashes and crumbs. Pauline is past caring.

Mrs Foster attempts to draw her into conversation on the subject of our land army experiences. Pauline lets herself go and, absentmindedly scrubbing the worst spots off her dress with her usual indescribable handkerchief, that in the hurry of leaving she has forgotten to change, gives a graphic description of the people and interior decorations of Spital Tongues.

'Of course things are much better here,' she says brightly. 'The Smiths' cottage is furnished quite well. Except for our bedroom which is terrible for some reason. You should just see it. Perhaps they ran short of money and picked the furniture up at a sale.' Pauline, of course, could not know that the furniture she is thus condemning has been provided for us by our hostess. She goes on brightly. 'It was awful the other night. The iron springs of my mattress were so rotten I went right through. You should have heard how the Smiths laughed. They were mean. They said I ought not to be so fat, but I'm sure it was really because their bed was so old.'

Mrs Foster is faced with two alternatives. She can either tell Pauline that she herself is the owner of the bed thus described, and laugh the matter off, or she can say nothing and risk Pauline learning the truth later from Mrs Smith. On the whole the first seems to her to be the most kind. She laughs gaily.

'I'm so sorry about the furniture, my dear,' she says. 'It actually belongs to an old shooting box that we don't use any more. The Smiths had nothing in that room as they don't ordinarily need it, so we lent them our stuff to use during your stay. I am afraid it does need a lick of paint.'

At this point if Pauline had been at home she would undoubtedly have covered her head over with her table napkin. She tells me afterwards that she only just remembered in time not to do it, and certainly so far as intelligent conversation is concerned Pauline might be counted out for the rest of the tea party. She never speaks again.

A few days after this catastrophic afternoon, we receive another invitation; or rather, I receive it, and I only accept it on the understanding that Pauline may come along too. This time, our host is Glen Douglas.

I have frequently seen Glen since I first met him at the mart and I like him increasingly. He intrigues me, and the more I know of him the more interested I become. The book that he spoke of lending me at our first meeting proved to be *Ben Hecht's Book of Miracles*. This is in itself a strange enough choice for someone like Glen to make, but when later on I stop my van and discuss it with him, some of his comments prove to be even more unexpected. He lends me more books, all of which I enjoy, and all of which are surprising. Some of them are by American and some are by Russian writers. I do not suppose anyone else in Wallbrugh has ever heard of most of them.

And then one day he asks me to go and have dinner with him at his farm. I am extremely intrigued to learn more about him, and dragging a rather reluctant Pauline along behind me, we get into Priscilla and drive off.

The farm proves to be a smaller holding than I had expected. It is purely a dairy farm and I imagine Glen is able to run the place himself with the help of a boy. He appears out of the garage as we drive up, wiping the oil from his hands and explaining that he has just been tinkering with his car.

We go indoors. The furniture of the house is a strange mixture of Victorian country mahogany and cheap twentieth-century plywood. Glen has, however, earned himself a good mark by dispensing with the hideously floral Victorian wall paper, that his father would no doubt have chosen, and the walls are now covered with white distemper. Hanging on them are some pleasant prints by Peter Scott.

Glen introduces us to his housekeeper, who is very much a part of the Victorian furniture and very shy of us. She shakes hands, and hastily retires into her kitchen. We have supper almost at once.

Over supper, I learn a little of Glen's history. It seems that his father was a farm labourer who inherited enough money from a deceased brother to be able to buy a smallholding and start farming on his own. Glen was brought up to be a farmer, and he had to leave the village school at fourteen. He had learned nothing by then, he tells me, and any knowledge that he may have now he has acquired since through his own efforts. When he was in his teens he went twice a week to evening classes in Wallbrugh. He also joined a library and he used to read anything and everything.

I am staggered by his general knowledge of literature, history, and politics. He is intensely interested in the growth of Russia, and he tells me many things about which I find I am profoundly ignorant. As the evening advances although he is entirely self-educated he puts my own expensive education to shame. Beside him, I find I know practically nothing. Dates and figures roll off his tongue as easily as the titles of books and their authors. We ponder over many and various things. We discuss the Ku-Klux-Klan and British Israelites, both of which I know very little about. We discuss Yoga and the building of the Pyramids. I have little to contribute on either subject, but Glen has read much about them, and can even quote me long paragraphs. I rapidly begin to develop an inferiority complex. 'I wish I'd had a little more education,' I sigh at last.

Glen is most comforting. 'Never mind,' he says, 'the education of the average person in Britain is negligible. Why don't you come to some evening classes? Will you be at Stoney Hall this winter? There are going to be some first-rate economics classes starting in November. I'd love to take you.'

I say hastily that I don't think my desire for education goes as far as economics classes in Wallbrugh.

'What were you training for if it hadn't been for the war?' asks Glen.

'I'd hoped to do commercial designing and a bit of shorthand and typewriting.'

'Good girl,' says Glen. 'I like a girl who wants to go out and do something on her own. Now, if the worst comes to the worst after the war, you will always be able to deliver milk.'

Pauline takes little part in the conversation. She has spent a hard day in the open air, and the warm room soon has its effect. For a few minutes she wrestles to keep track of the various hares that Glen starts, but they have soon loped out of her ken and it is not long before she sits back and allows the seas of slumber to engulf her. She is probably the most useless chaperone there has ever been.

On the way home she wakes up for a few brief minutes.

'What a funny man, Aunty Bee,' she says. 'What did he want to talk about Egyptian mummies for?'

'I don't know I'm sure Tubby. Perhaps he likes them.'

'Well, I kept on growing drowsy, Aunty Bee, and dropping off to sleep. And then I'd wake up and he'd be talking about Egyptian mummies, and then a few minutes later I'd wake up again and it would be performing seals or President Roosevelt!'

'We did talk rather a lot, I'm afraid.'

'Yes. And it didn't seem to make sense, if you see what I mean.'

The next minute she has gone to sleep again with her head lolling on my shoulder.

CHAPTER FIFTEEN
Like Ruth, Like Hell

WHEN I FIRST joined the Land Army I had no very clear idea of what I was going to do. I knew little about country life, in spite of the cottage in which my family used to spend their weekends. When I came across the word 'harvest', it always conveyed to me the one thing, corn. The corn I knew was always gracefully waving in a golden uncut sea beneath the heat of a summer sun. Occasionally I added to the picture the figure of Ruth, who appeared with her upper portion only visible, standing in the feathery stalks and holding a rather vague sort of knife in one hand. She always looked very pretty and picturesque, and was obviously posing for her photograph. When I joined the Land Army, I think in the back of my mind I saw Ruth and me changing places.

Of course I knew nothing of the sweat and toil that go into producing the gracefully waving sea of golden corn. I knew nothing of the manuring, the harrowing, the ploughing, the drilling, the sowing and the rolling. So much, at least, I have learned.

The binder is taken out and overhauled several days before the first field of oats is ready to be cut. I have to take bits of it into Wallbrugh in my van to have it fitted up with new bolts and pieces of canvas. My van seems to be regarded as general furniture and message lorry, and often by the end of the morning I can hardly find room in it for myself, it is so full of ploughshares and horse collars, sacks of potatoes and packets of tobacco.

As the time for reaping approaches Mr Foster is bitten with a bug of panic. As he sees his corn standing drying in the fields he is suddenly afraid that it will be ruined, and he will allow no one to rest and no sinew to be relaxed until every precious stook has been led in. Mr Smith tells us that he has known Mr Foster to rush extra hands from all parts of the country, to work in the cornfields at reaping time.

It is a big moment when one morning Mr Smith announces that he and Mr Weir will take their scythes and go and open up the wire-rail field. The rest of us watch them enviously as they set off. It is always exciting on a farm to be in at the kill of a new crop, particularly the corn. Paradoxically, we feel that Mr Smith and Mr Weir are in a way akin to those who are privileged to be the first to see the face of a new-born child.

Mr Smith and Mr Weir work unhurriedly, scything up the parts of the crop that have been beaten flat by the rain. As soon as they have cleared a way for him, Gideon follows up this skirmish of the infantry with a cavalry charge and with a clatter and a whirr, the binder launches the major attack.

A host of birds rise in alarm at the sudden noise, and skim in a lifting veil away over the golden grain. We watch as the binder claws its way with flashing sails among the sifting corn. Mr Weir is perched up behind Gideon, on the pillion, and every now and then, if anything goes wrong, he raps with his stick on the metal mudguard. The sheaves spit out sideways in a neat row of bundles their tops golden with grain, and their bases thick and matted with grass and clover leaves. Gideon calls to his horses and they mount the sloping field and disappear out of sight over the brow of the hill. But we can still hear the binder clacking.

By lunchtime, Gideon has cut his way round the field many times, and there are rows of plump sheaves waiting to be built into stooks. They all lie facing the same way, where the impatient binder has dropped them. Mr Smith sets Pauline and me to work gathering up the loose corn, which he and Mr Weir have scythed. He shows us how to make bands out of strands of corn, and how to tie it up into sheaves. This seems to be a pleasant enough job, and we set to work leisurely. We find however, that the corn is still very wet from its morning drenching in dew, and our shirt fronts are soon soaked through. Also we had not foreseen the thistles. At the bottom of the field the corn is fairly free of them, but as we work up the side to the field top, the thistles become thicker and our prickly armfuls become a positive agony to hold. These thistles are a great disillusionment.

When I used to imagine Ruth standing in the corn I had omitted to visualise any thistles at all. A few scarlet poppies perhaps, but thistles, definitely no!

'Ouch!' says Pauline, sucking her finger and trying to squeeze out a prickle. 'I do think Mr Smith might have warned us. I'm going to wear the thickest pair of gloves I've got tomorrow.'

'You probably won't be able to get a pair of gloves on tomorrow. My hands are twice as big as they should be, already.'

We work slowly and painfully along the top of the field, and begin to descend the hedge at the other side. Down at the bottom of the field, Mr Smith and old Grandpa Weir and Tommie are Building the sheaves into a first line of stooks. They make an odd trio. Mr Smith adds four sheaves to every two that the others can produce. The birds have long ago become accustomed to the noise of the binder and they have returned to peck in the tufted grain. It is very hot. The sky arcs overhead like an inverted blue basin, and there is not a cloud to be seen. The smoke from the chimneys down in the farm is twisting and curling straight up into the still air. There are hundreds of flies. They cling to our lips and eyes, and as we brush them off they swarm back angrily in ever-increasing clouds. The more we brush them off, like Pauline's Walter, the less they seem to take the hint. Pauline becomes infuriated by them.

'These flies!' she says, 'aren't they awful today! It must be going to rain or something.'

'Try not to keep swatting them. It only makes them worse.'

'Oh, oh!' says Pauline beating wildly at her face. 'Get away, you little beasts. Aunty Bee, you've hardly got any! Nice Aunty Bee! Look, flies, go and annoy nice Aunty Bee!'

She flings her arms round my neck and attempts to transfer her share of flies to my own orbit. When she withdraws, she has if anything, more than she had before. I cannot help pointing this out.

'Oh,' she says, stamping her feet in rage, 'why were they ever invented!'

'It's funny that flies always seem to like things with an odd smell,' I say unkindly. 'You can't have washed behind your ears this morning.'

The road runs down near the hedge and as I am wrestling to tie up a particularly prickly sheaf, I hear a car. I look up and see that it is Dicky. He hangs out of the window and waves. The car stops and

I see that he is getting out to speak to me. I wish very much that he had gone on, for I am well aware that with the heat and my exertion I am far from looking my best.

Dicky, however, must have an odd taste in women's dress for he grins at me admiringly over the hedge and says, 'Gee, darling, you're looking swell!'

I grin back and try to find a way of holding my thistly bundle less painfully to my bosom.

'Can you do a movie with me tonight, Bee?' says Dicky. 'I think I've got the petrol.'

I reply that there is nothing I would like better. And then it occurs to me that I have never arranged the party that I have long promised Pauline and I ask Dicky if he could bring a friend so that we could make it a foursome. Dicky is doubtful but he promises to do his best. It seems there is one, 'Dougie', who might be persuaded to come. 'The only thing is he may be busy,' says Dicky.

'Well get him if you can, Dicky. Pauline will be terribly pleased. Only you won't have to mind if she corners you and wants to know all about Hollywood. She's dying to ask you.' Dicky promises that he won't mind.

'What's he want now?' says Pauline resignedly as I walk back to my toil and Dicky drives away.

'Terribly exciting, Tubby! He wants us both to go and have dinner with him tonight. He's met a friend who doesn't know anyone around here, and he may be able to come too.'

'Aunty Bee, how absolutely marvellous! Nice Dicky! And now I shall be able to ask him if Harpo Marx really is dumb!'

Pauline sets to work at such speed that the sheaves are tossed out from her wake like the wash of a ship.

When we have finished tying up the last of the loose corn, Mr Smith sets us on to stooking. There is a knack in building a stook, and, like a house of cards, Pauline's and my stooks come tumbling down. We learn that it is hopeless to try to patch up a stook if it once begins to slip. The natural inclination of the builder is to slap on another sheaf quickly, to hold the thing up, but it nearly always collapses in the end. Stooking is pleasant but tiring. You walk considerable distances in the course of the day, going from sheaf to sheaf, and the sheaves, when they are first cut, are of considerable size. Later, when they have had time to dry, they shrink a lot, but when they are first stooked, many of them are as tall as Pauline and me, and certainly of equal girth. They are heavy to wield, and by the end of the day we are reduced to pulling them along the stubble by their bands, rather than carry them any more. The stalks of the sheaves are also extremely sharp, and we soon learn that it is not a good policy to work with bare arms when stooking. We roll down the sleeves of our shirts, but they only protect us from the corn, not from the thistles, which work their way through and pierce our swelling flesh.

By the end of the evening of the first day, the corn harvest has begun in earnest. Gideon has cut almost a third of the field and growing up all over the stubble, like the castles on a chessboard, are the squat little golden stooks. Everyone is weary. The horses plod back to their suppers with sweat-streaked hides and nodding heads. Old Mr Weir is feeling the sciatica in his back and he puts it down to the first nip of autumn in the air. Pauline and I are very glad indeed to stop.

We walk down the field to the gate, our shoes polished by the brushing stubble. My eyes are on the lookout for a four-leaved clover. I have a habit of finding four-leaved clovers that annoys Pauline intensely. One day I arrived back at the farm with a bunch of twenty-one of them, all of which I had found in different parts of the field.

'It's not fair, really it's not, Mr Smith,' said Pauline. 'She doesn't even try to find them! And here am I, with my nose glued to the ground all day, and I haven't found one!'

'Well, you ought not to be so fat, Miss Gardener,' said Mr Smith, knocking out his pipe on his heel.

'I can hardly see, Mr Smith,' said Pauline with icy dignity, 'the connection between my being fat and my inability to see four-leaved clovers!'

'Why, woman, your stomach is so big it casts a shadow on the ground all around you. Anyone can see that.'

Later on when Dicky drives up in his car we are both ready waiting for him, rigged out in all our finery. Pauline has been preparing herself with considerable care, and I suspect her of having designs on Dicky, for she considers that I do not appreciate him enough. She has no interest in the possibility of Dougie being a member of the party, and dismisses him with an absentminded, 'I hope you'll like him, Aunty Bee.' I cannot help being amused by her as she carefully powders her nose in front of our dark little mirror. She has to kneel on the floor to see into it at all, but she is obviously unaware of her surroundings and well away in dreams of her own. I guess that for the moment, Dicky has supplanted Gary Cooper as the man of her dreams. Does he not come from Hollywood too, and is he not undeniably handsome? As she puts on her hat, she is no doubt telling herself a story in which half-way through the evening Dicky draws her to one side and says, 'Say, sugar, help me dump this dame some place, and you and me'll have a little get together!'

There is no Dougie in the car. Dicky tells us that he won't be able to join us as he is out manoeuvring. Dicky fails to say manoeuvring what, and from what I know of some Canadians, perhaps it is just as well. Pauline hears of Dougie's failure to appear without interest, and settling herself back in the opulence of Dicky's car, she proceeds to put him through a searching interrogation. She starts off with Hollywood. Dicky is a slow chameleon. He is not yet used to having her in the back of his car, and he is obviously wishing her elsewhere. He replies politely, but no doubt more bluntly than he need, and I am afraid that several of Pauline's cellophane illusions begin to show signs of cracking. He puts his foot in it, finally, however, over the matter of Gary Cooper. In Dicky's opinion, Mr Cooper is a sap, and Dicky says so. I ought to have warned him.

When Pauline recovers her breath, she tells him pointedly and with some vehemence that Mr Cooper is not a sap. The tornado of reproaches continue for several minutes and poor Dicky cowers beneath them. After this he is more careful, but alas, the damage has been done. Pauline has revised her judgment of him, and I can see that she is thinking that if he is an example of the average 'script writer in Hollywood' there may be a chance for Elstree after all.

I feel that Dicky is disliking her with equal intensity, and as the evening proceeds, the atmosphere becomes more and more strained.

He doesn't even begin to understand her, and several times he rises to my defence when the poor girl is meaning me no harm at all.

'Don't you think Aunty Bee has the most revolting hair, Dicky?' says Pauline on one occasion, not meaning this literally, but only that its curly nature makes her envious. Dicky, however tries to defend me at once.

'Well, now,' he says indignantly, 'I think she has real pretty hair.'

Poor Pauline is so taken aback by the resentment in his voice it takes her quite a long time to recover.

Dicky asks us if we would rather go to a picture and trust to luck what we can get for supper afterwards, or have a proper meal and miss the picture altogether. Pauline is all for a picture so Dicky and I banish the vision we had of a nice dinner in our favourite hotel, and we set off for Wallbrugh. By the time we have parked the car and locked it, and put it out of action, Pauline, who has gone on ahead to discover what picture is showing, returns with the news that it is 'New Moon' with 'that man Nelson Eddy'. We gather that she does not approve of Mr Eddy, so back we get into the car and drive on. The next picture house that we try is very small and poky, and in a back lane of Wallbrugh; but there is no sign of a queue, and the film showing seems quite amusing, so once again we park the car, lock it up, disable it, and set off for the pictures. It is not until we ask for tickets that we are told there is a full house.

There are no more picture houses in Wallbrugh.

'Well I guess we'll just have to go on into Ashton,' says Dicky as we climb back into his car. 'You girls will sure have to see a movie now we've started out.'

Ashton is ten miles away. When we get there we find that one picture house is full, and the other has been burnt out and is closed for repairs.

By the time we get back to Wallbrugh it is half-past eight, and the only supper that we can find is some sandwiches and some bad coffee. Poor Dicky feels that as a host he has been a failure.

'Gee! What a party!' he says apologetically. 'I sure am sorry,

Pauline.'

'Oh, don't mention it, Dicky,' says Pauline as she climbs wearily into the car. 'This sort of thing always happens to me. Didn't you know my second name was Jonah?'

'No, is it?' says Dicky politely. 'Bee never told me.'

On the way home Pauline curls up into a ball and seems to be asleep. Dicky holds my hand. I watch Pauline in the driving mirror, however, and I am suspicious of this apparent slumber. I am not so trustful of her innocence as Dicky, and as he drives into the yard and stops the car, I resist the good night kiss that he attempts to plant upon my nose.

'Come on now,' I say jovially. 'Out you pop. Come on Pauline, wake up.'

Pauline wakes up so rapidly that my suspicions are fully confirmed. She has been no more asleep than I have.

'Popperty pop, popperty pop,' says Dicky, releasing me hastily and scrambling out of the car. 'Here we are then, girls.'

I stifle an unseemly desire to giggle.

'Good night Dicky. Thank you so much. It's been lovely in spite of missing the pictures.'

'Well, it's surely swell of you to say so, Pauline. You're a nice kid.'

'Good night Dicky,' I say. 'Thanks a lot.'

Dicky gets into his car and drives away. Overhead is a wonderful harvest moon, globular, and reminding me of a giant oyster.

'Popperty pop,' says the 'nice kid' as we watch Dicky's tail lamp disappearing down the road. 'Oh, Aunty Bee! Why didn't you let him kiss you? I was absolutely dying to know what you do with your noses. Don't they get terribly in the way?'

'Come to bed, Tubby,' I say. 'I'm sorry even that entertainment was denied you, you little wretch! I knew you weren't really asleep.'

'That was me being tactful.'

'I'm afraid it turned out a dull evening for you, Tubby.'

'Oh, it wasn't Aunty Bee! It was much better than being left behind while you are shaking a loose leg, even if we did miss the pictures.'

'How do you like Dicky?'

'I think he's the perfect limit! Calling my Gary a sap indeed! Gary could eat two like him for breakfast. Still – he's not bad apart from that. He's very good-looking. And he's very easy to tease. He rises beautifully.'

'Now you know what temptation we suffer when you are about!'

'Oh, I know,' says Pauline resignedly. 'I quite see I must be teasable. I mean I know I do things that ask for it; like telling Mr Weir not to tickle me. I don't believe he knew that I was ticklish before I told him.'

'Yes, that was unwise.'

'I knew it was at the time, Aunty Bee, but I just can't stop saying silly things. It's like doing silly things. I know if I pick up the cream jug, I will knock it over, and sure enough when I do, I do. It's an awful handicap to go through life with.'

'Poor old Pauline. P'raps you'll grow out of it.'

We take off our clothes and climb wearily into bed. Our arms are red and swollen from stooking, and Pauline decides that she will cover hers with hand lotion. This proves to be most unwise. I attempt to muffle her yells of pain by warning her that she will wake up the twins.

'Oh!' says Pauline, holding her arms close to her body, and rocking backwards and forwards. 'I'm dying, Aunty Bee! I'm going to do one of Anne's roaring pass outs.'

To comfort her I allow her to remain in bed while I take on her turn of switching out the light, and taking down the black out. I sink into my own bed again deliciously. It has long since ceased to be the hard horror it seemed on my first night at Stoney Hall, and now I find it all that could be desired in comfort and softness.

'Are you going to marry him?' says Pauline suddenly from the darkness.

'Good heavens, Tubby, who?'

'Dicky, of course.'

'Oh, don't be silly. He hasn't asked me for one thing, and I shouldn't want to if he did.'

'I think he would make a very kind husband,' Pauline sighs. 'He's got a beautiful car.'

'But you can hardly marry a man on the strength of that, Tubby. At least I couldn't. You'd better marry him yourself. He'd take you out to Hollywood, and you could meet Gary Cooper first hand.'

'I don't think he'd have me with you around, Aunty Bee. You know perfectly well that the silly ass adores you passionately.'

I find it difficult to visualise Dicky adoring anyone passionately, but I do not say so.

'Do you know what, Aunty Bee,' says Pauline sternly, just as I am about to fall asleep. 'You've got no heart at all. You ride over people like a perfect steam roller. I hope that one day you fall terribly in love with someone who won't even look at you. And I hope it breaks your heart. It would do it all the good in the world.'

'Says she, waving her wooden leg,' I murmur, and silence reigns.

As a milkmaid I have no private life at all. For all the privacy I get in my spare time, I might as well be Prime Minister. No doubt the Gestapo system of the dairy family has a lot to do with this. The day after I have been out with Dicky, every one of my customers seems to know all about it. They have often seen us together at the pictures, or having a meal in Wallbrugh; and they can tell to a second, how long I take in saying good morning to him when I take his men their milk at the Hall. Every morning I am greeted by people who look at their wrist watches pointedly and shake their heads. 'You're late today Miss Whitton,' they say. 'You've spent an extra few minutes talking to that officer of yours up at the Hall.'

Of course I am teased about Dicky unmercifully. I am repeatedly asked when the banns are being put up, and warned that if I can't be good I must be careful. I am also, often most unjustly, accused of sins which are not mine.

Priscilla is a black Ford with a local number plate. Everyone has seen me driving a black Ford with a local number plate, and every black Ford with a local number plate that is seen in suspicious circumstances is immediately presumed to be mine. Often a knowing and accusing finger is shaken slyly in innocent face.

'Now, Miss Whitton, where were you at twelve o'clock last night?' says Mrs Brown (or Mrs Smith or Mrs Telford).

'I don't think I was anywhere. Why?'

'Now then, Miss Whitton, you can't get away with that! You was seen with your young man sitting in that car of yours up on the moor, and there's no denying!'

'What an absolute slander! I was in writing letters all last night.'

'Oh no, you wasn't. Our Maggie was coming home from the hop and she saw you in the car, plain as plain, number plate and all.'

In the end I get very tired of all this. I do not profess to have a very milky white reputation at the best of times, but it is a little hard to have it painted quite so scarlet as mine repeatedly is, although there is no doubt at all that my customers enjoy it hugely. They seem to think it gives their milk an extra tang when they are able to imagine their milkmaid is a sort of civilised Jezebel; and they certainly appear to like me nonetheless for it.

One morning as I deliver my milk, I become unexpectedly involved in a celebration. I have two customers to whom I am particularly attached, a Mr and Mrs Riddle. They are a friendly old couple, and often when I go for their money on a Saturday Mr Riddle will cackle with pleasure and insist on pressing on me one of his peppermint cough sweets. Mrs Riddle treats me to a long recital on the ins and outs of her stomach, but she always has exactly the right change waiting for me, and for this I can forgive her much.

This morning, when I take them their milk, Mrs Riddle opens the door and mysteriously beckons me inside. The cottage is dark after the bright sunlight, but after a few seconds my eyes become used to the light, and I see on the kitchen table a huge cake of pre-war proportions and a bottle of elderberry wine. The sight of the cake excites my breakfast-eager stomach, and I find it hard to keep my eyes away from the table.

Mrs Riddle always refers to her husband as 'he'. He is sitting by the fire in his rocking-chair, rocking furiously and giggling away at me like a schoolboy. Mrs Riddle tells me that it is the anniversary of their golden wedding, and that they are 'having a bit of a celebration'. She shows me proudly the paragraph that has been written about them in the local paper, and a collection of cards and letters that have come from their children and grandchildren. She then pours me out a glass of elderberry wine.

'Drink to our health and happiness, dearie,' she says, beaming all over her kindly face. 'And I'm sure I hope you have the same. I'd join you with a glass, only a glass o' wine never did carry well in me stomick.'

I drink their healths, and my own stomach staggers beneath the impact of a burning solution of molten fire. I gasp; the world reels and I grope at the edge of the kitchen table for support. I have had glasses of elderberry wine given me before, but never such as this. I see not one Mrs Riddle, but a blurred kaleidoscope of Mrs Riddles, all smiling and nodding, and urging me to fill up my glass.

When my world has cleared again, however, and my stomach has picked itself up off its back, I begin to feel absolutely marvellous. The sun outside shines as no sun has ever shone before and all the birds burst their throats with a song entirely for my benefit. I watch in a roseate glow while Mrs Riddle cuts two slices from the cake and gives them to me, 'for you and the funny little lassie with the big eyes'. She assures me that if I sleep with the cake under my pillow, I will dream of my future husband. I thank her profusely and kiss her on both cheeks. I also thank Mr Riddle profusely, and very nearly kiss him on both cheeks too. I wish them all the happiness in the world, and Mr Riddle rocks and giggles more than ever. I wave my hand in farewell and blithely proceed on my way, carolling like a lark.

My high spirits last throughout the morning. By nine o'clock my customers are used to seeing a weary and drooping land girl who is still very sleepy and badly wants her breakfast. Today they are no doubt amazed to see the female equivalent of the advertisement, 'Who's been at my Eno's?' I should dearly love to know just what was in that glass of elderberry wine.

It is not every day that one participates in a golden wedding. A morning starting so well could not fail to have other tricks up its sleeve, and I have not long left the Riddles before my second adventure is upon me.

My route lies over a bridge, and as I drive up to it, I see that it is surrounded by soldiers. They are having a mock battle, and they have orders to stop all cars wanting to cross the bridge, and to demand to see their drivers' identity cards.

As I approach, a belligerent-looking youth with a drawn bayonet steps in front of me.

'I 'ave hinstructions to stop hall v-hikles wishing to pro-ceed over this 'ere bridge,' he says in a business-like manner. 'Hidenterty card please.'

I, of course, have no identity card. Neither, I discover, have I brought my driving licence with me, or anything at all by which the young man may distinguish me from Olga Polovski. I am forced to admit this to the perspiring face at the other end of the bayonet, and the face registers satisfaction.

'I shall 'ave to hask you to remain 'ere until ower hofficer can come and see you,' says the happy trooper, and he directs me to draw my van in to the side of the road. Four guards, all with drawn bayonets and wearing tin hats, are detailed to encircle me. We grin at each other and proceed to wait for 'Ower hofficer' to come.

The day is extremely hot. It is bad enough in the van with the smell of stale milk, but what it must be like out on the road my guards' faces show only too well. The troops who are not otherwise actively employed, are vastly amused by me and my bodyguard. We have to endure many wisecracks and my guards are warned to 'keep your eyes on your work, but do your duty all the same!'

The minutes pass and there is still no sign of the officer. I suggest breaking into a bottle of milk and having a little refreshment but although I see hope rise in the eye of the youngest of my guards, it is only a flicker. It seems that this would come under the heading of conniving with the enemy.

'Can't do that, missie,' says one of the men respectfully. 'You might produce a tommy gun and break out while we was doing bottoms up.'

We gradually assemble a little crowd of unattached personnel about us, and as the minutes pass, the atmosphere becomes more and more friendly. I am just learning that my right-hand foreguard is called Tiny because he is so big, when the crowd suddenly melts away and my guards leap to attention, and smartly present arms. 'Ower hofficer' is appearing at last.

After all this display of reverence 'Ower hoffice' proves to be a nice little boy with a college countenance and a very new yellow moustache.

'Oh, hullo,' he says smiling agreeably. 'I say, I'm frightfully sorry to have kept you waiting like this. We're having a sort of practice for the invasion. Rather fun, actually. I think we are all rather enjoying it. Wish a "Stop-me-and-buy-one" would come along, though!'

'I've been trying to sell your men some milk, but they seemed afraid I might shoot them with a tommy gun while they were drinking it.'

'Well, you never know do you? I hear you haven't got your identity card?'

'I'm afraid I haven't. I've always got so many papers in this van I'm afraid that I leave behind any I can possibly do without.'

'Well, do you know, so do I when I'm on leave. But that's unofficial.'

He takes down a few particulars about me and seems to be satisfied. He also takes my name and telephone number and I am uncertain if this is part of the interrogation or not.

'Will you be round this way again?' says the officer finally, as I am about to drive on.

'Not until this time tomorrow.'

'What a pity. We'll be gone by then I'm afraid. I mean it does give the men a kick to catch a car with no papers at all. However, perhaps we'll see you again some time.' He waves his little stick and I drive away.

For the whole of the next month Pauline and I stook corn incessantly. Hour after hour we gather up sheaves. We build the field into streets and corridors of neatly curving sooks, and before long the work becomes automatic. We take a great pride however, in building the stocks exactly in line. It is heart breaking to pass a field that has been standing stocked for some time, and to see some of the beautiful lines that we built so carefully, broken down and collapsed with the wind.

Gideon and his horses are replaced after the first few days by Charlie and his tractor. Charlie has been away for some time heaving timber in the woods. Back once more, the tractor mingles its phutting with the clacking of the binder as it drags it round the ever decreasing square of standing corn. Everyone who can be spared comes stooking. Reg and little Tommie are there, old Mr Weir and Gideon, Pauline and I, and sometimes even Mr Smith. Under this line of workers the scattered sheaves are gathered from the field with miraculous rapidity and in their stead the neat stooks clasp their hands as if in prayer.

Pauline and I have soon worn even our leather gloves into ribbons. The fingers are all in holes, and the sharp thistles find their way persistently into our mutilated flesh. The drying thistle leaves are brittle. They crumble off and fall inside the gauntlets of our gloves and work their way down into the lining inside, so that after the first few days our gloves are no real protection at all. In the evenings we spend hours perched at the windows of the cottage, attempting to dig the worst of the spikes out of our hands by the last light of day. Mrs Smith says that if the corn harvest goes on much longer she will go mad. She says she never sees us but we are digging away at ourselves with needles, our eyes screwed up, and expressions of agony on our faces. She is also, poor soul, nearly demented by the quantity of grain that we bring into her cottage in the folds of our clothes. She makes us empty out our shoes on the back door step, but it is impossible to keep the corn from flicking out of the rest of our clothing as we go upstairs. The bedroom floor is daily littered with corn, in spite of our attempts to undress standing in the fender. The result, of course, is mice, and we hear them rattling nightly in the wainscoting.

The first field of corn is almost cut, and there begins to rise a fever of excitement. As the square of corn in the middle grows smaller the excitement rises to a climax. The frightened rabbits that have retreated away from the blade of the binder are forced at last to break cover, and they make a wild dash for safety in the hedge. They run out singly, making bewildered zig-zags from stook to stook. On their heels shout and yelp a bevy of men and dogs. The men throw anything that they can lay their hands on, their knives or a stone or a clod of earth, and all too often Pauline and I cover our ears and turn miserably away from the cries of agony that the dying rabbits give. They look so pitiably small, after all, when the crowd of their hunters have parted, and we see their kicking bodies hanging limply from their captors' hands. The men hold them by the back legs and kill them quickly with a single rap on the back of the neck.

There is much conversation of a general nature as we are stooking, for although we stook in couples, we are all more or less within hearing distance of each other. Mr Smith, Gideon, and Reg are in the Home Guard, and it is always a subject for earnest discussion. It seems that there is a good deal of ill-feeling about the possession of the Company's one and only rifle.

'Man, who with any sense would give it to that Davy?' says Gideon indignantly, clapping his sheaves into place with unnecessary force. 'Everyone knows Davy's that blind he cannot see to pull the trigger.'

'Why, aye, man,' agrees Mr Smith. 'The whole thing's daft; mind, I'm telling you.'

'I did hear as how it was because old Davy and Willie Glendining were the first two to sign on,' says Reg putting in his oar. 'Davy got the rifle, and Willie got the respirator.'

'Well, if they promote that Davy major over the likes of me there's going to be trouble. Why, the lad only joined because he couldn't see what he was signing.'

'Oh, don't be silly,' says Pauline. 'He must have known what he was signing.'

'No, it's right enough,' says Mr Smith. 'I was down at the Plough one night having a pint and a game of darts, when the door opens and in walks Mr Foster. He makes a kind of speech, telling the lads all about the Home Guard, do you see, and asking if any of them would come up and sign on.'

'Aye! I was there that night,' puts in Gideon.

'Aye! I know you were,' says Mr Smith. 'And you were just about as blind as Davy! Well, then, Mr Foster turns to Davy and he asks will he be the first to put his name down. And Davy, being hard of hearing, puts his name at the top and thinks he's putting down for a ticket in the raffle. He asks me after Mr Foster had gone if I knowed what it was they were raffling.'

Mr Smith chuckles delightedly at the memory.

'You should have seen his face when I told him he'd just joined the Army!'

Gideon, however, does not seem to find this funny.

'But man, it's not right to hand him over our rifle for that,' he says, shaking his head gloomily. 'We may get the ammunition for it one day and then where will we be?'

The corn dries quickly, for the fine weather holds, and day after day the dawn breaks with a heavy dew and the promise of another scorching sun. Mr Foster urges Mr Smith repeatedly to get the corn led, and after a while even his caution is satisfied that it is dry enough.

Pauline begs Mr Smith to let her work with her beloved Bett and one of the carts. She points out that even if Bett does refuse to stand (and Pauline is sure she won't because she is such an angel, really she is), no serious harm will have been done because there will always be someone on the ground forking or leading her, to catch her head. Mr Smith is doubtful, but in the end he good naturedly consents to 'let her try'.

Pauline hitches Bett to the cart, and with an extra cage strapped to the top, so that the cart can take a larger load of sheaves, she sets out for the field. In the field is Mr Weir waiting with his fork to lift the sheaves up to her. However, he decides that Pauline must change places with him because he says that building the sheaves into a load firm enough to stay on as far as the farm; is a job that takes some skill! Pauline accepts the fork cheerfully, but after she has three times speared Mr Weir through the leg with it he says that he will risk letting her try to load and do the forking himself.

Loading is a fairly heavy job, for although the sheaves have shrunk considerably in drying in the stook, they are still of a formidable size. Mr Weir and I are recognised as the chief forkers, and Gideon and Pauline lead the carts. Mr Smith and Tommie work on the stack at the farm, and Charlie drives his tractor with a truck hitched on behind. Mr Weir and I are kept fairly busy. Some days old Mr Weir comes out with his fork to give us a quavering hand, but he tells us his sciatica has taken fright at a 'nip of autumn' in the air and he is obviously already preparing himself for his winter hibernation.

When Pauline has completed her first load, it is one of the oddest shapes that I have ever seen. It starts very well, but at the point where Mr Weir received his third jab, it takes a rapid turn for the worse and declines steadily to one side. She ties it on hopefully, however, with all the ropes she has, but we watch its wavering departure for the farm with grave doubts in our hearts. Seen from behind it is an even odder shape, and Mr Weir shakes his head over it. 'I doubt, I doubt, my Tubby,' he says. 'It wouldn't do for our sergeant major, my lassie.'

Mr Weir is perfectly right. At the first gate it shudders, slips, slides and collapses on to the ground.

'Eh, Tubby,' says Mr Weir, as we go over to help her put I back on again. 'I'm very much afraid you've a long way to go yet before you'll be a farmer's boy. You'll have to practise an awful lot before you can get your badge at loading. But never mind, Tubby, my lass, one day you'll be a man before your mother, never fear.'

Patiently, and very slowly, he shows Pauline how to build a load so that the sheaves are interwoven and do not come off at the first bump.

All this week we load corn solidly and the muscles on my shoulders swell to truly alarming proportions. I no longer feel that I need arm myself against homicidal lunatics with a quart bottle of milk. I feel that like Tarzan, I could wring their necks with my naked hands.

Mr Foster soon shows evidence of his speed fever. Night after night we are asked to stay on in the fields and work until it is dark. On Saturday afternoon we are both looking forward wearily to a holiday. We seem to have been working at full pressure for as long as we can remember, and we feel that if we do not have a holiday soon, something somewhere will crack. It is a very apologetic Mr Smith, therefore, who on Friday evening asks us if we will stay and work overtime on Saturday too.

'Mr Smith!' we moan. 'This is the end! Haven't we worked every night this week until it is too dark to see?'

'I know, I know,' says Mr Smith soothingly. 'But we've got to try and finish the field by tomorrow. You'll each get seven pence an hour overtime if that's any comfort. I'll see to that.'

We feel that seven pence an hour is small compensation for a lost Saturday afternoon, but we are sorry for Mr Smith's obvious distress, and we tell him that it is perfectly all right, and that we have had no plans made for the weekend anyway. I ring up Dicky for the fourth time that week, and tell him that I shall not be able to go out with him.

When we arrive at the field the next day, there are a perfect horde of people out. There are some strangers, but I recognise several of my customers, and we greet each other with laughter.

'Didn't think to see me out with a fork did you, Miss Whitton?' says Cecil's grand-da, the old rat catcher. He is almost as old as old Mr Weir.

There are many faces I know by sight through serving milk to their wives. There is the woodman with his two horses, and the contractor with his huge blue lorry. There is the carpenter and the chauffeur, the groom and young Billy, and there is a second motor bogie brought over from Glittering Stones. Every man in the place that can be spared seems to be forking or loading corn. During the afternoon the Foster children arrive with their Nannie and a pony and trap, and they have a hilarious time tumbling in the corn. The pony eats so much grain that it swells almost visibly.

In the middle of the afternoon, when the sun is at its hottest, Bett who has been behaving unusually well, takes it into her head to run away. She careers wildly up the field and makes a beeline towards the Foster pony trap, which is standing placidly unaware in her path. All would have ended in disaster if it had not been for the unpleasant Scots Nannie. To our amazement, we see her step into the path of the runaway and spread out her arms. Her nurse's cloak falls away from her, and she looks Bett full in the eye. In her forbidding Scotch voice she bids her stop. Bett recognises her at once for the Sterling stuff she is, for she slows down to a trot and finally stops and meekly begins to crop at Nannie's feet. Nannie leads away the pony and trap to the hedge, and Pauline comes up to reclaim her unruly angel.

'Oh Betty, darling; why did you do it?' says Pauline as she leads her back to complete her load. 'You are a wicked horse. Why do you always have to be bad when I look after you?'

We work until the light has faded and it is too dark to see. The streets of stooks have miraculously vanished, and only the stubble is left, bristling the cheek of the hill. Down at the bottom of the field are three stacks, built during the course of the day by Mr Smith and Mr Weir. They are silhouetted against the twilight sky. One of them is leaning over drunkenly, so great is the haste with which they have been rushed up, and Mr Weir, who is responsible for it, is subject to a good deal of good natured criticism.

The estate people climb into the back of a lorry, and they are driven off into the darkness with much clatter and calling. I climb wearily into the cart beside Pauline, and she sets the now docile Bett's head homeward to the stable.

In the bottom of the cart is an assortment of earwigs, beetles, and caterpillars, which have been shaken out of their homes in the sheaves. I feel them crawling up my legs, but I only brush them off again for I am far too tired to move.

As we turn in at the farm gate we see the stackyard filled with a new harvest of stacks. They stand like a strange city, massive and silent, and the little old cottages of the farm huddle close beneath them and seem to cower at their feet as if in fear. The stacks have grown with the night into monsters from another world, stolidly standing against the sky. They seem to crowd together, standing back to back in a menacing army that waits only for some unseen signal before launching their attack upon a sleeping world.

We go into the cottage, and somehow I am glad to be able to shut the kitchen door against them. Inside, with the electric light burning, and the friendly sanity of the two Smiths to reassure me, my sudden fear dwindles and becomes distant.

We say good night and go upstairs to bed. Mr Smith has been extremely nice to Pauline about the misbehaviour of Bett and has assured her that it wasn't her fault at all.

Pauline is only slightly consoled. 'But it would have to happen to me!' she says wistfully.

We undress wearily, and leave our clothing lying in a heap on the floor. I shudder to think of my early rise next morning, and envy Pauline, who will be able to stay in bed until late. I switch out the light, and take down the blackout. From the window, staring back at me from beyond the glass, I see a solid wall of towering straw. My fear returns with a rush, and as I climb into bed I am glad to have Pauline's regular breathing on the other side of the room. As I sleep I seem to feel closing in and pressing all about me the mighty power of the waiting corn.

CHAPTER SIXTEEN
Treading a Measure

THERE WOULD NEVER have been a hop if it had not been for us. Although in the past there was always a harvest dance at Stoney Hall, the old custom has lately been dropped.

'They used to have a good do,' says Mrs Smith reminiscing. 'They had the B.B.C. down broadcasting it one year. I'll never forget the carry on. They had a pig there to guess its weight and it got out of its pen and ran into the microphone. My mother was at home listening in and she said the announcer said he was sorry for the delay, but it had been caused by a technical hitch. Mother didn't half laugh when I told her the technical hitch was one of the young porkers!'

There are some wonderful granaries at Stoney Hall where the dances used to be held. It seems a great pity to Pauline and me that the old custom should not be revived.

I determine, however, that the suggestion shall not come from me but from Dicky. Dicky's soldiers, buried as they are in the country, have no form of entertainment provided for them, and I suggest to him that, as their officer, it is about time he did something about it. Dicky agrees, but says that he doesn't see very much that he can do apart from providing a bus to take them occasionally into Carmouth. It is now my chance to play my cards well, and I flatter myself that I do so. I suggest to him that they might like a dance. Dicky says they sure would, but where would he get a hall for them miles out in the country. I tell him of our granaries, and I suggest that he appeals to Mr Foster for the use of one of them. The proceeds could go to charity.

Dicky becomes quite enthusiastic and agrees to see Mr Foster immediately. Pauline and I hold our thumbs for the next few days but apparently Dicky's colonial powers of persuasion are good, for he finally rings me up and tells me that 'Mr Foster is a swell guy and has come across OK.'

The coming dance causes an enormous sensation. Dicky has some notices printed, and his men pin them up at various points about the country. Every one of my customers tells me about it and we discuss it from every angle.

Dicky's men are providing a band. It seems that my old friend the sergeant plays the trombone, and he persuades the school master to promise them the use of the school piano. As the day for the dance approaches, lorry loads of soldiers arrive at the farm with crates of beer and trucks of chairs, and pieces of plywood that are to be used to black out the many granary windows.

The granary that Mr Smith has allotted for the dance is thick with dust. It is also filled with rubbish of every conceivable description, and for many hours the soldiers are kept busy carting out rusty mangles and rotten sacks that have accumulated there throughout the years. I see Mr Smith gleefully watching their labours. He has chosen the one granary where a general spring clean is most needed.

When the day of the dance arrives, excitement on the farm is at fever pitch. The dairy family have given up all pretence at concealing their interest and they spend all day hanging out of their cottage window. Dicky spends the morning rushing about his work so that he will have the rest of the day free to direct operations, and by tea-time the preparations for the night's revelry are in full swing.

The children on the farm are almost crazy with excitement. They spend their time rushing wildly between the yard and the granary, and tripping up the heavily breathing soldiers at every corner. Only Mrs Smith works on steadily. She has no time to waste wandering round, for she and Mr Smith are having a party of people to supper, and she has her hands full preparing the food. Mr Smith pretends to hold the whole preparations in lofty and amused contempt, but we know that he is really as excited as any of us, and in spite of himself, he cannot stop his little blue eyes twinkling.

When we have had our tea, the last pretence of work on the farm stops. Charlie is ploughing up the bleaching stubble of the empty cornfields, and only he works on in aloof serenity. The red earth bleeds behind the dragging iron feet of his tractor and as I watch him idly, I suddenly realise with a shock that already the cycle for next year's corn has begun. Down the road and across the railway I can hear the throb of the thresher as it flays a harvest of grain. Next week, we too will be threshing, and after that the autumn will be upon us and the winter coming in the inevitable revolution of the seasons.

Pauline and I dress for the dance with especial care. Pauline is looking attractive with her high colour and her saucer eyes, and tonight she has managed to control her hair so that it is less wind-blown than usual. It has spent the last week in curlers, but the result is certainly fetching. Pauline has been teased a lot about these curlers. The last thing I have become used to seeing as I go to sleep at night, is Pauline sitting up in bed sticking curlers in her hair. The first thing I see when I wake up in the morning is Pauline taking the curlers out.

'I don't believe you ever sleep at all,' I tell her. 'I believe you no sooner get them in than it is dawn and time to take them all out again.'

However, I assure her that tonight she will be danced off her feet.

The Smiths are having a happy time entertaining their party of friends in the kitchen as we steal out of the cottage by the front door.

At the top of the granary steps there is a red lamp, and already there are several pairs of legs crossing in front of it. We climb up and push open the heavy wooden door.

Inside the granary there is a small card table with a soldier selling tickets. We buy ourselves a couple, and push our way past the sack curtain that hangs behind him.

The granary is very different from when we last saw it piled with sacks of cattle cake and white with dust. Dicky's soldiers have certainly made a good job of it and it reminds me now a little of a church at harvest festival time. The men have begged some sheaves of corn from Mr Smith, and these are fixed to the walls. Hanging from the rafters are a number of stable lanterns and strung from one to another, are a variety of Colonial flags.

The room is long and narrow with rows of chairs set about the walls. The band is at the end, sitting in a perfect arbour of corn sheaves, and already they are playing softly. Several early couples are dancing on the dimly lit floor, and the gently swinging lanterns catch their shadows and send them sprawling upward to the ceiling.

We have hardly emerged from the sack curtain before we are

collected by a couple of soldiers and asked to dance. The floor is smooth and springy, and the band at the end bangs away at a cheerful tin-pan alley ditty.

More and more people begin arriving. I find I know nearly all of them, and we shout and wave to them as they recognise us.

Mr and Mrs Smith arrive with Mr Smith's brother from Glittering Stones. Mrs Smith has treated herself to a water wave for the occasion and she looks very neat and trim. She smiles at us cheerfully across the room, and we laugh and wave back. I think what an absolute dear she is.

'She and darling Mr Smith are two of the nicest people I have ever met,' says Pauline.

Mr Smith himself is wearing his best Sunday suit and a collar, and he looks very unhappy in them. Half-way through the evening, I notice he loses patience with his collar and he removes it altogether. After this, he seems to feel much more at home.

All the estate people are here. Mrs Harris is shrieking with laughter and doing a dance all by herself in a corner with little Nancy for a partner. Young Billy is here, and he looks strangely waisted and angular without his familiar, blue serge apron. He asks me to dance. I accept gracefully, and sticking out his behind in a truly gigolo attitude, he proceeds to jerk and jig his way round the room. It seems that Billy is a jitterbug.

After the dance is over he grasps my hand. 'Come outside,' he says hoarsely, and wondering fearfully if I am about to have to defend my honour, I am rushed into the stack yard. However, it is only a pocket full of plums that Billy has brought with him, and we suck them happily in the safe cover of a stack.

The strains of music come to us softly, and the dull thumping of hobnail boots on the granary floor. A car drives up with a rattle that I think I recognise, and sure enough I see the gleam of a white mackintosh as it extracts itself from the driving seat, and makes unhurriedly for the granary step.

'Hullo, Glen!' I say. 'I didn't know that you were coming.'

'Yes, rather!' says Glen. 'Can't be left out of a show like this.'

I see him later leaning up against a wall and looking on, for it appears that his search for education has not extended as far as the tango. I sit out with him, and allow him to tell me all about the latest telescope that is being constructed in America.

Pauline is having the time of her life. She is being danced off her feet, and I see her scarlet face whirling by happily. She has a perfect stream of partners and as a result of her exertions she has split her dress down one of its seams, but she does not seem to mind in the very slightest. The room has become stiflingly hot, for the blackout screens at the windows allow little air to come in from outside.

Dicky arrives late. He scoops me out of the arms of one of his soldiers with a benevolent glare, and we fox-trot round the room warmly.

'I sure am sorry, sugar,' says Dicky. 'I can't stay long. There's some work cropped up tonight and I have to go see to it.'

'Oh, Dicky, how maddening. It would happen tonight!'

We dance on. Half-way through the evening Pauline makes friends with two medical students, who are camping out by the river. They are a pleasant-looking couple, and Pauline goes down well with them. They keep her dancing with them alternately, and as Dicky and I pass near, I hear her holding an earnest discussion with one of them about Gary Cooper.

As the evening draws to a close, the pace becomes fast and furious. Most of us dispose of those portions of clothing that we can dispense with, and the blood pressure of the band appears to be rising to boiling point.

'Come outside,' says Dicky. 'I'll have to go now, Bee.'

We stagger out into the cool of the air, and wind our way to Dicky's car amid a host of couples who are bidding each other fond good nights.

'Bee,' says Dicky. 'I didn't want to tell you before. We're moving. Word has just come through.'

'Oh, Dicky! Where are you going?'

'I don't know yet, Bee. May be any place. May be overseas.'

'Dicky, I'm so sorry. I'll miss you a lot. You are a good customer!'

'Oh well, maybe they'll change their minds yet. You never know with brass hats.'

'No, you never know.'

'Good night, darling.'

'Good night, Dicky.' He gets into his car. Suddenly we hear Pauline's ringing voice echoing across the stack yard.

'Oh, I'd simply love to see over the old water mill!' she says enthusiastically. 'It's perfectly sweet of you, really it is!'

'Pauline and her medical students,' Dicky says.

We laugh, and then we hear someone begin to whistle the refrain of an old tune:

There ain't no thrill,
By the water mill,
All by yourself in the moonlight.

It is, without any doubt at all, Mr Weir.

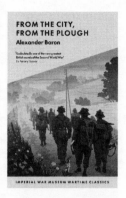

ISBN 9781912423071

£8.99

'Alexander Baron's *From the City, From the Plough* is undoubtedly one of the very greatest British novels of the Second World War and provides the most honest and authentic account of front line life for an infantryman in North West Europe.'

ANTONY BEEVOR

ISBN 9781912423163

£8.99

'Few other novels of the war describe the grinding claustrophobia, violence and lethal danger of being in a tank crew with the stark vividness of Peter Elstob... a forgotten classic that deserves to be read and read.'

JAMES HOLLAND

ISBN 9781912423095

£8.99

'Takes you straight back to Blitzed London... boasts everything a great whodunit should have, and more.'

ANDREW ROBERTS

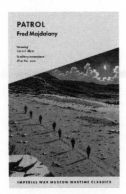

ISBN 9781912423156
£8.99

'When a man has been a soldier and seen action, he writes of war with true understanding, and with authority. When that man writes with with, elegance and imagination, as Fred Majdalany does in *Patrol*, he produces a military masterpiece.'

ALLAN MALLINSON

ISBN 9781912423088
£8.99

'A tremendous rediscovery of a brilliant novel. Extremely well-written, its effects are both sophisticated and visceral. Remarkable.'

WILLIAM BOYD

ISBN 9781912423101
£8.99

'Much more than a novel'

RODERICK BAILEY

'I loved this book, and felt I was really there'

LOUIS de BERNIÈRES

'One of the greatest adventure stories of the Second World War'

ANDREW ROBERTS

ISBN 9781912423279

£8.99

'A hidden masterpiece, crackling with authenticity that gives an unforgettable taste of the life of a fighter squadron in the summer of 1940.'

PATRICK BISHOP

'Supposedly fiction, but these pages live – and so, for a brief inspiring hour, do the young men who lived in them.'

FREDERICK FORSYTH